A NOVEL

Nicole Luiken

Great Plains Publications
1173 Wolseley Avenue
Winnipeg, MB R3G 1H1
www.greatplains.mb.ca

Great Plains Publications gratefully acknowledges the financial support provided
for its publishing program by the Government of Canada through the Canada
Book Fund; the Canada Council for the Arts; the Province of Manitoba through
the Book Publishing Tax Credit and the Book Publisher Marketing Assistance
Program; and the Manitoba Arts Council.

Design & Typography by Relish New Brand Experience

Printed in Canada by Friesens

Library and Archives Canada Cataloguing in Publication

Title: Feral : a novel / Nicole Luiken.
Names: Luiken, Nicole, 1971- author.
Identifiers: Canadiana (print) 20190110597 | Canadiana (ebook) 20190110600 |
    ISBN 9781773370316
    (softcover) | ISBN 9781773370323 (EPUB) | ISBN 9781773370330 (Kindle)
Classification: LCC PS8573.U534 F57 2019 | DDC jc813/.6—dc23

DEDICATION

In memory of Elmer Zumwalt. We were so lucky to have you in our lives, first as my father-in-law and later as grandfather to our children. You are missed.

CHAPTER

1

They'd left her behind.

A hot ball of shame and anger lodged in Chloe's throat as she ran along the dirt track through the forest. Bad enough Coach Wharton had bluntly told her to go home, that she couldn't keep up, but her so-called teammates had run off without so much as a backward look.

And maybe Coach was right. Maybe she couldn't run as fast as the rest of the track team, but it wasn't in her to give up.

They were too far ahead now to realistically catch, but if she took the shortcut and really pushed it she could run the last bit of the loop with them.

Chloe put her head down and increased her pace, until her feet flew down the trail, crunching on yellow leaves, until her lungs heaved and a bright stitch of pain pinched at her side. It felt good to push her body to its limits.

A furtive rustling noise alerted her that she was no longer alone. Half-hidden among the evergreen trees, a wolf paced her.

A surge of hope washed away the fatigue from her muscles. Had one of her teammates dropped back to run with her and encourage her? Judy, maybe?

But the wolf hung back in the trees, and her heart sank back into her cross-trainers.

Not a companion. What, then? A babysitter? Coach couldn't

possibly think she'd get lost. Unlike him, she'd grown up running these trails. Was this a test to see if she'd keep training on her own or wimp out and go home?

Chloe pretended not to notice the wolf and kept running, concentrating on keeping her stride easy and smooth. If this was a test, she'd pass it. If this was some kind of hazing, meant to scare her, then she'd endure that too and prove that she belonged to the Pack.

Because she did. She had all the extra werewolf strength and agility: her senses were keener than those of her townie classmates, and she'd had no difficulty qualifying for the high school track and field team. Her townie classmates simply couldn't compete physically with Pack. In human form she could outrun everyone but Dean. But her fifteenth, sixteenth, and seventeenth birthdays had passed, and she still had not Changed.

All the other teens in her age group had. Even Judy, the smallest and most nervous of them all, had Changed into her wolf form three full moons ago.

And when track and field started up again in September, Coach had wanted them to run in their wolf forms. Because while there were townie kids on the other sports teams, Coach Wharton had decreed a limited number of slots on the track and field team and filled them all with Pack. Practices were mostly just an excuse to spend time together. What they were actually learning from Conrad Wharton was how to control themselves as werewolves.

Chloe risked another glimpse at the wolf, trying to identify who it was by its colouring. Not all white like Coach. Not red like Judy. Other than that she couldn't tell. She got only flashes of white and grey and maybe brown between the tree trunks.

She ought to have known it wasn't Judy. Ever since her Change, Judy had started acting as if she were better than Chloe.

Judy's smugness and the veiled contempt in Coach

Wharton's eyes rubbed Chloe's ego raw. For most of her life Chloe had been the leader of the Pack teens, and now everyone was Dominant to her. Last week, Coach Wharton had told Dean that she might never Change because she was too afraid of the pain. Her! Who'd never so much as whimpered during one of Coach's brutal three-hour training runs.

And now that contempt had spread to the other kids like an infection. They closed their shoulders against her when she approached, as if she were a townie.

Tears burned in her eyes, blurring the trail. She accidentally stepped on a root and her ankle twisted beneath her. Pain shot up her leg. The bonfire raging inside demanded that she keep running through the pain, keep trying to catch them at the end of the shortcut, but her dad had lectured too many other Pack members about the stupidity of ignoring pain.

Chloe dropped onto a fallen log at the side of the trail and sucked down some of the water in her squeeze bottle. Her ankle would be fine in a moment. Werewolves healed fast—so fast it took something major to kill them—but she'd probably lost all chance of catching up with the Pack.

How could she have all the werewolf gifts and not have the ability to Change? It wasn't fair, but every generation there were a few Recessives, werewolves by heritage who were unable to Change. Also known as Duds.

Chloe's fists clenched. She was not a Dud. Glaring, she suddenly caught the blue eyes of a wolf staring out at her from behind a screen of underbrush.

Chloe shot to her feet, temper pumping through her. "Stop lurking. I know you're there. I'm not blind." Did her Packmates think they could scare her? *Puh-lease.* She'd grown up among werewolves.

The wolf faded back into the brush. Chloe nodded, satisfied, and sat back down.

But when she resumed her run, movement flashed in her peripheral vision. The idiot wolf had started tailing her again. *Fine, we can play it that way.* Chloe pretended not to notice, waiting until her sharp ears told her that her pursuer had ventured a little too close, then suddenly reversed direction and cut left into the trees.

A thick stand of young pine kept the wolf from retreating. It hunched its shoulders and growled. Chloe stopped in surprise. The wolf had a creamy chest and underbelly, black back and tail, blue eyes, and a distinctive black stripe bisecting its forehead. Who was it? None of the wolves in her Pack had colouring like this one.

The wolf couldn't be wild. Real wolves stayed far, far away from Pack territory, and this one was just standing there, staring at her head-on, unafraid. Unless the animal was sick? Chloe sniffed the air. Instead of the Pine Hollow Pack scent, the wolf smelled of wildness, musk and a hint of iron. No odour of disease. All the Pack kids got rabies shots as a matter of course, but Chloe's veterinarian dad had made sure she could recognize the signs of it, plus distemper and other canine ills. This wolf wasn't sick, so it had to be a werewolf.

Its pelt lacked the shine of a healthy wolf, and its ribs protruded. It was skinny and not full grown. Her nostrils flared. "That better not be you, Gail," she threatened. Judy's little sister was thirteen, a not unheard of age for the Change, but—

She stepped forward. The wolf snapped its teeth at her and broke left past her into the trees.

Instinct made her give chase, but she stopped after a few steps because—hello?—four legs were always going to be faster than two.

In frustration, she shouted after the werewolf: "I'm going to find out who you are and kick your butt!"

Sometimes having werewolf parents sucked.

Not because they were bad parents, but because they were

supernaturally good at knowing when she was upset and ferreting out the truth. Like now.

"Chloe, is something wrong? You've sighed three times in the last five minutes," her mom said.

Chloe stared down at her biology textbook and binder. She was in the kitchen. Her mom had been down in the basement doing laundry. A normal parent wouldn't have noticed Chloe's sighs, but, noooo, *hers* had to have super-hearing.

"Hmmm?" Chloe pretended to be absorbed in jotting down a note.

"Look at me." A note of warning sounded in her mom's voice as she asserted her Dominance.

Another thing that sucked about having werewolf parents: Chloe couldn't refuse the command of someone Dominant to her. She looked up.

"Now tell me what's wrong." Her mother was petite with pale skin, dark auburn hair tied back in a ponytail, and grey eyes, but her strength of will made her a force to be reckoned with.

Chloe shrugged, doing her best to downplay her answer without lying. Item three: lying to a Dominant was pointless; they could always tell. Fortunately, Chloe had a lot of practice at telling the truth while still omitting what she wanted to conceal. "Nothing new. Just the usual inability to Change." She was *not* going to complain to her mother about Coach being mean to her like some whiny child.

"Oh, honey." Her mother's expression softened, and she stooped to give Chloe a quick hug. "Be patient. It will come. I've been doing some research, and I've found some cases similar to yours. Come see."

Her mom beckoned her into the living room, where she pulled down a large 150-year-old book bound in red leather. As Pack historian, her mom kept the only copy of the Pack Lore.

Her mom paged past what Chloe thought of as the "fairy tale" part of the book, which was full of slightly twisted Slavic folktales, involving wolves and characters like Baba Yaga and Koschei the Deathless. The rest of the book was full of hand-written diary entries, records of genealogy and the occasional recipe.

"Here." Her mother tapped a line. Chloe squinted at the black squiggle until her mom took pity on her and read it out: "1944 —Ivan Andrews Changed for the first time, age 18."

Okay, that was a little encouraging. Except for the death entry that came immediately after: "Died in battle."

"And there's another one." Her mom turned to a second sticky note in an older section of the book. The handwriting here was in a different hand, but easier to read.

"1884—Andrei Peterov bathed in the light of the full moon and Changed, age 21," Chloe read aloud.

"What's this?" Chloe's dad strolled into the room. His grey sweatshirt and jeans hung on his lanky frame. He looked like the science geek that he was. Chloe might resemble him—they had the same brown eyes and wavy dark hair that became unmanageable if not cut short—but she was more social like her mother.

"Apparently, I can't Change because I haven't bathed in the moonlight," Chloe said ironically. After three years of trying, she was pretty sure she'd hit every phase of the moon.

Her mom swatted her shoulder. "I was just showing Chloe that she's not the first Pack member that didn't Change until they were her age or older."

Her dad peered down at the diary. "Sheer superstition. Look at the next entry: 'Mary Kosti wasted away from a witch's curse. Died, age 72.' At that age, werewolf good health starts to wear off. She probably had cancer. There's always a scientific explanation."

Her mom rolled her eyes. "Says the man who can Change into a wolf."

"Adaptive colouration—" her dad started.

Chloe had heard the arguments before. Time to change the

subject. She had a question for him anyway. "Dad, are there any werewolves visiting from other Packs right now?" Maybe that might explain the identity of the wolf who'd shadowed her in the forest.

Packs were territorial, and the handful that lived in Canada were widely scattered. Visitors weren't unheard of, but there was always an announcement because sniffing around a strange Pack uninvited was a good way to get your neck snapped. If not for the need to keep the Packs from getting too inbred, they would probably avoid each other entirely. Even then, mingling usually took place in neutral territory.

Chloe's dad was originally from the Churchill, Manitoba Pack. He'd met Chloe's mom at university. After they married, Chloe's dad had moved to Alberta and joined her mom's Pack. He'd been welcome because of his profession, but it was hard to switch Packs. A lot of times the couple would split apart after a few years and each return to his or her birth Pack, leaving one parent to raise the child. That was the case with both Dean and Brian's families.

"No one's visiting. Why?" He pushed up his glasses.

Maybe she shouldn't have brought it up. The werewolf had been a juvenile. If they weren't a visitor, then the werewolf was probably a runaway; Chloe didn't want to get a kid in trouble. "Oh, I thought I saw a strange wolf this afternoon. I was probably just mistaken." She tried to sound as if she'd merely glimpsed the wolf in the distance.

Anyone else in the Pack would have dropped it then, dismissing the word of a Dud. Her dad frowned, taking the matter seriously. "I'll phone around and find out if any alerts for ferals have been issued. I don't think they ever found Paul Riebel."

A feral. Huh. Chloe hadn't considered that possibility. She remembered hearing about Paul Riebel. The Thunder Bay, Ontario werewolf's brand-new car had been rear-ended and he'd gone berserk, Changing and killing the other driver. He'd run off into the woods afterward and gone feral. Real wolves were shy of humans and their guns. Feral werewolves, who'd rejected their humanity and stayed wolf for too long, were dangerous.

"It wasn't him." In the pictures Paul Riebel had been a big man and so had his wolf. Moreover, his wolf had a solid black pelt. The strange wolf might be a feral, but it wasn't Paul Riebel.

Mystery unsolved.

The wolf prowled around the snug house that the dark-haired girl had disappeared inside hours before.

Unnatural light spilled from the windows. He kept to the shadows. An anxious whine rose in his throat. Humans were stinky. Loud. Dangerous. He shouldn't have followed the girl. He shouldn't still be lingering here, but every time he started to lope away, something drew him back.

Slowly, it occurred to him that maybe he'd found what he was looking for. He'd been travelling for so long that he'd forgotten the reason behind his journey.

The days had blended into an endless grey Now, where he thought only about the weather, hunting prey, and shelter. Half-remembered instinct had kept him travelling south and slightly west. Skirting around towns.

Until the girl's scent had drifted across his path. She was what he'd been hunting for—if only he could remember why.

CHAPTER

2

Chloe's shoulders tensed as she walked the gauntlet into school. Three Pack boys leaned against the wall near the entrance and watched her with hooded eyes as if she were prey.

Kyle started it. "Dud," he coughed into his fist.

Brian echoed him. Cough: "Dud."

Chloe didn't blush, but she did burn inside with humiliation.

Dean stood closest to the door. He didn't bother coughing. He jostled her arm as he strolled past. "Hey look, it's Chloe the Dud."

Other kids milled around. Townies, not Pack. But in that moment Chloe didn't care. Red hazed her vision. She shrugged out of her backpack, turned and took a running leap onto Dean's back.

A normal boy would have been driven to his knees by the sudden attack. Dean staggered, but quickly recovered. "Get off!"

Chloe clung like a monkey while he spun in circles, shoving at her legs. She grabbed his ear and twisted hard. "Not until you take it back. I'm. Not. A. Dud." With each word she twisted harder.

He grabbed at her hands, growling. A twinge of worry shot up her spine, but they were at school. He couldn't Change to werewolf form. Her chest lightened with triumph. She should have done this months ago—

"Chloe Graham!" Rough hands yanked her off Dean's back and dumped her on the ground. Ow. Coach towered over her, his expression as dark as a thundercloud. A blond, muscular man in his mid-twenties, Conrad Wharton had a very fair complexion. When he got angry, as he was now, red crept up his hairline, making his blond eyebrows stand out as if highlighted. His nostrils flared. "Thirty push-ups! Now!" he bellowed. "Everyone else inside. This doesn't concern you."

Her euphoria fading, Chloe started rapping off push-ups, touching her nose to the concrete.

Coach crouched near her, his voice for her ears alone. "You forget where you are. This isn't elementary school."

She should take the rebuke in silence. She knew it, but— "They started it. I just finished it."

He flattened his hand between her shoulder blades, holding her down so that her arms ached with the strain. "You pushed one of your Packmates to the edge of control, and for what? Calling you a name that you know is true?"

Her throat constricted, making it hard to speak. "I'm not a Dud."

"I'll believe it when I see it." Coach straightened. He waited, muscular arms crossed, for her to finish her push-ups, even after the first bell rang.

Her arms were trembling by the time she reached thirty, but pride wouldn't let her collapse. She stood. "May I be excused?"

He nodded.

She snatched up her backpack and walked stiffly inside. She ignored the townies' stares with ease, but the Pack kids' glares ate at her. Bile flooded her stomach. Instead of the respect she'd wanted, cold contempt shone in their eyes.

"You're still a Dud," Judy said, then deliberately turned her back on Chloe.

Chloe wanted to grab her shoulder and make Judy turn around, but she gritted her teeth and turned away. Instead of putting her backpack into the locker beside Judy's, Chloe pushed through the wooden doors into the Girl's washroom.

She had the place to herself.

She hammered one of the metal stall doors with the heel of her hand. It made a satisfyingly loud noise, rattling on its hinges, so she hit it again.

And dented it.

This wasn't helping. She took deep breaths and leaned her forehead against the cool metal, trying to calm down.

She wasn't mad at Judy—okay, that was a lie, but she wasn't *only* mad at Judy—she was mad at herself.

Stupid, stupid, stupid. Once again her instincts had steered her wrong. She might not be a Recessive, but until she Changed, Pack Law slotted her at the bottom of the pecking order. She needed to get used to it.

Easier said than done.

New goal: get through the rest of the day without losing her temper. Prove that she was tough-skinned enough to be part of the Pack.

The door opened, and one of the townie girls came in. Ilona Novaskaya. She fluffed her hair at one of the mirrors.

Chloe moved away from the stall, hoping Ilona wouldn't notice the dent, and began to splash cold water on her hot face.

Ilona shot her a sidelong glance. "So why do they call you a dud?"

Chloe did not want to explain herself to the skinny, blonde girl. She lied. "I messed up at track and field practice yesterday. They're just being jerks."

"A teenage boy's one true skill," Ilona deadpanned.

Chloe smirked back, then busied herself getting some paper towels to dry her face. Ilona was all right, but she wasn't Pack. They could never truly be friends.

And the Pack kids would scorn Chloe even more if she started hanging around with a townie. She picked up her backpack and left the washroom.

Ilona didn't take the hint. She followed, keeping pace with

Chloe in the hallway. "Speaking of boys ... what do you think of Dean?"

"Besides that he's a jerk?"

"So jumping on his back isn't some kind of strange rural dating ritual?"

Chloe barked out a laugh. "No!"

"Rumour has it you two used to go out." Ilona leaned forward, grey-blue eyes intent.

"Nah," Chloe said. One make-out session behind the gym didn't count.

Ilona sighed. "He may be a bit of a jerk, but he's hot." The words sounded funny in Ilona's Russian accent.

Once upon a time, Chloe would have agreed. Dean was tall and muscular, with a devilish grin that had made her heart thump. She scowled, remembering her stupid dreams of marrying Dean and being the next Alpha pair. Last year Dean had thought she was pretty cool, too.

Ilona persisted. "Are you sure you don't like him?"

"I wouldn't take Dean Stravinsky served on a plate," Chloe said flatly. And wasn't that going to surprise him when she did Change? She pictured him groveling, begging her to go out with him. But he was dead to her now. Kyle and Brian, too. Not that Kyle, who was a year younger than Chloe, had ever really been in the running. She'd never date anyone who'd sneered at her and called her a Dud.

Maybe she'd meet someone at university like her parents had.

Thinking about university aggravated her anxiety. She'd been looking forward to campus life—taking courses that she chose, partying, being independent—but she'd always planned to return to Pine Hollow. If she was a Recessive, she'd be kicked out of the Pack after high school graduation. Forced to leave home, leave the Preserve, and live a mandated distance away from all werewolf packs, probably in some crowded city full of bad smells and strangers.

No. Not going to happen. Chloe fought to control the hitch in her breathing as she and Ilona entered the classroom. Chloe grabbed a seat in the middle, and Ilona sat adjacent to her.

"Well, if you're not into Dean, maybe I'll let him catch me," Ilona said.

Dean and a townie? Chloe's eyebrows shot up. She supposed Ilona was pretty, but she wasn't Pack, and she reeked of horses. Ilona's mom raised horses and peddled crystals and New Age kitsch.

Horses hated werewolves. The scent drove them mad. Her dad had to douse himself in cologne whenever he got a call to tend a sick horse. Cows and sheep were too dumb to understand the danger; pigs were smart enough to know her dad wasn't actually a wolf. Dogs could be dominated, and cats bribed, but horses weren't fooled, and their hooves could shatter bones.

A horse kicking Dean in the ribs. Oooh, up side. "Go for it," Chloe said. "But, fair warning, his dad hates townies."

Ilona frowned. "I live on a ranch, not in town."

"Doesn't matter. Anyone who doesn't live in the Preserve is a townie to Dean's dad." Ilona had only lived in town for a year or she would have known all the unwritten rules. Dating townies, non-Pack, wasn't forbidden, but the Alphas discouraged it. Some parents were more hard-line about it than others. For Chloe, it was a moot point. Boys who weren't werewolves always looked soft to her.

"What does he have against townies? Is it because of the logging deal?" Ilona asked.

"There is no deal," Chloe said sharply. "The Preserve is private property. They can't log it without our permission. The end." Her voice attracted attention and glares from the other townies—all seven of them, with the exception of one First Nations girl who refused to take sides.

The town of Pine Hollow was dwindling, its population falling below five hundred people, which was why the townies were so desperate for an infusion of jobs and money. Chloe sympathized, she did, but it wasn't going to happen.

She wasn't even against logging in general. If harvested and replanted properly, trees were a renewable resource. She just didn't want it to happen here, in their Preserve. Especially not clear-cutting, which was what was being proposed.

"Really?" Ilona asked. "I thought that was just a negotiating position. Judy's folks would really let the town die?"

Grrr. Chloe tried one more time to explain. "A logging deal won't save the town. Everyone talks as if opening the Preserve to logging will guarantee a sawmill getting built, but Pine Hollow is only one possible location that Diversified Forest Products is considering for the site. They're probably going to pick Delpin. It's bigger and more centrally located."

"Yeah, well we have no chance at all, thanks to you tree-hugging hippie freaks and your private commune," a townie boy said.

"Butt out." Chloe gave him a flat stare. He dropped his gaze and pretended an interest in his notebook.

"So are you hippies living on a commune?" Ilona asked. "You don't dress like it."

Pine Hollow had always had trouble classifying the Pack. Hippie commune was just one of the rumours swirling around. They'd also been accused of being a religious sect and of being witches who held orgies. The type of rumour changed with the decades, but being half-resented outsiders stayed the same.

Chloe shrugged. "You could call us conservationists if you want." That was what her dad said when hunters asked permission to go on their land. "But the bottom line is the Preserve belongs to us, and nobody but nobody is taking it away."

"Still," Ilona said, "it's going to suck for you guys, too, if the town doesn't survive."

The Pack would still be here long after Pine Hollow withered up and blew away. They'd owned this land since the werewolves first left Europe and came over to North America. (The Lore said they'd fled from famine caused by witches; her dad insisted over-crowding and deforestation was the true reason.) They'd gone West during the time of the fur traders, hoping for a place to settle, but found it already occupied. The Pack had bargained with the Dunne-za, a First Nations people, and with some sasquatches living nearby, then later filed for a government deed. The Pack owned the land jointly with Lady Sasquatch.

Chloe shrugged. "Yes, losing the town will suck. But we'll deal." Her dad would have to move his vet practice to Delpin and commute. The Pack kids would either have to bus in or be homeschooled. The Pine Hollow school population was already so small that grades eleven and twelve were in a split class and shared the same classroom. Even that meant a class of only twelve. Second bell rang. Dean, Brian, and Judy sauntered in, laughing. Although they looked nothing alike—Dean was pale and freckled and wore his russet hair in a crew-cut, while Brian, who was half-Chinese, had stylishly messy ink-black hair that flopped over his eyes—the boys were both over six feet with wide shoulders and had the same Pack swagger. They towered over tiny five-foot-two Judy, who looked pixie-cute in tight jeans and a purple tee, her light brown hair up in a ponytail.

Chloe tensed, but they ignored her, sitting together in a cluster beside Kyle.

Being ignored stung worse than being heckled. Chloe had to bite her lip to keep from saying something, anything, to make them notice her.

Last year, she would have been part of the group. Last year, she, Judy, and Abby would have sat together, and Chloe would've been the leader, the one planning movie marathons and skating parties. This year, Judy was queen, Chloe was a Dud, and Abby was dead.

Grief for her dead best friend rose in her throat and burned in the backs of her eyes. Chloe swallowed it down.

Their homeroom teacher, Mr. Presley, walked in. He took one look at the hostile atmosphere and sighed. He'd long since stopped trying to separate the grade eleven students from the grade twelve students and let Pack sit with Pack.

He'd just started taking attendance when a knock came at the door. The principal poked her grey-haired head in. "Sorry to interrupt, but I need to speak to Judy."

"Of course," Mr. Presley said.

Judy's face went milk-pale. She stood up, almost stumbling in her haste to reach the door. A surprising surge of protectiveness hit Chloe, an impulse to get up and provide support.

"What is it? Is my mom okay?" Judy asked, voice tight.

The closing door cut off most of the principal's answer, but the word 'hospital' floated in.

The Pack kids exchanged grim looks, briefly united with worry over this new crisis.

"What's going on?" Ilona whispered.

"Judy's mom is sick. Cancer," Chloe said briefly. Until they reached old age, werewolves were amazingly healthy. Alphas, especially, almost never got so much as a sniffle, much less a serious disease. But a year ago Judy's mom had been diagnosed with breast cancer. She'd had chemotherapy and a lumpectomy. Everyone had believed she was better and her natural healing powers had returned, but at her sixth-month checkup the doctor discovered that the cancer had spread to her stomach.

And now she might be in the hospital.

The wrongness of an Alpha being ill raised Chloe's hackles. The Alpha was strong. Had to be strong—or she wasn't the Alpha.

Judy didn't return to class, and when Chloe got home her mom's first words were: "If you have homework, get it done right away.

We're going to have a light supper—soup and sandwiches—then go to the Alphas' house." Her mom wielded a potato peeler with quick, deft strokes.

"No homework." Because she'd done it during her lonely noon hour. Chloe let her backpack slide to the floor. "I thought Judy's mom was in the hospital." Pine Hollow was too small for a hospital; patients had to travel a hundred kilometres to Delpin.

Her mom shook her head. "They sent her home."

"So she's better?" Chloe's heart lightened.

"No." Her mom grimaced. "The opposite. There's nothing more that can be done for her at the hospital." She paused and picked up a second potato. "They sent her home to die."

Chloe let out a small grunt, feeling as if she'd been kicked in the stomach. *Poor Judy.* "Die? I didn't know the cancer was that bad." She'd assumed werewolf health plus the extra strength of an Alpha would fight off the disease.

Her mom sighed. "No one knew it was this bad. The Alphas kept it from us."

Alphas weren't always married or even from the same generation, but Judy's parents, Olivia and Nathan Frayne, were the Pine Hollow Pack's male and female Alphas.

Chloe scowled. "That was dumb. They should've told us."

Her mom shrugged and began peeling the second potato. "Alphas can be … touchy about appearing weak. They probably didn't want to deal with Dominance issues on top of stress from the illness."

Chloe rubbed her chin, then shook her head. "Dominance issues from whom? I mean, that's the whole problem, isn't it? We don't have a female Beta right now." Because Abby's mom, Karen Jennings, had been the Beta, and she, along with her husband and two children, had died in a small plane crash last year. "And if the Alpha dies—" Her throat closed. She swallowed, tried again. "There's no one to step in, and Judy's dad will be grieving. The Pack will be weakened, which could make us prey to other Packs."

"You've been reading too much Pack lore," her mother said firmly. "Modern Packs aren't nearly as bloodthirsty, nor are they as vulnerable to drought and famine—things that used to force Packs to search for a new home. The Preserve may be on a coveted bit of land, but no one wants a war these days. We don't want to attract attention from humans." Then, without changing tone, "Can you grate some Swiss cheese for me? I'm making ham and potato casserole for the Fraynes."

Chloe got out the cheese and the grater. Was her mom right or was she just trying to paint things in a better light so as not to worry Chloe? "But we'd still be better off if we had a Beta ready to step in."

"Well, yes," her mother admitted. She started slicing the raw potatoes into a pot of boiling water. "The Pack is small enough that filling the spot didn't seem important. Which is going to bite us in the butt now."

Uncertainly, Chloe stopped grating and studied her mom. "Are you—?"

"Heavens, no," her mom said with a short laugh. "Your Aunt Laurie is Dominant to me. But even if she wasn't, I wouldn't want the job."

But who else was there? As a single mom, Aunt Laurie had her hands full taking care of the twins. Plus, she was in a long-distance relationship with a woman from another Pack and was considering moving to Ontario. Aunt Laurie would shun the responsibility. Dean and Kyle's mom had divorced their dad two years ago and moved to another Pack. Brian's mom was, bluntly, a ditz. Dean's sister, Heather, was twenty-one. Could they bring her home from college? Chloe tried to remember if Heather was particularly Dominant and couldn't recall, which probably meant she wasn't.

"Anyhow, we shouldn't be talking about this. Nathan has forbidden any speculation over who will succeed Olivia. It's disrespectful. The Alpha isn't dead yet."

So why are we bringing over a casserole like we do at funerals? Chloe didn't ask, dropping the subject. It's not like she wanted the Alpha to die—she liked Judy's mom. Still, it seemed stupid not to prepare.

They were the last to arrive. Vehicles choked the Fraynes' backyard and driveway, and werewolves crowded the house.

Chloe's mom put her hand on Chloe's shoulder, holding her back for a moment by the car. "Be kind to Judy tonight."

"I doubt Judy wants to talk to me."

Her mother sighed. "I know you and Judy have had a few ups and downs since Abby's death, but you've been friends forever, and she needs someone."

Abby's death hadn't driven the wedge into their friendship; Judy lording her ability to Change over Chloe and then calling her a Dud had done it. Though Chloe supposed if Abby were here she might have made Judy apologize.

Chloe made no promises.

Her mom patted Chloe's shoulder, then handed her a still-warm casserole dish. Balancing two plastic-wrapped plates of crackers, cheese, and homemade moose sausage, she led the way into the house to the kitchen where she joined the other women. Chloe's dad seated himself between Dean's dad, Rick, and Coach Wharton in the living room where a football game played with the sound turned low.

After putting the casserole into the already stuffed freezer, Chloe automatically tramped down to the basement where the kids always hung out. At the bottom of the stairs her steps slowed and trepidation expanded in her stomach. It might be easier to keep her temper if she stuck with the adults … But, no. She refused to let them run her off.

Still, she avoided Dean, Kyle, and Brian, who were pigging out on chips and snickering over YouTube videos on Brian's phone.

Aunt Laurie's twins and Brian's younger half-siblings were pestering Gail to let them have turns on the Xbox. Gail ignored them, grimly shooting aliens. She had earphones on and a dead expression on her face. There was nothing Chloe could say that would make Gail's mother better so she patted Gail's shoulder then took charge of the rugrats, organizing a game of hide-and-seek.

At first she was relieved that Judy wasn't downstairs, but after forty-five minutes, Chloe gave in and asked Gail where her sister was.

"Dunno." A shrug. "Probably still shut up in her room."

Crying by herself?

Pity stirred. Chloe looked around. Was there anybody else she could send to comfort Judy? But the boys were useless at that sort of thing, and Abby was dead. It was Chloe or nobody.

Sighing, she trudged up the stairs. Her last hope, that Judy had joined the adults in the kitchen, proved false.

She knocked on Judy's door. After a series of polite taps and no answer, she slipped inside the darkened room and leaned against the door.

Judy huddled on the bed, clutching a teddy bear. Tears made faintly luminous tracks down her face. "Go away." Her voice was raw.

Chloe didn't move. She forgot about the spiteful cat Judy had been lately and remembered the tag-along little girl she and Abby had played with on the swings. How many sleepovers had the three of them had? How many bowls of popcorn consumed, how many movies watched, how many secrets shared?

She cleared her throat. "I'm really sorry about your mom."

Judy's head lifted, and she glared at Chloe. "She's not dead yet. Everyone keeps acting like she is, but she isn't. She's not going to die today. If she dies, *then* you can tell me how sorry you are."

There was so much pain in Judy's voice that Chloe couldn't take offense. "Okay. I'm really sorry that she's sick," Chloe said softly. She sat on the edge of the bed. "Is that Abby's bear?"

Judy nodded.

"Poor old Hyde." Chloe stroked his plush head. "I'm glad he didn't get thrown out."

"Mom and I cleaned the Jennings' house ... after," Judy said in a small voice. "She said I could keep a few things. Most of it went to charity or straight to the trash."

The topic was kind of morbid, but so was the deathwatch being held. At least Judy was talking.

"So what happened to Jckyll?"

Judy pointed at the bureau.

Chloe opened the cabinet doors and took out the smaller teddy bear. While Hyde had dark brown fur, Jekyll's fur was white. A top hat was glued to his head at a jaunty angle, and he wore a red silk waistcoat. A watery chuckle escaped Chloe. "I'd forgotten about the monocle."

Abby had gone to great lengths to create the gold monocle and attach it to the bear with a ribbon. She'd also sewn the waistcoat herself when the original one tore. "She was really talented, wasn't she?" Chloe asked wistfully.

Judy nodded.

"I miss her so much," Chloe confessed, her grip tightening on the bear.

"Me, too," Judy whispered. It was the first time they'd agreed on anything in months.

The moment hung there, delicate as a snowflake. Chloe opened her mouth to say how much it sucked that Abby was dead and that Judy's mom had cancer, but before she could get the words past the lump in her throat, a knock sounded on the door.

Judy stiffened. "Go away."

Judy's dad, Nathan, poked his head in and flipped on the light, leaving them blinking. "She's asking for you." The Alpha wore his usual red plaid shirt and jeans, but his hair and beard were shaggier than usual. Maybe his wife was usually the one to nag him into getting a haircut. He exuded weariness like a cologne.

Judy put Hyde aside and stood up, her triangular face tight with anxiety.

"No," Nathan said, his voice a low rumble. "She's asking for Chloe."

A jolt went through Chloe, an instant spike of guilt. Had she done something wrong? Was the Alpha angry at her for letting Judy down? Had her dad told the Alpha about the feral?

"Uh, okay," Chloe said. One didn't refuse the Alpha. Especially not on her deathbed.

"I'm coming, too," Judy said. Her jaw set in stubborn lines.

Her father shrugged. "If you want." He paused, one hand on the doorknob. "She's tired. She needs ease."

Chloe nodded. "We won't stay long."

He shook his head. "Not what I meant. She's tired of this. Of the cancer."

Of living? Chloe's stomach rolled over.

"Set her mind at ease." His eyes met hers, asserting Dominance until she nodded and respectfully dropped her gaze. Before she could ask him what he meant, he left the room.

Chloe started to follow him, but Judy shoved her way in between. Right. Judy was Dominant to her now. Chloe didn't think she'd ever get used to that.

An old-fashioned wedding-ring quilt covered the Alphas' bed. Olivia reclined against a pile of cheery yellow pillows as if holding court. Chloe breathed a sigh of relief. At first glance, Olivia didn't seem to be at death's door, but the pink on her cheeks was rouge. She wore a black wig, her hair having fallen out during chemo.

Chloe bowed her head.

"Come sit on the bed," the Alpha said, patting the mattress.

Judy sat on one side and Chloe on the other. Judy fussed with the quilt. "Are you warm enough, Mom? I can get another blanket."

Olivia made a tiny gesture, waving her off. "I'm fine." Her hazel eyes had a glassy sheen to them. She'd probably been given drugs to dull the pain.

This close, the scent of cancer—repulsively sweet and fruity—was overpowering. Chloe breathed in very carefully through her mouth. How did Judy and her dad stand it?

And she'd thought Ilona's horse scent was strong.

"Chloe." The Alpha took her hand. Her skin felt cold, her grip weak. "This is very important: have you Changed yet? Even a partial Change?"

Chloe hesitated. Under normal circumstances it would be impossible to lie to an Alpha, but Nathan had all but commanded her to lie. Perhaps because of the drugs, Chloe met Olivia's gaze easily. "I'm getting closer," she said.

Instead of looking eased, a different emotion flashed across the Alpha's face. Disappointment? Frustration? But that didn't make any sense. Surely Olivia couldn't want Chloe to be a Recessive? Chloe must be mistaken. Olivia had probably just grimaced in pain.

Judy snorted. "Oh, really? If you're close, how come I didn't so much as see a claw tip when we practiced yesterday?"

Blood rushed to Chloe's cheeks.

The Alpha patted her hand, but seemed distracted. "You mustn't give up hope, Chloe. But a Dud can't … There really is no one … " Her voice drifted off, her gaze unfocused.

Chloe stiffened and pulled her hand away. Her chest burned. She wanted to shout, "I'm not a Dud!" But underneath the anger lay cold fear. If the *Alpha* thought she was a Dud, maybe it was true.

Chloe shot to her feet. "Can I go now?"

"Yes, of course." Olivia continued mumbling to herself, as if unaware the rest of them could hear her. "There's no one else. It has to be me. It's the right choice … "

Gut clenching, Chloe stumbled to the door, glad to leave the Alpha and the smell of death behind.

CHAPTER

3

"Everybody out."

Nathan's brusque order startled everyone in the kitchen. Chloe froze in the act of making a cracker, cheese, and sausage sandwich. After her visit with the Alpha, she hadn't had the heart to go back downstairs and play with the younger kids.

"The Alpha's too tired for company. Go home." Nathan underlined the order with a hostile glare and a baring of teeth.

As one, the Pack dropped their gazes and quietly left, though Chloe's parents exchanged puzzled glances. Not everyone was given a chance to say goodbye to Olivia.

In the driveway everyone milled around for a moment, some of the woman exchanging hugs.

Coach Wharton jogged over to where Kyle, Dean and Brian stood. "Early practice tomorrow, you three."

The boys groaned. "But it's Saturday," Brian said, unwisely.

"I expect to see you at the trailhead by six on the dot." Coach was an inch shorter than Dean, but his body was built like a tank. His wide shoulders shut Chloe out of the conversation. Was that on purpose or had he just not seen her?

"You guys are wusses," she said cheerfully. "Morning runs are the best."

Coach barely glanced at her. "We'll be running in wolf form. Stay home and get your beauty sleep."

Brian smirked. "Yeah, Chloe."

In her pocket, Chloe balled her hand into a fist, but she kept her tone respectful. "Then I'll run on my own. I'm still on the team."

Now Coach looked directly at her, his green-eyed stare Dominating. "Maybe it's time you quit."

Chloe took a step back, as if he'd slapped her. "No." Her voice sounded hoarse. He couldn't cut her.

"If you want to stay on the team" —and by team he obviously meant Pack—"then I expect to see serious effort from you. No more whining."

Whining? She never whined. Chloe's upper lip lifted from her teeth in an unconscious snarl.

"I need to see some guts," Coach said harshly. "Show me you want to be one of us. If you aren't in wolf form, don't bother coming out tomorrow." He strode off, leaving Chloe reeling.

Dean, Brian and Kyle stared at her. Kyle's mouth hung open as if he couldn't believe what Coach had said either.

"See you *Monday*," Dean emphasized. He put his hand on Kyle's shoulder and steered his little brother toward their pickup truck.

Stone-faced, Chloe rejoined her parents. Her dad was giving Aunt Laurie advice on what to feed her elderly cat, but her mom gave an exaggerated shiver and climbed into the van. Chloe gratefully followed.

"What was that about?" her mom asked.

"What was what about?" Chloe stalled.

"Chloe." Her mom turned in the seat and gave her the Dominant stare. "I can tell you're upset. Did one of the boys say something?"

Chloe slouched down. "Coach said not to bother coming to practice tomorrow unless I'm in wolf form. He all but said the reason I can't Change is because I'm a coward." Her throat hurt.

"Oh, did he?" her mother said in sudden cold fury.

"What's that?" her dad asked, clambering into the driver's seat.

"Conrad Wharton, in his infinite wisdom and experience, thinks Chloe's delay in Changing is due to cowardice," her mother said. From her deadly tone, she and Coach Wharton would be having a little chat soon. Chloe's mom might Change into a small brown wolf that Coach's white wolf outweighed by at least a hundred pounds, and he might rank fourth in Pack hierarchy, but Chloe would bet on her mom. Hell had no fury like a Mama wolf protecting a pup.

Except Chloe wasn't a pup any more. She prickled with embarrassment.

Before she could object, her dad snorted. "Our Chloe, a coward?" He ruffled her hair, before starting the engine. "If anything, she has the opposite problem. She's not scared enough."

Warmth kindled in Chloe's chest. She'd been getting more and more anxious about the Change as the months dragged on, but she'd never been afraid of Changing itself. Something deep inside her relaxed.

At midnight Chloe slipped out the door.

She'd spent all evening poking at her problem. If she took it as a given that she *wasn't* a coward, then maybe what she needed to spur the Change was to connect with her wolf nature. What better way than a run outdoors in the moonlight?

And what better time than tonight? Then she could show up to Saturday practice in wolf form and make everyone eat their words.

She inhaled the crisp autumn air and began at a slow jog to allow her night vision time to adjust. Even though the darkness held no danger—werewolf scent kept away all big predators, she had a cell phone in her pocket, and she could heal any accidental injuries—something about being abroad at night made her blood pump a little faster. Her already acute senses sharpened. An owl hooted. Branches rubbed together. The fresh pine scent of needles blended with the richer loam of the forest floor.

Just to make things perfect, the white orb of the moon shone through the treetops. Her dad insisted it was nonsense, but Pack Lore was full of stories of werewolves Changing for the first time beneath the full moon.

Maybe tonight it would be her turn.

Jittering with excitement, Chloe increased her pace. She followed a faint deer trail for a while then let her feet choose the route, weaving between the trees, trusting in her sense of direction.

Although she was at least a mile from where she'd encountered the wolf last time, Chloe had only jogged for about ten minutes before something rustled off to the side. A true wild wolf would have stayed far away. Put one more check in the werewolf column. Not wanting to spook the wolf, she kept her eyes forward and kept running.

Her strategy worked. The strange werewolf grew bolder and began to run beside her, only a few paces away, a companionable presence.

She tried to blank her mind, to run free, be wild, be a wolf ...

At first, joy and anticipation buoyed her up, but when she tried to Change—first coaxing, then willing with all her might— nothing happened. After ten minutes, disappointment crept in, and her pace slowed.

She would *not* cry.

To distract herself, Chloe sneaked glances at her companion from the corner of her eye, still trying to place the werewolf's bisected facial markings and failing. After a moment she did confirm that he was male. Definitely not Gail then. And the next oldest un-Changed Pack members after Gail were Chloe's eight-year-old twin cousins, a flat-out impossibility.

The werewolf must come from another Pack then. Runaway or feral? Since she hadn't been attacked, she was betting on runaway.

But just when she relaxed, the werewolf suddenly cut in front of her and barred the way, hackles raised, snarling. Feral behaviour.

Pulse slamming in her ears, Chloe slid to a stop. Her throat dried as she became acutely aware of how alone they were. She hadn't told anyone where she was going. No one would miss her until morning. She could phone for help, but it would take at least twenty minutes to get here.

Just because the werewolf wasn't the killer Paul Riebel didn't mean he wasn't dangerous.

If it was a wild wolf, she would assume he was protecting his young or a den and back away slowly, but that didn't apply to a feral.

Ferals had human cunning, coupled with the violent instincts of wolves. Looking at his sharp teeth, she began to understand why they were so feared, why all the Lore warned against them.

Running might trigger an attack, so she scanned the ground for a stout branch, a weapon. Anything to equal the odds. A fight between a wolf and an unarmed human could only end one way.

The feral stopped snarling. But as soon as she tried to move around him to the left, he blocked her, baring his canines.

Crap.

She didn't know exactly where they were, but she'd been looping back toward her house. The wolf stood between her and safety.

If only she could Change! Then she and the feral would be on equal footing. She could fight him or have a chance at out-running him.

A move to the right provoked another fierce snarl. The wolf's blue eyes met hers, trying to Dominate her. What was he planning? To eat her? Add her to his harem?

Screw that. "You're not Pack," she told him. "These woods

don't belong to you." She sidled left, keeping a wary eye on the feral, ready for attack.

There. A knobby branch lay on the ground. A little longer than was ideal, but the right thickness.

She scooped it up, then spun to face the feral. But instead of lunging at her with open jaws, he merely blocked the direction she needed to take.

Lips drawn back in determination, she charged him, holding the branch out in front of her like a spear.

He skipped back, avoiding the blow. She didn't pause, just kept running, angling in the direction she thought her house lay in. Her night vision was good, but not good enough to tell one group of trees from another.

She held the branch crosswise in front of her face, using it like a shield to keep from getting blinded by branches. Some whippier poplar boughs still got through and stung her forearm, but she gritted her teeth and kept running. Simultaneously, she dug the cell phone out of her pocket, though reception in the woods was spotty—

Behind her the werewolf howled.

Suddenly her feet dropped out from under her, pitching her into a fall. The cell phone flew from her grasp. She broke branches and collected bruises, as she slid, bounced, rolled, into a deep gully.

She hit the bottom with stunning impact. Her shinbone broke with an audible crack, and she lost all the air in her lungs. Rivers of fire streamed up Chloe's leg. She gasped, trying to get enough oxygen. Oh, God, oh, God …

Her face contorted, and she dug her fingernails into the dirt and evergreen needles. A wheezy scream escaped her.

For a long time she concentrated on breathing through the agony. *Red. Fire.* The pain didn't go away, but it did dull enough that she could think again. Her dad had often speculated that werewolves had a higher tolerance for pain than normal humans.

More branches broke, and the feral slid to a halt beside her, jaws parted to show his sharp teeth.

Chloe froze in place. Her pulse beat in her ears. She was completely vulnerable, crippled by her broken leg. And she'd lost the cell phone near the top of the ravine.

Instead of attacking, the feral whined. He crept forward, his belly hanging low on the path, as if trying to make himself smaller to show he was no threat.

Tears of pain ran down her face, but she kept her gaze on the wolf—on the danger. The moon peeked between the high branches, highlighting his bisected face, creamy throat and pale eyes.

"Well?" she rasped with false bravado. "What are you waiting for? You herded me here—" Except that wasn't true. The feral had tried to turn her off the path leading to the gully. "Oh. Sorry." She gritted her teeth against another surge of pain. "You were trying to warn me, weren't you? I didn't understand." Without thinking, she held out her hand.

The wolf inched closer and sniffed her fingers.

So he wasn't planning on eating her. That was good, but she was still in a jam. She tried to move her leg and inhaled sharply as fresh pain speared her.

Baring her teeth, she counted to one hundred, and the pain subsided once more.

She shivered, the chill night air biting deeper now that she'd stopped exercising. The sweat on her skin turned icy. Was she going into shock?

No. She was Pack, and werewolves were tough. She wasn't in any danger of dying. Still, she really wished she hadn't been holding the cell phone when she fell. She patted the ground in case it had rolled down the hill with her, but five minutes of careful search produced only some mushy leaves. The phone could be anywhere on the slope. She'd never find it without a massive infusion of luck.

"Just need a little time for the break to heal," Chloe said, talking to herself more than the werewolf. The sides of the gully looked dauntingly steep.

Her eyes widened. "I'm so screwed." Her leg would heal, but if she wasn't found soon it would heal crookedly.

Although her dad was a vet, he often dealt with broken limbs within the Pack, both saving his Packmates the 100 km trip to the nearest hospital and preventing the human doctors from noticing just how fast Pack healed. She vividly remembered a time Nathan had limped into their house on a leg that had broken and healed crooked during a hunting trip. When human bones healed wrong they could have surgery to correct it—the subject was put under with anesthesia, the orthopedic surgeon cut the bone with a saw and used steel pins and plates to hold it in place. Nathan hadn't wanted to risk revealing his super-healing to a regular doctor and her dad's veterinary practice wasn't equipped to use anesthesia on humans, so Nathan had ordered her dad to rebreak it with a maul.

The maul … Shudder. And breaking a healed bone was tricky, because the healed spot became stronger than the rest of the leg, and the bone could break in a second spot.

She appealed to the strange werewolf. "I need you to Change back to human and fetch my parents."

He whined, hunkered down beside her and licked her hand.

"Please? You don't have to show yourself, just howl at them or ring the doorbell. Wake them up so they realize I'm gone and start searching for me."

The wolf didn't move. He wasn't going to help.

Chloe swore. She made an imprudent movement, and a wave of pain rolled back over her. Greasy sweat popped up on her forehead, and she grew lightheaded.

She kept from screaming by force of will, counting in her head.

When she reached thirty she could talk again. "Okay, if you don't want to show yourself to my dad, why don't you transform into human and set my leg yourself?" As options went, it sucked. Setting bones wasn't for amateurs, and it would mean more pain for her and less chances of success, but it was still better than the maul.

The wolf whined and wouldn't meet her eyes.

Her temper surged like hot lava. "So who are you anyway? Are you a runaway? If something is really bad about your home Pack, we won't make you go back. But if it's something small ... well, think of this as your chance to go home a hero."

No response.

She shivered, which triggered another spike of pain. The wolf nestled closer to her, and she buried her cold hands in his fur.

At least she wasn't alone.

The wolf's presence was oddly comforting, curiously like Pack. His smell wasn't quite right—both wilder and muskier than Pack—but usually when Chloe met a werewolf who wasn't part of Pine Hollow, they smelled wrong. The feral didn't raise her hackles like those wolves had.

Once again, Chloe found herself ticking off Pack families, trying to come up with a name. She was quite familiar with Dean and Kyle's wolves. Dean's dad was too old. Could Dean's sister have brought home a werewolf boyfriend from college? But Chloe hadn't seen Heather at the deathwatch. The feral wasn't part of the Alphas' family. Not Brian or his two younger sibs. Not her aunt or cousins. Definitely not Coach Wharton, whose wolf was pure white.

She was missing someone … but who? She counted Pack families in her head. Aha. The number only seemed low because of the hole left by the death of the Jennings family—

Chills cruised down Chloe's spine. Her eyes widened, and she stopped petting the wolf. It couldn't be. Could it? The wolf had pale blue eyes, just like Abby, just like—"Marcus?" she whispered.

The wolf pushed his head into her hands, tongue lolling. His blue eyes asked why she'd stopped.

She cautiously sat up straighter, wincing at the stab of pain caused by the motion. "Marcus, is that you?"

He stiffened.

Chloe breathed through her mouth, trying to think.

Holy crap. Abby's brother, Marcus, was—or had been—ten months younger than Chloe. At the time of the plane crash he hadn't had his first Change yet. This could be Marcus. If he'd somehow survived the crash.

Werewolves could heal almost anything, but they burned a lot of energy doing it. The Jennings' plane had gone down for unknown reasons in the Northwest Territories, almost 1000 km from Pine Hollow, over a year ago. Chloe supposed a wolf could have travelled all that distance, but why do it as a wolf instead of Changing into human form and using the telephone? Her dad would have hopped a plane in a flash and brought him home.

The answer came at once: *because he can't Change.*

"Oh, no, no, no…" she breathed. All Pack kids were warned, over and over, of the dangers of remaining in wolf form for days on end. Stay too long and the werewolf went feral. Wild. Dangerous.

Tears pricked her eyes. "Marcus? Is it really you?"

Another whine. She resumed petting him. Soon, the cream and black wolf was snuggled up against her side. Chloe kept stroking his head, near tears, as she thought of how far he'd come, of what he'd been through.

She hated to ask, but she had to know. "Did anyone else survive?" *Abby* ...

The wolf whined. The pain in his blue eyes was far too human.

On to the next obvious question. "Can you Change back? Try, Marcus," she urged, holding his head between her hands. He couldn't have gone fully feral, not if he allowed her to get this close.

The wolf closed his eyes and hunched his shoulders. She held her breath, but nothing happened. Just like nothing happened every time she tried to Change to a wolf. She laughed bitterly. "Well, aren't we a pair?"

The wolf whined. She'd called him Marcus, and the name felt both terribly right and terribly wrong. Marcus was the name that had belonged to him before, but he was a wolf now, not a boy. The boy was gone forever, lost.

Part of him wanted to do as she asked and Change back into a two-legged human. She was injured, and it hurt something deep inside him to see her in pain. He would have run to the moon and back for her. But this he could not do.

A shudder ran through him. Become a boy again: a creature with soft, vulnerable skin, no fur to keep warm at night, and useless, too-blunt teeth? No.

The wolf was better, stronger, than the boy.

And he needed to be strong, because he now remembered why he'd crossed hundreds of miles to come back home.

There was something Evil here in the heart of his former Pack's territory, something that had killed his family. Something he needed to protect the girl from.

CHAPTER

4

How the heck was she going to get out of here?

The walls of the gully were too steep. Even completely healthy it would take a bit of a scramble to get out. With a broken leg? Not happening. Which meant waiting until her leg healed crookedly or hoping to find a gentler bank.

Even with better than human night vision, she couldn't see more than five feet ahead of her. She squinted. Okay, the ground sloped slightly uphill in that direction.

Sitting up, she leaned back on her arms, then used her arms and her good leg to lift her bum and ease backward a foot. Her breath hissed in as her broken leg dragged on the ground.

The wolf whined at her distress, as if wanting to help her. Unfortunately, she didn't have the materials to make a travois.

"You want to make yourself useful?" she asked him, hitching herself a second time. Ouch, that hurt. "Scout me a way out of here."

She wasn't sure if he understood, but he trotted up the gully and disappeared in the dark.

With her cell phone gone, she had no way of telling the time, and she began to regret speaking so harshly—she hadn't meant to drive the wolf away—before the shine of animal eyes in the dark announced Marcus's return.

Monstrous relief swamped her chest, making it impossible to speak for a few moments. She blinked back tears. He'd come back. She wasn't alone.

The wolf nosed her chest. She hugged him, then said briskly, "So did you find a way out of this hole?"

He whined, took a few steps down the ravine, then returned for her.

"I'll take that as a yes." She started hitching along again.

After another timeless period, the wolf jumped onto a sort of ledge. Chloe groaned. The ledge appeared to wind out of the gully, but getting herself onto it was going to be a Grade A pain.

Hitching or crawling simply wouldn't work. But the ledge was only four feet high. If she could stand up, she could roll herself onto it.

Her leg already blazed with pain. Her skin crawled at the idea of trying to put any weight on it or worse, falling again.

Harshly telling herself that if she rebroke the leg it would just make it easier for her dad to set, Chloe maneuvered herself next to a tree and tried to stand. Bolts of agony punctuated each small movement. Roll onto her good knee—*gasp, twitch*—grab the tree trunk and pull—*wheeze, moan*—lurch into an upright position—*curse, pant for breath*.

Clinging to the tree trunk, Chloe tried to gauge how far away the ledge was. Two hops or three? No point in waiting. She took a deep breath and started hopping.

The jolting sent lightning streaking up her leg, so bad she almost passed out. She stumbled and automatically tried to catch herself on her bad leg. It folded under her. She screamed and would've fallen if Marcus hadn't seized her jacket sleeve in his jaws. Growling, he exerted a steady upward pull.

Swearing continuously, Chloe ignored the pain messages flashing up her nerves and awkwardly rolled her upper body onto the ledge. Her broken leg dangled painfully, and again the wolf came to her tugging on her pants until it had support.

She lay on the ledge, kissing dirt, waiting for the shrieking agony in her leg to fade. She started to count to one hundred, lost count and made herself start again. By her third attempt, the pain abated enough for her to breathe better.

The wolf whined at her.

"I know, I *know*," Chloe snarled back. "Not a good place for a nap." She started crawling the rest of the way up the path to the top of the gully.

By the time she pulled herself over the top, dirt crusted under her fingernails and streaked across her face, and she trembled in every muscle. She lay on her back and rested again. Her leg throbbed.

The feral lay beside her, offering his warmth to share.

She wished she had fur. In desperation, she tried again to Change—Changing sped healing, but right now she was willing to risk the maul if it meant she made it home faster and less painfully. But nothing happened. The moon looked down on her from above, aloof and judgmental.

"I'm Pack," Chloe whispered to herself. "Pack are tough." Groaning, she resumed hitching along.

The wolf stayed at her side the whole time. He gently corrected her course a few times; Chloe followed him without question. It still took forever before her house came in sight; thank god she'd left the porch light on.

Ominously, by then her leg had gone from a jackhammer throb to a mere dentist's drill of pain as her werewolf-assisted healing kicked in. If she'd gone through all this and still had to face the maul, she was going to scream.

At the edge of the forest, Marcus whined and pulled away from her.

"Come to the house with me," Chloe pleaded. "My dad's a vet. Maybe he can do something. Help you."

No response. The wolf just looked at her.

It was Marcus though. Chloe was sure of that now. She would never have made it without him.

She started across the yard alone, then looked back and lifted a hand in farewell. Marcus yipped once, then faded into the forest.

Chloe curled her lip at the stretch of lawn separating her from the house. Yes, she could probably drag herself over there, but her body ached with exhaustion, and it wasn't like she could hide this little adventure from her parents anyway. Time to face the consequences. She sucked in a lungful of air and bellowed. "Mom! Dad! A little help here!"

Within moments a light switched on and her mother called, "Chloe? Where are you?"

"Outside! I need help!"

Her parents appeared at the door together, her mom wrapped in a housecoat, auburn hair all tangled, her dad in pajama bottoms and glasses. Her mom gasped and rushed toward her. "Chloe! What happened?"

"I fell into a gully and broke my leg."

"Why on earth—?" her mom started.

"That can wait." Her dad carefully picked her up and carried her inside. Yay for werewolf strength. "How long ago did you break it?" he asked, laying her down on her bed.

Chloe grimaced. "I sneaked out for a run at midnight. I fell probably twenty minutes later. What time is it now?"

"Almost three." Her mom abandoned her questions, falling into crisis mode. "It's already been healing for two and a half hours. Is it too late?" she asked her husband. She worked at the vet clinic with him and often assisted in surgeries.

"I don't know. Let's get those pants off."

Fortunately, Chloe had chosen a comfortable old pair of sweats to run in, so her mom could pull them off without resorting to scissors. She covered Chloe's lap with a blanket. Chloe bit her lip and squeezed her mom's hand while her dad examined the break.

"We've got to convince the Pack to spring for an X-ray machine," her dad complained.

"What about the one in your office?"

"It's a fifteen minute drive, which will just give the bone more time to heal. I'd prefer to rebreak and set it now if I can. Plus, Mickey said he'd do a kennel check on one of our patients."

Mickey was another of her dad's employees, a patient, gentle giant of man who was awesome with animals but wasn't Pack.

"Okay," her dad said after a moment. "I don't think it's as healed as I feared, probably because you've been moving and stressing it out. You shouldn't need surgery. Do you want me to try to rebreak it now, or wait until we have an X-ray and I can get you a local anesthetic?"

"Do it now," Chloe said.

No mauls, no saws. Her dad simply had her mother hold onto her upper body while he grabbed hold of her lower leg. "This is going to hurt. Try not to kick me in the face. Ready, baby?"

Chloe nodded. He yanked.

The crack of breaking bone wasn't quite as loud this time, but the pain still struck swift and hard. Tears poured from her eyes, and she bit her lip bloody. Her mom braced her upper torso while her dad carefully straightened the bone. Agony sizzled up her leg. She clenched her jaw, her fists, willing her body to stillness.

"Almost … There." The pain eased off. "It should be set," her dad said briskly. "Though we'll still need X-rays to verify."

Chloe lay back on the bed, gasping and trying to recover.

Her mom felt her forehead. "She's cold."

Splints, aspirin, hot chocolate and even a rag to wash the dirt off her face and hands followed. But all too soon Chloe was in the back seat of the SUV on the way to the vet office and the inquisition started.

Her mom: "Why were you outside running at night?"

Her dad: "Why didn't you let one of us know or take the cell phone?"

"I did take the cell phone, but I dropped it when I fell into the gully." Explaining her superstitious theory about moonlight spurring the Change made her cheeks hot with humiliation. And then came the question she'd been dreading.

"How did you break your leg?" Her dad was watching the road and didn't make eye contact.

"I got disoriented in the dark and fell in the gully."

Until the words came out of her mouth, confident and smooth, Chloe hadn't decided if she would tell them about the feral or not. She was ninety percent sure that the feral was Marcus and thus didn't pose a threat, but the second she mentioned that a feral had been hanging around, her parents would go into a flap.

She had no proof that the feral was Marcus, only his eye colour and intangibles like the way he felt like Pack and had tried to help her. Her parents might believe her, but his identity wouldn't outweigh the fact that he was a feral—and Pack Lore considered ferals deadly dangerous. Her parents would feel obligated to notify the Pack, and the Alphas would be a lot less willing to take the word of a Dud about the feral's identity.

They would hunt him down and shoot him on sight.

Chloe shuddered. She couldn't, wouldn't, allow that to happen. How could she give up on Marcus without giving up on herself first? She had to believe it was possible for her to Change, and if she believed it for herself then why not for Marcus, too? How was being stuck as a wolf that much different than being stuck human the way she was?

A year had passed since the Jennings' plane went down, but it didn't necessarily follow that Marcus had been trapped in wolf form for the whole time. Maybe he'd managed to Change a few times, but hadn't been close enough to civilization to phone for a rescue. There were lots of possibilities, but if she told anybody, the Alphas would take action to protect the Pack, and Marcus, after all his suffering and long journey, would be just as dead as Abby.

Not. Going. To. Happen.

So Chloe lied. She held her breath. Lore held it impossible to lie to a more Dominant Pack member. But in the dark they couldn't make out her face, and the lie passed.

By Sunday evening Chloe wanted to climb the walls. She'd slept through most of Saturday, but her dad insisted on complete rest for the weekend, either in her room or on the living room couch. The enforced inactivity was driving her mad.

She desperately wanted to know what was happening. If anyone else had seen Marcus. If the Alpha had fallen into decline. Who would be the next female Alpha.

Neither a family movie marathon of *The Lord of the Rings*, nor the good news that her dad recovered her cell phone, unbroken, could distract her.

On Sunday evening, her dad said she could go back to school the next day if a second X-ray showed the bone to be healed. After supper, the three of them bundled out to the SUV to drive to his office.

A cold, relentless drizzle smeared the windowpanes. The ceaseless motion of the SUV's windshield wipers hypnotized Chloe.

Did Marcus have a den somewhere out of the rain? She was impatient for her leg to heal so she could go back to the woods.

There had to be a way she could help Marcus Change. "Dad, can the Change be triggered by adrenaline? Would a traumatic event"—like a plane crash—"trigger it?"

Her dad glanced over at her, alarmed. "Possibly. But, Chloe, promise me you won't put yourself in danger. Your Change will come in its own time."

"I'm not stupid," Chloe said sharply. "I didn't break my leg on purpose."

"Glad to hear it," her dad said.

Chloe continued to think out loud. "So, if adrenaline can trigger the Change from human to wolf, do you need to be extra calm to Change back?"

Her mom pursed her lips. "It helps. When I first Changed back, I did it while I was asleep. It took me a while to master the trick consciously."

Disappointment tightened her chest. If Changing back were as easy as falling asleep, Marcus would have done it on his own already.

CHAPTER

5

Chloe's stomach clenched when Judy didn't get on the bus Monday morning. Did the Alpha still cling to life or had she slipped away?

But minutes before the second bell rang, Judy bounced into homeroom. She seemed so cheerful that Chloe risked nudging Kyle.

"Is her mom better?"

He forgot his scorn and grinned at her. "Word is she turned a corner."

Chloe's spirits rose, but caution tinged her hope. *Please let this last-minute reprieve not be followed by an even swifter collapse.* People didn't generally 'recover' from terminal cancer. But maybe werewolves, especially Alpha werewolves, did.

Surprise turned to shock when Judy went up to Ilona and hugged her.

Ilona's pale eyebrows flew up. Her arms hung loose as if she didn't know what to do with them. Finally, she gave Judy a small pat on the back. "What's going on?" she mouthed at Chloe.

Chloe shrugged.

Judy released Ilona, beaming. "That's for your mother. I'm sorry I acted so skeptical before. Please apologize for my rudeness. I thought all that holistic stuff was nonsense, but the crystals your mom gave my mother are working! She's sitting up and smiling. She even ate toast this morning!" Judy danced away as if toast for breakfast was better than rock concert tickets.

Chloe would feel the same way if her mother had cancer. She shuddered.

Chloe eyed Ilona thoughtfully. "I didn't know your mother practiced holistic medicine." Chloe didn't believe in crystals herself, but illness could be affected by a person's mood—placebos proved that. So if the crystals made the Alpha feel better, Chloe was all for them. Plus, they were pretty.

"She's not my mother," Ilona muttered under her breath.

Probably only someone with werewolf senses would have heard her, but Chloe's curiosity sparked. She leaned across the aisle. "What do you mean she's not your mother?"

Ilona's eyes widened. "Nothing. I was just kidding."

"No, you weren't." Chloe pushed harder—from concern now. Anything touching on the Alpha was automatically Pack business. "Who is she, if not your mother?"

"Not so loud!" Ilona grabbed her arm. Chloe allowed herself to be hustled over to the window where they wouldn't be heard over the class clamour.

"So?" Chloe repeated.

Ilona squirmed. "My mother's dead. Basia is my ... aunt. She looks exactly like my mother."

"Her identical twin?"

"Yes." Ilona bit her lip. "When we emigrated, there were some legal issues. My aunt didn't want to wait for paperwork, so she used my mom's passport. Look, would you mind not spreading that around? As far as the principal knows, she is my mother."

"Uh, okay." It was still weird, but it wasn't any of her business.

Class started, ending the conversation.

Chloe kept her head down and ignored the Pack teens as much as she could. They returned the favour—until last period of the day. Gym class. Which was, of course, taught by Coach Wharton.

In the locker room, Chloe changed into sweats. She followed the others outdoors to the sports field with a stone face. Whatever taunts came her way, she wasn't going to let them know she cared.

Coach stopped her halfway through her warmup lap. "Chloe, why weren't you at practice on Saturday?"

Fury engulfed her. *Because you told me not to come unless I could Change.* "I bro—*hurt* my leg." At the last moment Chloe remembered their townie audience and substituted hurt for broke.

"And are you all healed up now?" Coach asked, disdain in his face.

She fought to hold his stare. "Yes," she said, even though her dad had warned her to take it easy today.

He waited until she dropped her gaze, then said, "Get a jersey and go to the other side of the field. You're on team blue."

Judy, Kyle, Dean and Brian were all team red. He'd slotted her with the townies.

Chloe clenched her hands into fists and tried not to snarl. *Be stone.* She spied Ilona sitting cross-legged on the sidelines, still in her regular clothes, reading a book. Ilona often sat out of gym. Chloe didn't know why—Ilona seemed healthy otherwise. "Why aren't you playing?" she asked.

Ilona glanced up. "I'm anemic."

In the bright sunlight, she did look a touch pale. Chloe's lip curled. So much for the healing powers of the crystal charms provided by Ilona's aunt. If they actually worked, then Ilona wouldn't be sick.

Pride forced Chloe to play soccer as if her life depended on it. She chased the ball relentlessly. Despite her efforts, Blue team quickly fell behind. Though she did get the satisfaction of faking out Dean and scoring on him. Chloe smirked. "Nice try."

His face turned red. "I hear you reported a feral. Funny how no one else has seen this mad wolf."

Crap! She hadn't mentioned the feral since she'd figured out it was Marcus, but her dad must have told the Alpha about her first sighting. Now everyone would be looking for a strange werewolf.

"Maybe it was a coyote," Brian said.

She was on the verge of faking a laugh and agreeing—anything to get the pressure off Marcus—when Judy chimed in. "I bet she just made it up. We all know how Chloe likes to be the center of attention."

Words curdled in her throat. Hurt stabbed her.

You were my friend last year.

But apparently the Alphas' daughter couldn't be friends with a Dud.

Chloe skipped track and field practice and boarded the bus to go home. Not because she was sick and tired of being treated like a leper—though she was sure everyone would assume she'd crawled off to lick her wounds—but because her problems were an anthill compared to Marcus's Mount Everest. She needed to focus on helping him before he got shot.

She leaned her head against the windowpane, studying the school yard as if fascinated, to ward off anyone who might try to talk to her. Some bushes moved and Dean pushed his way out, his hair mussed. A minute later, Ilona emerged from behind the screen of branches. Her smile looked self-satisfied. Well, well. So Ilona had caught him then. Happily, Chloe's main feeling was amusement. She was so over Dean.

A pang went through her as she remembered how she, Abby and Judy had naively assumed they would marry within their own Pack, mentally pairing Chloe with Dean, Abby with Brian, and Judy with either Kyle or Marcus. Then Conrad Wharton joined the Pack and they all conceived massive crushes on him, even though he was at least ten years older. Chloe's infatuation had only lasted until Coach's first brutal training session. Abby's had lingered.

Thinking about Abby reminded Chloe of her teddy bears, and she grinned as an idea hit her.

After scrupulously leaving a note for her mother, Chloe jogged through the woods to the Alphas' house.

She'd expected Marcus to appear and tag along. When he didn't show, her belly fluttered. What if he'd left? What if someone had seen him lurking and raised the alarm?

She took a deep breath. *Stick to the plan. Get Hyde.*

Judy was at practice. Nathan's pickup was gone, but, of course, Olivia was still too weak to be left alone. Two cars sat in the driveway, a candy-red old Chevy that Brian sometimes drove and a teal-green Mazda with a crystal dangling from the mirror.

Luck favoured her. Brian's ditzy mom, Kristen, opened the door. She squinted at Chloe as if not quite recognizing her. "Chloe? What are you doing here?"

Ditz or not, she was still Pack and outranked Chloe. Chloe lowered her gaze respectfully. "I'm here to pick up something from Judy's room, and my mom will want me to ask if the Alpha needs anything." There, no lies.

Someone else might have asked questions. Brian's mom just waved her on in.

To Chloe's surprise Olivia was sitting in the living room. Swaddled under an afghan and wearing pajamas, but still a far cry from Friday's bed-ridden condition.

A large red crystal hung on a silver chain around the Alpha's neck, which looked odd with the jammies. Underneath her black wig her cheeks had actual colour in them.

Sitting in the easy chair across from the Alpha was a stranger, but judging by the crystals she wore this must be Ilona's mother. Aunt. Whatever. She had the same wheat-blonde hair as Ilona. Her skin was tanned, and she wore an embroidered peasant blouse and a long, flowing skirt. She glanced at Chloe with disinterest, then picked up a polished green stone—jade, maybe?—and handed it to Olivia. "Hold this against your heart chakra. Meditating on it will promote physical healing."

Chloe suppressed a snort. The Alpha had stomach cancer. There was nothing wrong with her heart.

Olivia accepted the jade stone, but didn't put it to her heart. "Just a moment, Basia."

Basia sighed, clearly not liking the interruption.

"Chloe," the Alpha said. "Was there something you needed?"

Chloe smiled cheerfully. "Just dropped by to borrow something from Judy. Is there anything my family or I can get you?"

"No, no … I'm fine." A small smile. "We still haven't eaten the casserole your mother brought on Friday. Though it looks delicious."

Chloe bobbed her head, then turned away. As she edged down the hall to Judy's room Basia said imperiously, "Your flow has been disturbed. We must start over from the beginning."

Chloe opened the door to Judy's bedroom.

Hyde, Abby's teddy bear, sat on top of Judy's dresser. Unlike Jekyll, who'd mostly sat on the shelf, Hyde had been part of the girls' games for years. Chloe couldn't help cuddling him for a moment. Grief for Abby clogged her throat.

Chloe wasn't sure if she believed in an Afterlife—heaven or reincarnation or anything—but in case Abby's spirit could hear her, she made a promise. *I'm going to save your brother, I swear it.*

Except now, a pang of doubt hit her. Would Marcus even recognize Hyde? Would it be enough? After so much time in Judy's room, would the toy even smell like Abby? Maybe she should try to find an object that Marcus had owned.

Kyle and Marcus had been best friends. Chloe pictured herself going over to Kyle and Dean's house and asking for one of Marcus's possessions. Yeah, not a good plan. Kyle would laugh his ass off then shut the door in the face of a Dud. Would anyone else have something of Marcus's?

She doubted it. Hyde was it then.

Hmmm. She should have brought a bag to conceal the bear. She didn't want the Alpha asking questions.

One couldn't lie to the Alpha.

She held the bear casually down at her right side and kept her left side to the living room. Fortunately, Olivia and Basia ignored her, still doing chakras. Brian's mom was surreptitiously checking her phone and barely nodded. One small wave and Chloe hurried out the door, home free—

A car door slammed as Dean dropped Judy off. Crap. Practice must have ended early. Chloe stepped back into the shadow of a juniper. Dean drove off, but Judy marched up the walk straight toward her.

Wanting to move any conversation farther away from the house and the Alpha's ears, Chloe met her halfway. "Hey, Judy."

Please let Judy assume she was here running errands for the Alpha.

Chloe tried to just keep walking by, but Judy blocked her path, scowling. "What are you doing here? Why weren't you at practice? Are you quitting?"

Wouldn't Coach like that. "No," Chloe said, "my leg was starting to twinge by the end of gym. I figured I should give it a rest."

Judy lifted her eyebrows. "Oh, right. Your *broken* leg."

Chloe ground her teeth. "Look, call my dad if you doubt me. He'll show you the X-rays."

"Oh, I'm sure you did hurt your leg," Judy said. "Coach said you probably did it on purpose. To get out of practice," she added helpfully. "So, you'd have another month's worth of excuses for not Changing."

Chloe gasped in outrage. "That doesn't even make sense! First Coach says I can't Change because I'm too afraid of the pain, and then he claims I purposely broke my leg? Hello, broken bones are kind of painful!"

Judy frowned uncertainly.

"Jeez, can't you think for yourself?"

Judy narrowed her eyes. "I'm Pack. Maybe the reason you can't Change is because you aren't. You don't belong, Chloe. You never have."

Her words stabbed like an icepick.

Chloe sucked in the hurt, refusing to show weakness. "You're wrong," she said coldly. "I am Pack." She started to move past her ex-friend, but just then Judy saw the teddy bear.

"Hey! What are you doing with Hyde? He's mine."

"Calm down. I'm just borrowing him. I'm doing a kind of memorial for the Jennings."

"A memorial?" Judy wrinkled her nose. "Why now? I mean, the one year anniversary passed three weeks ago."

Chloe shrugged. "Because I want to."

Apparently, that was the wrong answer. Judy held out her hand. "Give him back. You can't take him unless I say so."

Since Judy was now technically Dominant to her, Chloe was supposed to bow and scrape and beg her permission.

Screw it. She didn't have time for dominance games. She pushed past the smaller girl. "I'll bring him back tomorrow."

Judy grabbed for the teddy bear. But Chloe had half a foot of height on her and easily held him out of reach.

Judy's face turned bright red. "You have to listen to me! I outrank you."

"Oh, yeah? Well, if you really are Dominant then take it

from me," Chloe challenged. "No calling on the Alpha for help," she added. "Just you and me. Let's go."

She stared into Judy's eyes. The other girl tried to Dominate her, bend her to her will. Chloe expected to have to fight her own instincts, but in truth she didn't feel the slightest urge to hand the bear over.

Weird. Chloe's stomach squirmed. Was Judy right about her not belonging to the Pack? Did being a Recessive put someone outside Pack power games?

In any case, she wasn't about to back down. While Judy stared open-mouthed, Chloe put on an expression of unconcern and sauntered away.

The girl's scent on the wind brought the wolf to his feet.

He left the small hollow where he'd been drowsing, waiting for her return, and trotted forward. His tongue lolled. He was so happy to see her that he wanted to roll on his back and show his belly. Happy, happy! His tail thumped.

She dropped to her knees and took his head in her hands, an intimacy that would have made him shy away only days ago, but now felt so right. He closed his eyes in bliss as she dug her fingers through his ruff.

He opened them again when she stopped.

"Hey, Marcus, I brought something for you. Remember this?" Reaching behind her back, she pulled out something small and furry. It wasn't alive, nor did it smell dead.

Curious, he nosed it, breathing in deep.

Memory burst over him. Abby. The stuffed toy had been Abby's. Something detonated in his chest as pictures of his sister flooded back ... along with the knowledge of her death. Grief crushed him, its weight rolling over him like an avalanche. Remembering pushed splinters of glass under his skin.

This was why he'd chosen to stay a wolf—not because of his human physical frailty, but because the death of his family had crippled the boy.

Being human meant pain. He'd only survived these long months by becoming wolf.

The overwhelming emotions needed an outlet. The wolf threw his head back and howled.

CHAPTER

6

Chloe tossed the teddy bear aside and threw her arms around Marcus's furry neck. "Hush! It's okay," she lied, frantic to quiet him before his howls attracted too much attention.

Stupid, stupid, stupid. Instead of reminding Marcus of why he should turn human, Abby's bear had reminded him of his grief. The wolf shuddered in her arms, keening.

After a moment she started talking, trying to dredge up better memories. "Hey, do you remember that time my mittens got soaked and my fingers were freezing? I sat between you and Dean on the bus so I could stick one hand in each of your jacket pockets. The seat wasn't wide enough, and you had to sit half in the aisle. Every time we went around a corner you almost fell off." At the time, Chloe had mostly been interested in snuggling up to Dean and had paid little attention to Marcus.

Under her hands Marcus stiffened, his snout lifting to sniff the air.

"What is it?" Chloe asked, getting to her feet.

The feral's lips peeled back, his shoulder tensing. Deep growls ripped from his chest.

Dean jogged around a bend in the path. "Has Little Chloe finally Cha—" he broke off.

Crap.

Dean sniffed. "Who's that? He's not Pack." Dean bared his teeth.

Though Dean had at least twenty pounds on the feral, Marcus didn't retreat. Any second now, Dean would Change, and the two werewolves would tear into each other.

"Out of the way, Chloe."

"No. Leave him alone." Chloe kept her hand on Marcus's back.

The feral growled again and moved in front of her. Did he think Chloe was part of his Pack?

"This is our territory. Leave." Dean bared his teeth and stripped off his hoodie, a hair away from Changing.

"Stop it!" Chloe yelled, but neither werewolf listened. Coach Wharton had trained them for situations like this; otherwise wolf instinct took over. And Dean had only been a wolf for twenty months. ... If only she could Change.

An itchy prickle ran over her skin, but no fur came.

The feral feinted left, snapping his teeth.

Dean danced back out of the way, kicking off his jeans.

Chloe pushed between them, shoving the feral away. "Stop it! Just stop it!" If her dad had been there he would have blistered Chloe's hide—only an Alpha could get away with that kind of move—but she didn't know what else to do. She clouted Marcus's ear. "Go!"

Marcus backed up and whined. Dean growled at him. Chloe stepped forward, blocking him. "Run!" The feral loped off, but he stopped at the top of the hill and looked down at her in—confusion? disappointment? —before vanishing out of sight.

Dean got right up in her face, trying to glare her down. "What were you thinking? Never get between two wolves in a fight. You know that, Chloe."

Chloe suppressed the instinct to cringe before a Dominant wolf. She did know it, but—"It worked, okay?"

Dean stared at her, disbelief written on his square face.

"That wasn't me and Kyle tussling, that was a werewolf who isn't Pack, either an intruder or a feral. You could have been mauled. What were you doing with it in the first place?" He started to pull on his jeans. "Who was it?"

She shrugged.

"Was it someone from Quesnel Pack sniffing around our territory?" he demanded.

She had to nip that idea in the bud before he started a war. "Quesnel wouldn't send a juvenile. I think he's a runaway. From Saskatchewan," she added.

Dean scoffed. "A runaway would go to the city, not here. A runaway would have Changed so they wouldn't risk getting shot as a feral. "

Chloe shut down her expression.

"That's it, isn't it?" Dean curled his lip. "Only you would try to make friends with a feral. I bet you're just doing this to get attention. Everyone knows how much you've missed being teacher's pet."

Teacher's pet? Indignation fizzed in Chloe's veins. She opened her mouth to protest, then stopped. Because two years ago she had been a bit of a teacher's pet. In Coach's eyes she could do no wrong—just like Dean couldn't now. Had she been this arrogant then? Well, if she had, she'd been more than punished for it these last fourteen months.

"You're lucky it hasn't ripped your throat out," Dean continued. He pulled his hoodie over his head.

"He wouldn't do that."

Dean raised his eyebrows. "It won't get the chance, because as soon as I get home I'm going to tell my dad, and he and the rest of the Pack will drive off your little pet feral." He turned away.

In desperation, Chloe caught his arm. "He isn't feral," she ground out. "He's Pack. It's Marcus Jennings."

Dean's eyes widened. "What? Marcus is dead!"

"All they found in the wreckage were burned bones," Chloe said stubbornly. "He could have escaped."

"But you haven't actually seen him, right? He hasn't Changed into Marcus?"

"No, but the feral is the right age and—"

Dean made a scoffing noise. "No way is that Marcus. The Jennings are dead. Your dad flew north and checked the wreckage for survivors himself."

Chloe shrugged. "Maybe Marcus was wounded or crazy with grief." Because his whole family died. Her throat tightened. Abby's death had hurt bad enough. Add on two more deaths on top of that ...

"You're delusional," Dean declared. "If that was Marcus, and he could Change, he'd be chowing down in your kitchen right now. But he isn't. So either it isn't Marcus, or Marcus has been a wolf long enough to lose the ability to Change, and he's a feral who needs to be killed before he hurts someone. Either way, my dad or Coach will put a bullet through his brain."

"*No.*" Chloe grabbed his arm again, voice fierce. "You can't tell anyone."

"Says Chloe the Dud. Why would I listen to you?" Dean asked.

Blood pounded in her ears. So what if she hadn't Changed yet? Last year she would never have let Dean get away with talking to her like this, and she wasn't going to any more either. She looked him dead in the eye. "Because if you don't listen to me I'll tell your dad you've been sneaking around to see a townie."

Dean's mouth hung open for a moment. "Have you been spying on me?" He sounded incredulous.

Chloe rolled her eyes. "Get over yourself. I haven't the least interest in who you date. But the two of you weren't exactly discreet."

"You wouldn't dare tell." He stepped close, trying to Dominate her again, but she locked her knees and kept her chin up.

"Try me."

Dean sneered, but backed away and left.

The feral rejoined her as soon as Dean was out of sight. "Oh, Marcus." Chloe dropped to her knees and cupped his furry face, trying to make him understand. "He may not keep his mouth shut. You have to hide. Don't come near me for a few days. It's too dangerous."

He whined, blue eyes uncomprehending. And when she walked home, he followed right to the edge of the driveway.

Her mom was waiting for her when she returned. Arms folded. Mouth grim. Uh-oh. But surely it was too soon for Dean to have tattled on her …

"I just had a phone call from the Alpha—"

Chloe winced. Oh, right. That.

"I was going to ask if you took something of Judy's, but I can see the teddy bear in your hands. What's going on, Chloe? Why would you steal a stuffed toy?"

"It's Abby's old bear." Chloe clutched it tighter. "I wanted to have a kind of private memorial for her. And I didn't steal it. I borrowed it."

"Taking something without permission isn't borrowing," her mother said acerbically. "Why on earth didn't you just ask Judy?"

Because it was too important, and she would have said no just to spite me. Chloe shrugged. "I'm done now. I'll give it back tomorrow."

"No," her mom said, voice hard. "Not good enough. You will march back over there right now and return it. Furthermore, you will grovel."

"What?" Chloe burst out. "I'm not going to grovel! Judy's been a total snot to me lately."

Her mother remained firm. "I'm sorry you and Judy aren't getting along, but it doesn't excuse your actions. No, you listen to me, Chloe Katherine."

The use of her middle name and the Dominant stare stopped the hot words bubbling up in Chloe's throat.

"I don't think you understand what you've done. You walked into Judy's room—her territory, and *by extension the Alphas' territory*—and took something that didn't belong to you. We're wolves, Chloe. You might as well have peed on her bed."

"Oh." Her stomach sank.

"So you will return the bear, immediately, and you will humbly beg Judy's forgiveness and the Alphas'. Then you will accept whatever punishment they deem necessary." Her mother took a breath. "Because if you don't, you will be setting yourself outside the Pack, and that's a very dangerous precedent for someone in your position."

By which she meant someone who might be a Recessive.

"Is that what you want?" her mom finished.

Chloe shook her head, blinking back tears. No. Judy was wrong. Chloe was Pack. She didn't want to be an outsider. Just the thought made her panicky. She wanted to belong.

Her mom put her hands on Chloe's shoulders. "I know this will be unpleasant, but it needs to be done. In half an hour it will be over. Now run. You're already late."

Unpleasant didn't even begin to cover it. The next half hour standing before the entire Frayne family was the most excruciating one of Chloe's life, made worse by the constant worry that Nathan would get a phone call from Dean's dad about Marcus.

Chloe started out by giving Hyde back to Judy, who snatched him away as if Chloe's touch might contaminate him. "Judy, I'm sorry for taking Hyde without your permission and for entering your room while you weren't there." She kept her gaze lowered in the proper submissive posture, for the count of three, then checked to see how her apology was being received.

From the thin line of Judy's lips, not well.

Chloe then turned to the Alpha and lowered her head still further. "Alpha, I apologize for coming into your home with bad intentions." Was that enough? She stole another glance up.

Olivia had no expression on her face. Chloe couldn't read her at all, and her heart gave an extra little thump. What if the Alpha didn't accept her apology? What if the Alpha kicked her out? Minor transgressions might be tolerated from a Pack member, but would chafe more from someone everyone regarded as a Dud.

Chloe swallowed and tried again. "I humbly beg both your pardons."

Still silence.

Sweat broke out under her arms. The other werewolves would smell her panic. "Please assign me a punishment so that I can make amends for my offense of trespass."

"Oooh, make her cook meals for us for a month and serve us dinner," Judy said.

A flick of anger went through Chloe. All she'd done was borrow Hyde! She started to lift her head to protest, but the Alpha shifted, and Chloe quelled the impulse. "I will do as the Alpha commands," she said instead, forcing the bitter words out.

"She could scrub the floors," Judy suggested. "On her knees. With a toothbrush."

Spiteful cat.

Keeping her gaze subservient went against every instinct Chloe possessed. Her muscles locked, arms quivering with the effort of not storming out the door or yelling at Judy.

I need to prove that I am part of the Pack.

Finally, after an eternity, Olivia spoke: "I think something outside the house would be more appropriate. Chloe, be here this Saturday an hour after dawn. Bring work gloves. You can show your contrition by raking leaves and working in the garden. I will expect a full day's work from you and hard effort."

"Yes, Alpha. Thank you, Alpha." Chloe bowed again.

Olivia lifted a hand in dismissal, but before Chloe turned to go Nathan spoke for the first time. "Wait."

As she stood still, he walked right up to her, invading her personal space. She cast her eyes down again, hands fisted at her sides.

He growled at her, something he'd never done during all her and Judy and Abby's years of mischief. "Your standing invitation to our house is hereby revoked." He turned away as if he couldn't stand the sight of her.

She'd always gotten on well with Nathan, and his new lack of trust punched home. Tears leaked from Chloe's eyes. She stumbled home in a fog of misery.

The only good thing was no one had asked her why she'd taken the bear in the first place. Chloe hadn't had to lie, and the feral remained a secret.

Of course, if Dean told, a mountain was going to crash onto her head. All evening she waited in suspense for the phone to ring—but it didn't.

Perhaps Ilona meant more to Dean than she'd thought.

Chloe knew Judy would have spread the word about her disgrace, so she'd braced herself for the Pack kids to treat her as a pariah. What she hadn't anticipated was Ilona's hostility. The townie girl glared at her and deliberately sat in a different seat both on the bus, then again in homeroom, in order to be farther away from Chloe.

Chloe was mystified and a little hurt. What on earth had she done to Ilona?

Ilona didn't leave her wondering long. On the way to their first class she blocked Chloe's path and demanded: "What do you have against me and Dean?"

Ah. Dean must have told her about Chloe's threat—without telling her why Chloe had threatened him. "Me? Nothing." Chloe seized the chance to get a little of her own back. "Dean's the one keeping your relationship a secret. Doesn't that bother you?"

For a moment Ilona seemed stumped, then her chin lifted. "Maybe I like the illicit thrill of a secret romance."

A tic started by Chloe's eye. Illicit thrill? Really? "Whatever."

Some of her skepticism must have bled through, because Ilona raised her voice. "Hey, Dean!"

He stopped fiddling with his locker and turned, his expression wary.

"Call me next time your dad's away and you're feeling lonely." She shot him a smoldering glance.

Dean looked first worried, then pole axed. A broad grin swept over his face. "I'll do that."

Brian nudged him. "Dude! You are so going to get some."

Dean began to wrestle with Brian. Ilona shot Chloe a so-there look and vanished down the hall. Chloe shook her head in disbelief, but all she cared about was Dean keeping his mouth shut. And Ilona had just given him a large incentive to keep quiet.

After school, Chloe gritted her teeth and went to track and field practice. Until Coach actually cut her, she would act as if she were still on the team. However, she did her warm-up stretches at a careful distance from her Packmates. Which was probably why she smelled the strange werewolf first.

Sweat. Musk. Lake water. Not Pack. Danger!

CHAPTER

7

Chloe shot to her feet and homed in on the interloper. A biker in black leathers had crunched into the school parking lot. He put down the kickstand, took off his black-and-red helmet and shook out a long mane of sweaty, dirty blond hair. Goatee. Earrings. Tattoos.

Coach and the boys weren't in sight. Of her Packmates only Judy was anywhere close by. Figured.

The biker climbed off his motorbike and moved toward Judy.

Instinct sent Chloe on an intercept course. Apparently, part of her still regarded Judy as the smaller, weaker Pack member who needed protection.

The biker grinned at her, showing crooked teeth. "Hello, there. I'm guessing you're Chloe."

He knew her name? Wariness replaced aggression. She tilted her head. "Maybe. And who are you?"

"Scout. I'm from the La Ronge, Saskatchewan Pack. I was supposed to arrive tomorrow, but the roads were beautiful and I ended up here a day early. Thought maybe I should stop in town and call ahead before entering your Pack's territory."

"And you just happened to end up at the school?" Chloe asked skeptically.

He laughed, a pleasant growly sound. "No. You caught me. I heard you were a sharp one."

That didn't make sense. Why would a werewolf from a Saskatchewan Pack know or care anything about her?

Before she could ask, Judy jogged up. "Who—" she broke off and took a step back. "You're a werewolf!"

Well, duh.

But Scout nodded politely. "Yes. I'm Scout from the La Ronge Pack." He unzipped his leather jacket enough to pull back the collar and show his Bite mark. It marked him as belonging to a Pack and not a feral.

Most of the stuff people 'knew' about werewolves was total garbage. The full moon was nice for hunting, but, as Chloe had proved, it didn't cause the Change. Silver didn't poison them— heck her mother got a rash if she *didn't* wear silver or gold. Garlic? Chloe and her dad had it on ice cream every Garlic Festival. And she'd been born a werewolf. If a werewolf bit a human, they might get infected (the same as if a human bit a human) but that was all.

However, every werewolf able to Change received a special Bite from their Alpha as part of their initiation into the Pack. Unlike normal wounds, an Alpha Bite always scarred.

Judy responded in kind, tugging aside her T-shirt to show her three-month-old Bite. "I'm Judy Frayne."

"The Alphas' daughter," Scout finished. He nodded respectfully, then turned expectantly to Chloe.

Heat flushed her cheeks. "I don't have my Bite. I haven't Changed yet."

"Oh?" Scout looked oddly disappointed.

Judy laughed harshly. "She's a Dud."

Cat. Chloe fought back a snarl. "Pack Lore says some wolves don't Change until age eighteen. I'm only seventeen."

"Waiting for your first Change is tough," Scout said diplomatically. Really, he was a lot smoother than his appearance had indicated. But he'd need to be to represent his Pack.

He sniffed the wind. "More of your Pack are coming. So I'm just going to ease back a few steps and stand over there. To prevent misunderstandings." He retreated to his bike.

Coach and the boys rounded the corner at a fast clip. From the sand clinging to Kyle's shins Chloe gathered they'd been practising long jump.

"Who's he?" Coach demanded.

Scout lifted his hands. "Calm down. Your Alphas are expecting me."

Coach stopped a few feet away, hands on hips so that his biceps bulged. The three boys ranged behind him.

"I'm Scout from the La Ronge Pack." He showed his Bite again.

Coach didn't reciprocate. "You're early," he said.

"By a day," Scout said easily. "The weather was so nice, I couldn't resist opening up the throttle a bit on the highway. You have some very pretty country here. Everyone's heard of your Preserve." Was that a touch of envy in his voice? "So, can you escort me to your Alphas?"

Sudden alarm flared in Judy's eyes, and she smelled of fear. Chloe took a step closer to her to cover the betraying odour. *Of course. If he stays at her house, he'll see how weak the Alpha is.*

"I have a better idea. You go sit your ass in a hotel for a day and arrive when you're supposed to." Coach bared his teeth.

Scout stiffened, the laid-back persona suddenly slipping to show the wolf beneath. His posture switched to a readiness to fight, and his lips drew back from his teeth. "And who are you to give me orders? You're not Alpha or Beta of the Pine Hollow Pack. In fact, I don't know you at all." He squinted. "Or maybe I do. Bill Josephs, isn't it?"

"No," Coach growled. "It's Conrad Wharton." He glared at Scout, asserting Dominance.

The moment hung there. Scout and Coach were both

well-muscled, both young and strong, though Coach had an edge in mass. Chloe couldn't breathe for the tension. Would they fight?

Scout glanced aside, then got angry for the betraying gesture. "I'm an official representative from the La Ronge Pack. I will be treated with respect!"

The brewing fight made Chloe glance around nervously. There was no one in sight, but they were still in town. Anyone could drive by.

She elbowed Judy. *Do something*, she mouthed.

Judy cleared her throat. "Mr. Scout? We weren't expecting you so early. Why don't you do as Coach suggested and chill for a few hours, maybe have a bite to eat, while my parents make arrangements to billet you."

Judy was good at smoothing things over when she wanted to be.

Scout cast one more fulminating glance at Coach, then addressed Judy. "I'm sorry if my early arrival is inconvenient. I can stay in a hotel if need be."

"I'll talk to my parents," Judy said again.

Scout nodded to her, pointedly excluding Coach, and threw a leg over his bike. The engine roared to life, and he motored away.

Judy sagged with relief.

Coach turned on them, blue eyes glittering. "Listen up, this is a serious matter. Outsiders can't be permitted to find out how weak the Alpha is. That means no talking to Scout on your own. He'll be trying to catch you in a mistake. If you see him sniffing around where he isn't welcome, inform me or Nathan. Got it?"

They all nodded.

"Go home. Practice is cancelled."

Three hours later, Chloe and her family arrived at the Alphas for an impromptu barbeque in honour of the visiting werewolf.

Apparently, the Alphas had decided to bluff it out. Judy's mother wore a heavy sweater—not too out of place on a cool fall evening—and sat on some cushioned patio furniture close to the firepit. She looked like she was relaxing while her husband grilled the meat, instead of being too weak to do anything. Her black wig still seemed super-obvious to Chloe, but maybe a man wouldn't notice. The other women fetched for Olivia, making a subtle show of deference to her rank instead of fussing like nurses.

Chloe's mom took one look at the aggressive postures of Scout, Coach, and Dean's dad, who was Nathan's Beta, and tsked. "Curtis, you better go over there and defuse things. Ask about something neutral before those idiots ruin everything."

Chloe's dad ambled over. "Scout, good to see you." After a brief handshake, her father said, "Any news on Paul Riebel?"

No, no, no! Don't bring up the feral! Now everyone would be reminded that ferals were dangerous and should be shot on sight.

"You could say that," Scout said. "A mauling occurred up near the Manitoba-Ontario border. A hunter was attacked by a wolf while field dressing a deer. A wild wolf would have fled at the sound of rifle fire."

Her dad winced. "A black wolf?"

"Yup. The hunter says it came out of nowhere, took him down and ripped away his gun. Left him bleeding. He thought the wolf was going to tear out his throat, but the wolf went after the deer carcass instead, and he managed to crawl away."

Chloe's horror grew. Not just for the poor hunter, but for what this meant for Marcus.

"When the Churchill Pack Alpha heard about it, he sent out a hunting party to take Riebel down. But there's a lot of bush and wild land up there so they were spread pretty thin. It took them two weeks, but they found Riebel and cornered him in his den. By all reports he was thin as a rail and mad as a rattlesnake. Riebel went for the weakest of the Pack and mauled her pretty bad. She almost bled out before Mitch broke Riebel's back and finished him off." Scout shook his head. "Ferals are nasty business."

"At least they got him," her dad said grimly.

Sick to her stomach, Chloe moved away, not wanting to hear any more.

Her mother beckoned her.

"What?"

"Go pay your respects to the Alphas." Her mother gave her a little push.

Right. Since she'd screwed up so badly over the teddy bear incident, she needed to be ultra-circumspect and polite.

Chloe said her hellos. Olivia replied graciously. Nathan grunted at her—still angry about the infringement on his territory. Chloe ducked her head and quickly excused herself. She wandered around to the backyard.

The other Pack kids, including the rugrats, were playing a game of lawn darts, which she normally enjoyed. Today, she didn't even try to get in on the game, leaning against the wall of the house instead. She prepared to be bored out of her skull for the next hour, fiercely wishing her parents hadn't insisted that her cell phone stay in her pocket.

To her surprise, Kyle excused himself from the game and marched up to her. Chloe straightened, his body language making her wary.

"Can I talk to you? Alone?" Kyle jerked his head toward the woods.

Oh-kay. Curious, Chloe followed.

Kyle vibrated with anger, but he waited until they'd walked a quarter mile from the house before stopping in a small clearing. Hmmm. Should she be nervous? But this was Kyle. She remembered him as chubby tagalong.

"Is it true?" Kyle demanded. "Dean said you think Marcus is alive." He looked torn between hope and anger.

No point in denying it. "Yes," she admitted, "but he's having trouble Changing—"

"We never saw Marcus's wolf. How do you know it's him and not Paul Riebel?"

Chloe bared her teeth. "Didn't you hear? Riebel's dead, killed up by Churchill. Plus he's the wrong colour."

"If you're so sure it's Marcus, why didn't you tell me?" Kyle demanded.

"Gee, let me think. Could it be because every time I've seen you for the last five months you coughed 'Dud' into your fist?"

Kyle flushed. "Sorry," he mumbled.

She waited.

"Could you take me to him? Please?" His voice verged on a wolf's whine.

She relented, her throat aching in sympathy. Abby had been her best friend; Marcus had been Kyle's. She knew what it was like.

"I can try. He's not always around."

They started down the path to her house.

"Do you have anything of his?" she asked. "I'm trying to spark his memories, give him a reason to Change back to human."

Kyle wrinkled his brow. "Not really. A hockey biography I borrowed."

That wouldn't work. "Anything more personal? Anything with a scent?"

"Sorry, no." Kyle frowned. "Wait a moment. Is that why you stole Abby's teddy bear?"

"Yes."

"Judy made it sound like you were trying to get her goat."

"I'm sure she did." Chloe couldn't care less about Judy. She focussed on Marcus. There had to be some way to reach him ...

Inspiration hit her. "Do you know if Marcus ever had a girl-friend?" A girlfriend could give Marcus a reason to Change back.

Kyle raised an eyebrow. "No girlfriend, but he did have a crush on a girl. He got all googly-eyed whenever she was around."

Huh. Chloe didn't remember that. "Who?"

He snorted. "That would be you."

The wolf lifted his head from his paws. She had come.

Only one female mattered in the wolf's world: She. He could get drunk on her scent alone. She was beautiful, her voice lilting. Her hands in his fur made him want to roll on his back.

But this time She had brought another werewolf with her. A male.

The wolf's hackles rose. He didn't want other males anywhere near her. He rose to his feet and loped forward, deter-mined to drive off his competitor.

CHAPTER

8

Marcus had had a crush on her.

Chloe's throat thickened with guilt: she hadn't paid enough attention to him to even notice he liked her that way.

When she thought back, she could see the clues—he'd often hung around when she was visiting Abby—but they hadn't registered. He'd just been Abby's brother to her, Abby's *baby* brother. And besides, Chloe had been infatuated with Dean at the time.

She shook her head and straightened her shoulders. Marcus had bigger problems now. His feelings for her didn't matter. Or, rather, they only mattered in that they might make his wolf trust her more and enable her to help him.

Chloe slowed her steps as she and Kyle reached the stand of pine where she'd most frequently encountered the feral. "Marcus?" she called softly. "Kyle, maybe you should give me some space. He might be shy."

But in the next instant a growl ripped out, and the feral rushed toward them.

"No!" Chloe stepped into the wolf's path. He tried to deke around, but Chloe threw herself on him bodily and hugged his middle until he stopped. Here's hoping, she hadn't just done something monumentally stupid.

He continued growling at Kyle, but didn't snap at her.

"Marcus?" Kyle's voice cracked. "Marcus, it's me. Kyle."

"Stay back," Chloe said. "Give him a moment to catch your scent."

"Maybe it isn't him." Kyle's face had turned so pale his hair looked even redder.

"He howled when I showed him Abby's bear. He helped me when I fell into the ravine and broke my leg. It's him," Chloe said with conviction.

She stroked the werewolf's fur, then turned his head toward her. Holding his gaze, she closed his jaws like dog trainers did.

"Jeez, Chloe," Kyle said. "Do you have a death wish?"

"Marcus wouldn't hurt me." She met his pale blue eyes. "Marcus, this is Kyle. Don't growl at him. He's Pack." Then to Kyle: "Give me your hand."

"And let him bite it off?" Kyle muttered, but he gave her his hand.

"What are you worried about? You're a werewolf," Chloe teased him. "You'd heal." Slowly, she moved their joined hands up to the feral's nose and let him get a good sniff.

Under her arm, the wolf's muscles went suddenly rigid. She tightened her hold, fearing he intended to bolt. But after that one quiver he relaxed and politely licked their fingers. His back haunches went down and he sat.

"I think we're okay now." Chloe released Kyle's hand, but continued to stroke the wolf's head and back. After so long alone he had to be starved for touch.

"Well, there's definitely no way a wild wolf would let you pet him like a dog," Kyle said.

Duh.

"Talk to him," Chloe said impatiently. "See if you can convince him to Change."

Kyle knelt in the leaf litter. "Hey, buddy, it's me, Kyle. Your friend. We used to play baseball together. You'd pitch and I'd hit. Remember the time you accidentally beaned me in the forehead and I got a concussion, and we were too scared to tell so we pretended I had the flu?"

Marcus tilted his head as if listening to Kyle's anecdote. He stretched his jaws in a wolfish smile while Kyle told stories about some of their stupider mischief.

After a few minutes, Chloe glanced at her phone's clock. "We have to get back soon or we'll miss the barbeque."

"Change and come with us, bro," Kyle pleaded. "Just think, juicy hamburgers loaded with bacon and cheese. You can eat until you're stuffed. Come on, Marcus."

The wolf whined. Another shudder went through him, then he suddenly turned and ran off, tail down.

"Crap." Chloe stood, brushing off the knees of her jeans. "I thought you were getting through to him."

"Yeah, so did I." Kyle's shoulders slumped. "He didn't even try. What if he's stuck forever? What if he really is feral?"

"We just have to keep trying," Chloe said sharply. "He's not hurting anyone."

"Okay," Kyle nodded. "I'm not giving up. Let's—" He stopped and tilted his head.

Faintly, in the distance someone called their names: "Chloe, Kyle, supper!"

They broke into a run.

Everyone had formed a line, dishing up. Chloe tried to slide in, unnoticed. She grabbed a paper plate, but before she could do more than plunk a bun on it, her dad called her. "Chloe, come here a moment."

Her dad was sitting beside the guest of honor, Scout, and their plates were full. "Scout, this is my daughter, Chloe."

"We've met," Scout said, smiling. Gold glinted off one of his earrings.

"Chloe, tell Scout about the feral you saw last week."

Crap.

She needed to be so careful here, to mislead without lying. Chloe deliberately relaxed her muscles as if the question meant little to her. "Actually, I'm not sure it was a feral." Because she believed Marcus could be saved. "And I only saw it for a few moments." The first time.

"Just tell us what you saw," her dad said. "Scout travels a lot for his Pack and may have heard gossip about missing members."

"It was a juvenile."

"Was it white?" Coach asked, unexpectedly inserting himself into the conversation.

Chloe blinked, astonished that Coach was taking her claim seriously. "Not white. He had a black back and a cream underbelly." She shrugged again as if she weren't sure and didn't mention Marcus's most distinctive feature: the line bisecting his wolf's face.

"So it was a male, then?" her dad said.

Whoops. "I think so."

"Juvenile male with black and cream fur," Scout repeated. "It's not ringing any bells, but I'll ask around, see if anyone has any runaways."

Coach scowled. "If the werewolf is from another Pack, they'd better get their asses down here and pick him up. We won't tolerate intruders."

Chloe bit her lip to keep from defending Marcus. She met her dad's gaze. He nodded permission to leave. She started to return to the buffet line, but Scout's next words stopped her dead.

"If it wasn't a juvenile, I'd worry that your territory was being probed." Scout instantly had all the adults' attention. He paused to sip his beer.

"By who?" Dean's dad demanded.

"Word is that the Quesnel pack may be fracturing."

"Because of their size?" Chloe's dad asked.

"Partly," Scout said. "The Quesnel Pack must be at least three times the size of your little Pack here."

More tension as inner wolves pricked up their ears. Two subvocal growls vibrated in the air.

Scout pretended not to notice; maybe he enjoyed stirring the pot. "But most of the problem is their land. Remember how they were forced to pull up stakes and move when the government proposed a hydro dam that would flood their territory?" Everyone nodded. "I don't know if you've been following the story on the news, but after years of being stalled by Aboriginal groups and environmental protesters the dam's construction is underway. Some of the Pack, led by the female Alpha, want to go back, blow things up and declare all-out war against the government, and some want to go north or east and find better territory. Nobody seems to be happy with the new site: it's too close to the city. The only thing holding them together right now is the male Alpha. But Thomas is getting on toward fifty and has a couple of strong Dominants nipping at his heels."

All of this made very bad news. If the bigger pack fractured, they might well decide to take over a weaker Pack, or drive them away entirely. It became critical that Quesnel not learn about Olivia's illness.

Her dad cleared his throat and changed the subject, asking how his old Churchill Pack was dealing with the problem of polar bears being driven southward by the melting ice caps into their territory.

Chloe went back in line and filled her plate. Brian, ahead of her, was on his second helping. By the time she found a place to sit, the adult talk had drifted to old news: the 'information session' the logging company was holding at the school, the boycott some of the townies were talking about instituting against the

Pack—as if they could afford to lose so much business. Blah, blah, blah. Chloe finished her food and disposed of her paper plate.

Restless, Chloe wandered around the backyard. The other teens had gone down to chuck rocks at the pond. As Chloe passed by, Dean declared, "I'm bored. Let's race."

Judy pouted. "Where's the fun in that? You have the longest legs, you always win. Let's play a game."

"Like what? Hide-and-seek?" Dean scoffed.

"How about a decathlon?" Chloe spoke without thinking. Silence fell like a door slamming in her face, a forcible reminder that she was still persona non grata. A blind need to make them accept her made her push on. "We could do running plus high jump, etcetera."

Judy wrinkled her nose as if she'd bitten into something sour.

"How about an obstacle course?" Kyle said, carefully not looking at Chloe. "Run, climb ropes, dive through the tire swing, that sort of thing."

"Ooh, good idea," Judy said.

That's practically the same as my idea. Chloe didn't say it. In fact she kept her mouth shut while the others hammered out a course. Excitement began to pump through her veins. She was the best hurdler and pretty good at rope climbing. She might not be able to beat Dean, but she wouldn't come in dead last. She had a chance to prove herself.

"Excellent idea," Coach said from behind them. "Let's show our guest Pine Hollow style. I'll be the official timer. Everyone goes through the course twice, first as a human, then as a wolf."

Judy groaned, but Kyle's ears perked up. He had a faster Change than Dean and might gain an advantage. No one protested.

Bastard. Red hazed Chloe's vision. Her hands clenched into fists, and she wanted to spit. He'd changed the rules on purpose to humiliate her and get her to drop out. Well, screw that. She'd run the route, beat everyone's time and show them.

Everyone worked together to lay out the circular course and all too soon it was time to start. The adults drifted over to the start/finish line to watch.

Chloe's mom looked furious, her pale complexion flushed, her back rigid. She beckoned Chloe over to her, but Chloe just shook her head. She wouldn't be shut out. She was doing this.

"I'll start everyone out at one minute intervals," Coach announced. "We'll do it in age order. Dean, first, then Brian, Chloe, Judy and Kyle."

Shirtless, Dean toed the line.

"On your mark, get set, go!"

Dean sprinted fifty yards to the homemade timber and tire swing across the yard. He lifted the tire over his head and let it drop down, then stepped out. Jumping up, he caught hold of the adjacent rope and climbed hand-over-hand.

"On your mark, get set, go!"

Brian took off down the track. He was a little slower and had only covered two-thirds of the distance when Dean reached the top of the rope. Dean dropped down, landing in a crouch and gave the tire a hard swing before Brian got there. First slowing it, then trying to crawl through, wriggling his wide shoulders, cost Brian precious seconds.

I can catch him. Chloe bent and toed the line.

"On your mark, get set, go!"

Chloe sprinted forward.

Dean cleared the mud puddle/long jump and then two makeshift hurdles.

The ground flew by under her feet. Her breaths came hard but deep and regular. Halfway there.

Brian had almost reached the top of the rope. His arms and shoulders were well-muscled, but he had more bulk to haul up. He touched the top beam, started to slide down then "youched" when he gave himself rope burn and jumped the last four feet. His hair flopped over his eyes.

Almost there—

Gasping for breath, Brian gave the tire a spinning twist before lumbering off.

Chloe didn't slacken her speed, mentally timing the tire swing. Now! She dived forward, threading the tire, then somersaulted up. She'd scraped one arm a little, but otherwise gained time. Grinning, she jumped for the rope and muscled her way up as fast as she could. Slapped her hand on the beam. Let go. She landed with her knees loose and springy.

Judy had only covered half the distance to the swing. Good. Dean was partway through his Change for round two. Not good. Chloe gave the tire a shove and dashed on to the long jump.

From the muddy ruts, Brian had fallen into the puddle. She sailed over it, her cross trainers only slipping a little on landing. She ran on, legs pumping, fierce joy singing in her heart as she closed in on the luckless Brian.

He broke off his approach to the first hurdle and simply stepped over it, but managed the second one with poor form.

Chloe was a good jumper, but the on-its-side barrel they were using as one of the hurdles was a little wide. She took the first barrier with ease, but clipped the second one with her leg. Stumbled. Managed not to fall.

Her lungs laboured, gasping, but she put her head down and powered toward the finish line. Ahead of her—but not by all that much—Brian tore off his T-shirt and threw it aside.

She crossed the finish line only five strides behind him. Her mom and dad cheered.

Brian kicked off his shoes and stripped down to his underwear.

Stomach twisting in sudden dread, Chloe followed suit. Practising smooth, fast Changes was part of their Pack training.

Stripping was part of it, something they'd dared each other to do since age fourteen. The boys got a chance to look—and Chloe had done her own share of ogling back. True Pack weren't embarrassed by nudity.

And if she repeated that a hundred times maybe she'd start believing it.

Maybe if she could actually Change instead of just standing there with sweat chilling on her skin, she wouldn't be so self-conscious.

Training her gaze forward, Chloe saw Judy almost reach the top of the rope, then give a cry and let go. Kyle had caught up to her and squirmed through the tire like an eel. Dean raced to close the gap in wolf form. He, of course, would get to skip the rope climbing on the second lap.

Beside her, Brian grunted in pain and dropped to the ground. Fur sprouted on his arms, then swept across his flesh in a wave. His nose pushed out into a muzzle, his legs shortened and a tail popped out.

Come on, you can do it, Change. Chloe closed her eyes and willed the Change with every atom of her being. She strained every muscle.

She tried to shut out the cheering audience, tried to ignore the knowledge that her lead was tick-tick-ticking away, and the blush that wanted to surge because she was standing before everyone, including non-Pack, in her sports bra and panties.

Nothing.

Deep breath. Try again. She ran over every helpful hint she'd ever heard. Unfortunately, many of them contradicted the others. *Be loose. Keep your focus. Think like your wolf. Don't think about it, just do it. Concentrate on one part of your body, like your paw. Always start with your skin.*

Cheering made her open her eyes. Judy had finally made it to the top of the rope. Brian's wolf form was stuck halfway through the tire. Dean and Kyle were in a race for home, Kyle still on his first lap, Dean as a wolf.

The wind blew, and she shivered. Despair squeezed her heart as Dean and Kyle sprinted closer.

Change!

Still her body remained stubbornly human, except colder.

Dean crossed the finish line. Then Kyle. Both started to Change, Dean to human, Kyle to wolf. Kyle cast her a pitying look, then began his second lap. Soon after Judy puffed up and stripped down.

Chloe tried to copy her, tried to *see* the moment when the Change began.

Judy wasn't as smooth as the boys. She whimpered as the Change swept over her, slowly but inevitably . And then Judy's small red wolf gave a derisive sniff and headed out on her second lap. Leaving Chloe standing alone in her underwear.

Chloe could feel the press of eyes on her. Of pity and contempt.

Rage flickered inside her. Instinctively, she fed the feeling, nursing it along to ease the sting of total humiliation.

She let it build, feeding oxygen to the ever-present coals until the rage burst into red-hot life. Then she took the rage and imagined it blasting through her skin, Changing her—

A hand pushed on her shoulder. "Give up and get dressed. The race is over," Coach said.

Startled, she opened her eyes, ready to growl at him to back off. But Judy's wolf had crossed the finish line and was halfway back to human.

Her shoulders slumped, but she didn't allow herself to cry as she quietly dressed herself.

"Dean is the winner," Coach declared. "Kyle came in second, Brian third, Judy fourth. Chloe Did Not Finish." As if everyone couldn't see that for themselves.

A round of polite applause followed. Dean and Kyle's dad congratulated his boys, and the party broke up.

Chloe's mom crossed the lawn, sympathy in her eyes, and handed Chloe her jacket. She gave her a quick hug. "Excellent first lap, especially the dive through the tire. You had the second best time on the first lap. I'm so proud of you for not giving up."

Chloe just nodded.

They trooped out to the SUV in silence. Chloe slumped in the back seat, incredibly weary. Tears pricked her eyes, but she refused to give in to them. Instead she started dissecting the race. The rage might have helped; she'd felt close. If Coach hadn't interrupted her, maybe—

Her dad suddenly thumped his hand on the steering wheel, startling her. "Damn Conrad Wharton anyway!"

"I never liked that man," her mom said icily. "He's far too arrogant. Two years ago he came to our Pack a beggar, and now he's acting as if he's Beta. And I'm not impressed with Nathan either. He should have stepped in and squashed the contest before it went that far. He never would have let Conrad humiliate Judy that way."

Chloe's eyes widened, feeling slightly alarmed, but also warmed by her parents' support.

"It's probably my fault," Chloe said. "Because of the whole invading the Alphas' territory thing."

"You're not the first teenager to ever push the boundaries, dear," her mother said. "You apologized and accepted your punishment; that should have been the end of it."

"Actually," her dad said, "I think some of the blame falls on me."

"I doubt it," Chloe said.

"Nathan's preoccupied with protecting his mate. He was desperate for anything to distract Scout—and Scout's visit here is my fault." He sighed and slowed the SUV to turn down their driveway. "Chloe, Scout got his name by doing just that—scouting. Packs who need to recruit someone with a particular skill set—a lawyer, a carpenter or what have you—ask him to be on the lookout for prospects. That's why he's welcome at any Pack in North America, despite belonging to La Ronge at least nominally. When I was in Winnipeg for that convention two years back, I bragged you up a bit to the other Packs. As a potential Alpha. That's why Scout was here, to check you out. His visit had nothing to do with rumours of our Alpha being sick." Her dad parked the car. "It was just bad timing."

Chloe sat back against her seat, stunned. "You thought I had the potential to be an Alpha?"

"Yes. The other kids have always followed your lead. And I was very impressed with the way you took charge and made sure everyone was safe when your bus slid in the ditch that time."

Chloe remembered that. It had been deeply cold, -30 plus windchill, and Mrs. Patil had been dazed from hitting her head on the steering wheel. "All I did was a little first aid."

"You kept the kids on the bus, bunched them together for warmth, and made sure no one got carbon monoxide poisoning. I was very proud of you."

Well, of course he was proud of her. He was her dad. Chloe didn't think she'd done anything that special, just used common sense.

Two years ago she would have been thrilled at being talked up as a potential Alpha. Now she just found it sad. According to Pack Lore, Alphas were better at everything—including the ability to Change. Even if she wasn't a Dud, there was no chance she was an Alpha.

She didn't want to be Alpha anyhow. At this point her only ambition was to become part of the Pack.

Determination gathered in her chest; she envisioned it hardening into rock. *They can humiliate me from here until eternity. I'm not giving up.*

CHAPTER

9

Pebbles hit Chloe's window, waking her just before midnight the day after the barbeque. Who? Could Marcus have Changed?

But when she rushed over to the window, Kyle stood on the lawn below, wearing a safety-orange hunting vest. He beckoned furiously and then faded back into the shadows of the elm.

Chloe started to ghost down the hall, but slowed when she heard her father moving around the kitchen. Although by preference he was early-to-bed early-to-rise, his job meant he often received emergency calls after hours. From the pauses in his conversation, he was speaking on the phone.

"Are you sure this wouldn't better wait until morning?"

The way he'd couched the question gave her pause. With an animal owner he was soothing, but decisive.

Intuition prickled. *He was talking to one of the Pack. Someone Dominant to him.*

"Yes, of course Chloe is home. It's a school night."

She turned and tiptoed back into her bedroom. She barely got the covers pulled up when her dad peeked in the door. She struggled to keep her breathing even and regular while her pulse was racing. This had something to do with why Kyle had thrown pebbles at her window, something to do with Marcus.

As soon as her father's footsteps retreated to the kitchen, she got out of bed in a flash. She found ballet slippers in her closet—not as good as her cross-trainers, but far better than bare feet. Then she popped the screen and went out the window, dropping six feet to the ground and landing in a crouch.

"What took you so long?" Without waiting for an answer, Kyle grabbed her arm and pulled her along. "Hurry. We have to find Marcus before Coach and Dean and my dad do. They're out looking for the feral right now with rifles."

Chloe stumbled as if she'd been slugged in the stomach. "Dean told your dad?"

"Dean sneaked Ilona into his bedroom yesterday. Dad smelled a stranger and got on his case about dating a townie. Apparently, Ilona's mom is involved with the boycott movement, which really put things in the toilet. Then Dean started yelling back about how you were the one who was really endangering the Pack by harbouring a dangerous feral."

Chloe bared her teeth. "I told Dean it was Marcus."

"I tried to tell Dad, but, well," Kyle grimaced, "he doesn't listen when he's mad. He grabbed his rifle and stalked out of the house. He phoned Coach on his cell and now there's a hunting party."

They'd reached the stand of pine where she sometimes met up with the feral, but she couldn't see him. "Marcus?" she called softly. Her night vision might be better than a regular human's, but clouds hid the moon, and the shadows lay as thick as blankets. Her chest felt tight. They had to find him. Warn him.

She squeaked in surprise as a nose nudged the back of her knee. Marcus lolled his tongue at her in a lupine grin. He seemed pleased with himself for making her jump.

Another time she might have laughed, but tonight her nerves were strung too tight. "Marcus, you're being hunted. You need to get out of here. Run!"

The wolf stared at her, either uncomprehending or unwilling.

"She's right." Kyle added his voice to hers. "You need to make tracks. They have rifles. They'll shoot you."

She dropped to one knee, so that she could look directly into the wolf's gleaming eyes. "Run, Marcus. Once you leave the Preserve, they'll stop chasing you."

Marcus whined as if he didn't want to leave her.

"You can come back in a week or so," she promised. Did the feral understand units of time like weeks? Her eyes grew hot. What if he left then forgot about her?

A distant howl split the night. The hairs on the back of her neck lifted. She recognized the wolf's voice as Dean's and the note of triumph in it. "He has your scent. He'll be tracking you, and the others will follow him with guns. You have to go," she said urgently.

The wolf tugged at her sleeve, wordlessly asking her to accompany him.

Her heart twisted because part of her wanted to go with him, run free into the night. She shook her head. "I can't Change. I'd slow you down." The admission tasted like ashes.

The wolf tugged again.

"Chloe, it won't take Dean long to track him." Kyle bounced on the balls of his feet like he did before a race. "We don't have time to stand around arguing."

She stood. "Okay, Marcus you win. But if you won't run, then you have to hide. We need to cover your scent." Too bad she couldn't run back to the house for some mint extract or bleach to overpower Marcus's scent, but her dad was doubtless still awake.

Running water? A tiny trickle flowed at the bottom of the gully—but that was half a mile away. It had, however, rained yesterday.

"Roll in the mud," she told Marcus, giving him a shove for emphasis.

He obediently lay down. While he rolled back and forth in the mud, her mind raced, coming up with, then discarding hiding places. Not her garage or anywhere close to her house. Definitely not anywhere near the Alphas' house. Maybe the gully itself?

Marcus stood again, his fur thoroughly caked with mud.

"Good. That ought to help. Now let's move." Chloe broke into a jog, quickly pushing her pace up as much as she safely could without crashing through the trees. Silence was just as important as speed right now.

They ran for about ten minutes. Chloe took deep breaths, falling into a rhythm. Just as she started to search for the ravine, another howl came from behind them—closer this time.

Kyle swore and stopped dead. "Dean is probably following my scent and yours."

Chloe winced. She was an idiot. She'd figured Dean would dismiss Pack scents because they regularly ran through the Preserve, but the recent rain meant that he would know that her scent was fresh.

She kicked soggy leaves away from a muddy spot and reluctantly wallowed in it. Ugh, she hated getting mud and twigs in her hair. It didn't help that both Marcus and Kyle smirked at her. She glared at Kyle. "Your turn."

He shook his head. "I have a better idea. I'll draw them off. They won't shoot me."

He had a good point. Dean and his dad would know his scent, and his orange safety vest stood out like a lighthouse in a prairie. She nodded and Kyle veered left while she and Marcus continued toward the gully.

A minute later, the feral pulled up suddenly, turning across her path so that her thighs hit his back. She stopped and squinted. A deeper blackness lay ahead. They'd reached the edge of the ravine, but the bank here looked too deep to scramble down without breaking another limb—no, thanks.

They were forced to turn and pick their way along the top.

"Stop!" a voice called out. Coach.

Chloe froze, not because Coach was talking to her, but because he was obviously close enough to hear them. She put her hand on Marcus's furry head, and he obediently stilled.

"Tell me where the feral is." A growl vibrated in Coach's voice as he used Dominance to inflict his will on Kyle.

Kyle whined in distress. "That way. But Chloe's with him. Don't shoot her."

Crap.

"Stay out of my way," Coach ordered Kyle. Then he started toward them.

Chloe bolted, legs and arms pumping, head tucked down, barreling down a dim path. Branches scratched down her cheek, and she hurdled a fallen sapling, but she didn't slow down, desperate to get out of rifle range.

Marcus loped just behind her, though he could easily have passed her and escaped. *Stupid, loyal wolf.* He obviously considered her part of his Pack. He didn't understand that he was the only one in danger.

Frustration bit into her with sharp teeth. Two legs were too slow. Her weakness was going to get Marcus killed.

A rifle shot cracked out.

Her heart stuttered as Marcus yelped and fell back. She couldn't see much in the greyscale of night vision, but thought he'd been hit in the shoulder.

After an agonizing pause, he gamely kept running. His stride now hitched.

Too slow. He was going to die, killed by his own Pack. The bitter unfairness of it filled Chloe with rage.

A wolf howled and a black shape hit her in the chest, knocking her to the ground. Dean.

His weight pinned her down. He growled in her face, but kept his jaws closed. *He was taking her out of the field of fire so Coach could shoot Marcus.*

Ironically, if Marcus had actually been feral, he would have run. Instead Marcus circled around and drove Dean off of her. Dean fought back and in moments the two wolves were wrestling on the forest floor at her feet, snapping and snarling.

Dazed, Chloe pushed herself to her feet. Drying mud flaked off her arms.

Coach jogged into sight, raised the rifle to his cheek then swore. "They're too close together. Chloe, move back." His voice rang with such authority that Chloe involuntarily took a step back.

Marcus snarled. Though smaller, he was holding his own against Dean, nipping and then retreating, with no wasted motions.

Not that it would matter in the end. If Dean won, Marcus would be dead. If Marcus snapped Dean's neck, he would cross the line and become a true feral and Coach would shoot him like a rabid skunk.

She clenched her teeth until her jaw ached, the rage flaring up like a smoldering fire doused in gasoline. Rage that this was happening at all. Rage at her inability to Change. Rage that the Jennings' plane had gone down in the first place. Fury at her own helplessness to save Abby's brother scorched her bones.

Anger and adrenaline stormed her body. Desperation seized her: she had to help Marcus! For the first time she didn't merely want to Change, she *needed* to Change.

Fur prickled her skin, and Chloe's back bowed on a wave of pain as she collapsed to the ground.

Suddenly, the night transformed to almost daylight brightness. Her hearing sharpened, and smells exploded in her nose like a bomb. She sawheardsmelled her Pack under attack.

Clothing tangled her front legs, the constriction unbearable. She ripped at the cloth with her teeth, squirmed free of her pajamas.

While she Changed, Dean had gained the upper hand. Marcus was down. Chloe threw herself into the fray, growling. *Mine! Stay away!*

Surprised, Dean retreated. Chloe stood over Marcus's fallen body. He lived, but the rich scent of his blood permeated the air.

"Chloe?" Coach smelled shocked for a moment. He kept talking, but she couldn't focus on the words when all her other senses were demanding her attention; they became noises without meaning. Chloe waited for him to Change and attack, but he only raised a long stick to his shoulder, pointing it at Marcus.

No. Not a long stick. *A gun.*

Crack. Another bullet hit Marcus, in the leg this time.

Instinct took over. Chloe charged. She hit Coach's torso with her whole weight. He fell on his butt.

Coach bared his teeth and swung the rifle at her head. She dodged the blow and seized the wooden stock in her teeth, ripping it free from his grip. She threw the rifle into the forest and stood guard, blocking his path toward it.

She spared a brief glance at her Packmate. Marcus licked at his rear leg, though the bleeding had already slowed. He yipped a warning.

Coach had begun to Change. Already, his nose had pushed forward into a snout, and a rash of black fur broke out on his back. A silent snarl of pain formed on his now-black lips as his tail sprouted, bones popping and rearranging themselves.... . Then it was done. A white wolf twice as heavy as Chloe faced her.

The other wolf—*Dean*—hung back, content to let the more Dominant white wolf handle things.

Arrogantly, the white wolf stalked toward Marcus, expecting her, the lesser wolf, to get out of his way.

The white wolf was fourth in the Pack hierarchy. Chloe didn't have a chance, but she could give Marcus a few extra moments to heal. She blocked the white wolf, growling.

He snapped his teeth in warning. She flinched, but stood her ground, legs trembling with the effort of protecting her Pack.

The white wolf lunged forward and bit her haunch, drawing blood. Her flank burned, but she didn't show her belly, didn't back down. She growled her defiance.

Behind her, Marcus climbed back on his feet, partially healed but moving stiffly. He tried to stand by her, but she snapped at him. *Run!* She wasn't in danger, he was.

Again, the large white wolf tried to go around her. Again, she blocked. His scent changed from impatience to puzzlement. He loomed over her, growling, but this wasn't about being bigger or even stronger. Dominance was about will.

Maybe if her Change had come easily two years ago she wouldn't have been able to do it. Maybe those months of being called a Dud, of persevering, had all led up to this moment. Chloe stared him down.

He dropped his gaze—only for a second, but everyone knew what it meant.

And then another two-legs—*Dean's Dad*—jogged up, Kyle at his heels. The man also held a long stick, but he pointed it at the ground. "What's going on?" he demanded. "That's not a feral, that's Chloe. Can't you tell from her scent?" The Beta moved between Chloe and the white wolf.

The white wolf growled in frustration.

"Why isn't the feral attacking?" the Beta asked.

"I told you. It's Marcus," Kyle said.

Silence, then: "Run that by me again. Marcus Jennings?"

Talk, talk, talk. Chloe took advantage of her enemies' confusion to retreat into the shadows. She nipped Marcus's flank, urging him to escape with her. She started to stretch out her legs and run, but Marcus fell behind, still wounded. She slowed until they could run shoulder-to-shoulder.

No one pursued them.

Marcus howled in triumph. *Mine!*

Mine! She howled back.

The two of them ran together through the dark pines, paws hitting the earth in tandem, hearts beating as one. They were Pack!

The she-wolf was beautiful, just as the wolf had known she would be: a creamy gold wolf with amber brown eyes and a gorgeous flirty tail.

They ran together beneath the starry sky, and happiness burst inside him, a feeling so much greater than the absence of pain he'd mistaken as contentment before.

He had a Pack again, was alone no more. He lifted his voice and howled his triumph to the moon. The she-wolf lifted her head and howled, too, creating a melody.

Another wolf howled in the distance. She turned her head and fear speared through the wolf. Would she return to her old Pack?

But then she nuzzled his nose and took off after some mice scurrying under the leaf litter. She was a naturally quick hunter, but neither of them was truly hungry. They played, then let the mice escape.

She danced and frisked with him, filling his heart with pure joy.

Then her nose lifted, and he smelled it, too. The stink of bad magic and rank fowl.

The wolf had smelled the Evil in the Forest before and

followed it to the house as its source. When the she-wolf tried to track the stench, he nipped at her in warning. It was a place to be avoided.

She took a few steps toward it, but stopped when he whined his distress. She tilted her head, then acceded to his wishes. They ran through the night once more, away from the Evil.

Hours later, panting and happy, they denned together in the hollow he'd made underneath the root of a large tree. Noses touching, soothing warmth, smell of Pack.

The tantalizing odour of apple pie drifted out into the forest.

Chloe's wolf self didn't find the smell appetizing, but it brought forth strong memories of home and warmth and love. Marcus nudged her, puzzled, but she trotted towards the scent, compelled.

The house was stuffed full of important smells and so was the fox-haired woman who stood in front of it, another werewolf in human shape. The house and the woman and the smells both drew Chloe and made her uneasy. She hung back at the end of the driveway.

The woman spoke in a low voice. "It's time to Change. Come back to me, Chloe."

Change? But she'd only just found her wolf form. Chloe wanted to run some more on four legs. She wanted to pounce on a pile of fall leaves and hunt squirrels and howl at the moon with Marcus. She whined.

"It's dangerous to stay wolf for too long, especially the first time." The woman held out her hand. No, not the woman. Her mother. "There will be plenty of time to run as a wolf later, I promise. Please, Chloe."

Chloe's wolf had only a dim understanding of 'later', but she wanted to please her mother. Chloe hunkered down and started to Change. Her fur rippled.

Marcus whined and pawed the dirt, morose.

Acting on instinct, she flirted her tail over his muzzle, giving him her scent, then Changed.

Despair threatened to drown him. *He was losing her.*

He ought to have known the she-wolf wouldn't abandon her family, but in the joy of her Change he'd forgotten.

All his dreams of running through the forest with her, of being her mate, of being free and wild, crashed and burned.

The she-wolf was his world. The thought of being shut out when she walked through the door to the wooden house gutted him. He howled, but his anguish remained. A balance tipped inside him. The pain of remaining a wolf outweighed that of becoming a boy.

So he threw himself into the Change and mirrored her, Changing from wolf to boy, pulled along by a mating instinct even stronger than the call of the wild.

They finished Changing at the same moment and lay panting together in the dew-wet grass, almost nose-to-nose. And then mouth-to-mouth, lips meeting in a flurry of wildness.

CHAPTER 10

Although only their lips touched, the kiss engendered heat deep in Chloe's body. The kiss could easily have turned into something more if her mom hadn't rushed up just then.

Instantly, Marcus rolled into a crouch, as if expecting an attack.

"It's just my mom," Chloe soothed.

His eyes remained wary.

Her mom stopped several paces away and held out two blankets. Chloe wrapped one around her nakedness, then draped the other over Marcus' shoulders. When she stood up, he copied her. She linked hands and smiled triumphantly. "Mom, you remember Marcus."

"Thank goodness you're all right." Her mom gave her a swift hug, then turned to Marcus. "Marcus, welcome home."

She didn't try to hug Marcus, fortunately. As it was, a quiver ran through him, like a wild animal in the presence of dangerous humans.

Chloe kept tight hold of his hand and held the blanket together with the other.

"Let's get you two in the house before you get chilled," her mother said.

Chloe tugged on Marcus's hand. "Come on."

Silent, wide-eyed, he let her pull him up the driveway.

"What happened after I left with Marcus?" Chloe asked. "Did they cancel the hunt? Mom, you have to call them and tell them Marcus isn't feral." In case he bolted and Changed back to wolf.

"I will," her mother said steadily. "First things first. Clothes and hot food." They entered the kitchen, and Chloe's mouth watered at the cinnamon smell of apple pie. Her stomach growled. No breakfast, and she'd expended a lot of energy last night, playing and hunting.

She frowned, trying to remember. She hadn't eaten any little critters, had she? Gross.

"So where's Dad?" Chloe asked.

"Out searching for you, where do you think?" her mother said tartly. "And he's in wolf form, so I can't phone him. Hmmm." Her mother studied Marcus. "Chloe, you stay with him. I'll bring the clothes here. I suspect Marcus will be more comfortable if the room has an exit."

Marcus watched her leave, then sniffed around as if—Chloe's stomach curdled—he'd never been inside a house before.

As if he were still feral.

He had yet to speak a word.

No! She shoved the fear down. Marcus had Changed back to a boy, that meant he wasn't lost, wasn't feral.

It just might take him a while to lose the habits of a wolf, that was all.

Her mother returned with jeans, a long-sleeved shirt, underwear and socks for her. For Marcus she offered some drawstring sweatpants and a large T-shirt of her dad's. "Those are fresh from the laundry, so I'm hoping they won't have Curtis's scent on them."

Feeling awkward, Chloe dropped the blanket. Marcus whined when she tugged her hand free. She dressed quickly, not looking at him, aware that her cheeks were flaming. *Werewolves aren't embarrassed by nudity.*

Some day she'd get the hang of it.

"Your turn," she told Marcus. She held out the sweatpants, keeping her gaze on his face.

His top lip wrinkled in disgust, but he took them and put them on.

Chloe breathed out a sigh of relief. Mute or not, he at least remembered clothes. She held out the T-shirt.

He ignored it.

She didn't push it. Maybe the shirt smelled like her dad's property.

Now that he had pants on, her gaze slipped down to his chest. She blinked. He was lean to the point of gauntness, his belly concave, but, wow, what flesh he did have was ripped. He put Dean to shame, and Dean did serious weight training.

Then there were the scars. Most noticeable was the puckered red wound where the rifle bullet had hit his shoulder—thankfully there was an exit wound on the other side. But there were a lot more white marks, some in the shape of teeth and claws, most burns. Because of their amped-up healing ability werewolves almost never scarred. Only massive trauma left marks.

Her breath caught. It was driven home again: the plane crash had almost killed him.

She bit her lip on a sudden wave of emotion. *Abby.*

Sensing her distress, Marcus moved closer to her so that their sides brushed. Chloe gave his fingers a quick squeeze, then sat down at the kitchen table. "Can I have a slice of pie? I'm starving."

"Under the circumstances ... " Her mother smiled tenderly. "Congratulations on your first Change, darling. We knew you could do it."

The relief of not being a Dud, of being Pack, made Chloe grin like a dork.

Her mom set a scoop of ice cream on top of the still-warm apple pie and served it to Chloe. "Marcus? Would you like ice cream on yours?"

He didn't answer, but gazed out the window at a bird chirping.

Brow creasing, her mother set down a plain slice on the placemat beside Chloe.

His nose wrinkled, and he made no move to sit and eat.

"Maybe something with meat in it?" Chloe suggested.

"I'll warm up some leftovers," her mom said.

Marcus flinched at the noise of the microwave buzzer, but sniffed appreciatively at the beef stew when it came out.

"Sit," her mom said firmly.

Marcus perched on the very edge of his chair.

See? He does remember being human.

"Use the fork, or you'll burn your fingers," her mother cautioned.

Marcus picked up the fork correctly and began to shovel down the food. He finished his heaping plate at almost the same time Chloe finished her smaller piece of pie—and she'd started first.

At least he knows how to use a fork.

A noise from outside startled Marcus. He popped up from his chair and backed against the nearest wall. A moment later, Chloe heard it, too: paws on gravel.

Her mother went to the window. "It's your father. I'll cut him off and bring him around the back so Marcus doesn't feel trapped." She hurried out.

Chloe got up and reached for Marcus's hand. She smiled reassuringly. "It's okay. It's just my dad. Dr. Graham. You remember him, right?"

Low voices in the yard, then grunting as her dad Changed. Marcus tensed.

"It's okay," Chloe repeated. She tried to catch his gaze. "Marcus, it's okay. There's no danger."

But when the back door opened, Marcus stripped off his pants and Changed. By the time her parents reached the kitchen, Marcus was once again a cream and black wolf. He growled. Chloe threw her arms around him and hugged him tight. "Stay with me."

Her father stopped at the sight of them together. He crouched down to their level, making himself less threatening. "That's the feral?" His voice was low and soothing, the voice he used with injured animals in his clinic.

"He was a boy a moment ago," her mother said anxiously.

"Marcus Jennings, you said?"

"Absolutely, without question," her mother confirmed.

Her father rubbed a hand over his face. "Well, there's no doubt that this is an unholy mess, but I swear to you, Marcus, and you, Chloe, that I'll stand by Winston and Karen's boy. Make sure he has every chance to recover. Welcome back, son."

In the circle of her arms, Marcus relaxed a fraction. She stopped worrying that he was going to escape into the forest. She didn't let go, but arranged her legs in a more comfortable cross-legged position.

"Now that your father is here, I'd like to hear the full story, please."

And after that would no doubt come the lecture. Chloe cleared her throat. "I already told you about the first time I saw the feral. I didn't realize it was Marcus until the night I broke my leg … " Chloe related everything that had happened.

The lecture that followed was stinging. Chloe winced through parts of it, but her parents didn't yell and they didn't make her grovel like the Alphas had when she did wrong.

"All right," her father said, when they finally wound down. "It's time to take this to the next level. I'll phone Nathan and call off the hunt."

Chloe waited tensely through that phone call. Her dad eventually hung up and announced: "The Alphas will see you both tonight after Scout has left."

Chloe let out a slow breath and turned to Marcus. Still a wolf. "You'll have to Change back for tonight, but you can stay as you are for now. Mom? No school?"

Her mother gave a short laugh. "You've already missed most of the morning. No school. And Mickey is covering for me at work so I'll stay home, too."

"Marcus and I will go watch a movie in the den then." The sofa there was long enough for a wolf to sit beside her. If she picked the right movie, maybe she could induce some nostalgia.

Her mom paused in the doorway. "Chloe? Did I mention how very proud your father and I are of you for going to bat for Marcus?"

They shared a warm smile.

Chloe held Marcus's furry head cupped in her hands and stared into his pale blue eyes. "It's time to see the Alphas. It's very important that you Change back into a boy before we go." Should she tell him why? Yes. He wasn't a child. "If you don't, they can declare you a feral and kill you. You have to prove that you're still civilized, that you're really Marcus Jennings."

The wolf's muzzle wrinkled, and he growled softly, but Chloe eyed him sternly. "Change, Marcus, I mean it."

He chuffed, sounding resigned. She set down the sweat pants and turned her back. She didn't let herself hold her breath, but inside she quaked. If this didn't work—if they had to bring him before the Alphas with only her word and her mother's that it was Marcus—

A grunt issued from behind her.

In a surprisingly short time, a human hand reached for the sweatpants. When she turned, Marcus stood before her, a boy with ragged brown hair, wary eyes and a scarred chest.

"Good." Chloe studied him critically. "You need a haircut, but that can wait. Clothes are more important."

She and her mom had put their heads together and scrounged up a quilted winter vest. Chloe held it out to Marcus, but he refused to take it.

"Come on," she coaxed. "You can leave it unzipped and shrug out of it in two seconds flat, but you need to look as normal as possible." She lifted his hand and pushed it through the vest's armhole. Marcus allowed her to slide the vest onto him, but he didn't exactly help.

"Now, the most important thing: can you talk?"

He stared at her face with total attention, yet at the same time Chloe wasn't sure he comprehended her.

"Try saying your name: I am Marcus Jennings."

He opened his mouth, but no words came out. He whined.

"It's okay." Chloe patted his arm. "Just keep trying. Maybe clear your throat." She demonstrated.

He tilted his head to one side. Crap. There was a scar on his Adam's apple. What if his voice box was damaged? She traced the raised line with her fingers. He stood perfectly still under her touch. "Is this why you can't talk?"

No reply.

"I'd like my dad to take a look at this. Can I call him or will you freak out again?"

He tensed.

Chloe blew out an exasperated breath. "Okay, I get that you can't talk, but you can still nod your head, right? There's nothing wrong with those muscles?"

After a short pause, he shook his head.

"Will you let my dad examine you? I'll stay here the whole time."

He nodded, then shook his head.

"Does that mean you're not sure?"

Nod.

Chloe bit her lip. It wasn't worth the risk of Marcus going wolf again. "Okay, we'll try later."

Similarly, they walked over to the Frayne's house together rather than risk a nervous werewolf panicking inside the confines of the SUV. Chloe led the way, Marcus silently followed. Her parents hung back another ten paces, giving them space.

Marcus's feet were bare. He'd refused the pair of shoes her mother offered. "I'll buy slip-on sandals the next time I'm in town," her mother had said, frowning. But, honestly, he didn't appear to notice either the coldness of the ground or the scattering of rough twigs and pebbles.

As the Alphas' large bungalow came in sight, Chloe's heartbeat picked up, drumming a rhythm in her throat. This ought to be her moment of triumph. She'd Changed and proven she wasn't a Dud. Her place in the Pack was secure. She'd succeeded in bringing Marcus, thought lost forever, back to the Pack. But instead of jubilation, anxiety tightened her chest.

She no longer trusted the Alphas—and that was bad.

She didn't know when they'd lost her respect. When they'd kept secret the extent of Olivia's illness? When they hadn't curbed the other teens and Coach from making her life hell? When they'd forced her to grovel without once asking why she'd taken Hyde?

Maybe all those things together.

Chloe hated the freefall feeling of not being able to depend on the Alphas. She hoped tonight would restore her faith in them, but in the meantime her muscles remained tense, ready to run.

CHAPTER

11

She laced her fingers through Marcus's before stepping into the yard. "Okay, we're going to take this slow and easy. Just remember, everyone here is part of our Pack. They'll be happy to see you. Don't spook. Don't turn wolf. Stick close to me and nod or shake your head if people ask you questions. Got it?"

Marcus was staring at the house.

She cupped his chin and made him look at her, then repeated her instructions. "Got it?"

This time he nodded.

"We'll be right here," her father added from behind them. "You're safe."

Like the barbeque, Pack meetings were almost always held in the backyard around a blazing firepit. Because what true werewolf would want to be inside when they could be outside under the sky and moon? (Unless it was minus twenty or colder, then the Pack seemed willing enough to tolerate a roof.)

Though the autumn air was still five degrees above zero, Olivia was bundled up in a winter jacket, gloves and boots. At least she didn't have a toque. Nathan hovered nearby, but she was standing instead of sitting in the padded patio chair.

Chloe's family was the last to arrive. The Pack stared and murmured. She resisted the urge to stick out her tongue at Dean, who kept blinking and shaking his head. Kyle had a huge grin on his face.

"Come forward." Olivia beckoned.

Chloe squeezed Marcus's hand and drew him forward.

A long moment passed as the Alpha pair studied him.

"So it's true," Olivia said, her face full of wonder. "Marcus Jennings, know that you are welcome back among your Pack." She held out her hands.

Her graciousness eased Chloe, but Marcus didn't budge. She elbowed him, and he laid his hands briefly on top of Olivia's.

"I can see you've had a hard time of it and a long journey," Olivia said softly. "What can you tell us about the crash?"

Marcus took a step back and glanced around nervously. Chloe reached for his hand.

Olivia's expression grew puzzled. "I know it must be painful to talk about, but you must understand how anxious we are."

Chloe's heart lurched. She spoke up on his behalf. "He doesn't talk. His throat was damaged in the crash. But he can answer yes or no questions," she added quickly.

"Ah." Olivia's brow creased. "Marcus." She waited until he met her Alpha gaze. "Are there any other survivors?"

Instead of nodding, Marcus threw back his head and howled. The mournful quality of his cry left no doubt as to his answer, but Coach muttered: "Damaged throat, my ass."

Chloe's nerves tightened. Marcus looked wild: howling like a wolf, barefoot, vest unzipped. The way the two Alphas were frowning sent prickles of dread up her spine.

She wrapped her arms around Marcus's waist, soothing him until he stopped, then addressed the Alpha. "I'd say that's a no."

Coach stepped forward, and Marcus snarled at him. Great.

"He may have managed to Change back to a boy, but his mind obviously didn't survive the trip. He's still feral." Coach glared at Marcus. "He's dangerous and should be put down."

Marcus lifted his lip, showing his teeth.

Don't Change now. "Marcus, stop it."

"He obviously has no control over his wolf," Coach continued.

"Why? Because he doesn't like you?" Chloe went on the offensive. "You put two bullets in him, and you're a bully! I don't like you either. Marcus Jennings was born to this Pack. You're the Outsider."

"Your father is an Outsider, too," Judy said.

"My father has been part of this Pack for eighteen years; Coach has been here for only two," Chloe protested.

But everyone was muttering now and closing in around Marcus, which only made him shake harder.

Chloe bared her own teeth. "Back off! Give him room!"

Olivia lifted her voice in echo. "Give him room!"

Marcus panted, his eyes flashing every which way, alert for threats. Chloe grabbed his chin. "Calm down. Everything is fine. Do not Change."

He pulled in a deep, ragged breath. His shoulders stopped hunching, and he stood proudly at her side.

Nathan stepped forward. "Everyone but Marcus and the Graham family withdraw to the driveway."

Coach stiffened, as if intending to ask to be included, but retreated under Nathan's hard glare.

"We need to hear the full story," Nathan said.

So Chloe told it all again from meeting the feral in the woods to how Marcus had been pulled along when Chloe Changed back.

Nathan shook his head when she finished. "I never heard the like."

"Me either," her dad said. "I think the Change may have hormonal triggers."

Olivia fingered the crystal hanging around her throat. "So the feral's Change into a boy may be a matter of instinct rather than will?"

Her dad looked up sharply. "I never said that. I'm speculating—"

She held up a hand. "Granted. However, please understand our position. We must take the welfare of the Pack as a whole into consideration. There has never been a case of a feral Changing back after so long in wolf form—that I know of. Rachel?"

Chloe's mom shook her head. "I can't recall anything, but I'd need to research it further and consult other historians before I can give you a definitive answer."

Chloe tried not to feel betrayed. But, of course, her mother couldn't lie to the Alpha.

Olivia continued, "He has the form of a boy, but right now his mind is still wolf. Still feral."

"You can't kill him!" Chloe burst out, horrified at where this was going.

The Alpha ignored her, and Chloe's mom put a warning hand on her arm, meaning *Don't interrupt*. Chloe quivered with suppressed fear and indignation on Marcus's behalf.

"Curtis, you're the medical expert," Olivia said. "What do you think?"

Her dad spoke carefully. "If you're asking me if the boy can be saved, I believe there's a strong chance. It's far too early, in my opinion, to make a medical decision."

"He travelled so far. Please," Chloe begged. Tears clogged her throat.

The Alpha's gaze became distant. "Very well. Marcus was Pack. He deserves some time. We shall reconvene on the matter in one week and hope to see improvement." Though she said 'we,' she didn't consult with her husband.

"And if you don't?" Chloe asked, fists clenched, throat raw.

Another squeeze from her mother, meaning *Don't challenge the Alpha*.

"Let's leave that decision until then," Olivia said firmly. "In the meantime, he must remain out of public view."

In case you decide to kill him later?

"For everyone's safety." Olivia fixed her Alpha stare on Chloe.
Her mother's grip grew bruising.

Chloe forced herself to lower her gaze.

"He'll need to stay with someone," Olivia continued.

"We'd be happy to have him," her mother said at once.

Nathan frowned. "I don't know if that's safe. Are you confident he won't attack you?"

"Yes!" Chloe said. Her parents echoed her a heartbeat later.

"Winston and Karen named us guardians in their will," her father added. "Let us do this for their son."

"Very well." Olivia leaned back against her husband with a sigh. "I'd intended to hold Chloe's Pack ceremony tonight—"

A jolt went through Chloe. In all the excitement of Marcus's return she'd forgotten what it meant that she'd had her Change. She could finally be inducted into the Pack and receive her Bite.

"—but I'm tired and emotions are high. Let's postpone it, hmmm?" Olivia continued.

"Fine by me," Nathan said neutrally.

Chloe eyed him curiously. Tradition held that the Bite be given by the Alpha of the same gender as the receiver. To give the Bite, the Alpha had to be in wolf form. Did he fear his wife was too ill to Change?

Olivia waved a hand. "Then it's settled. Take me inside."

Without another word, Nathan scooped her up in his arms as if she weighed nothing and carried her into the house. The rest of the Pack starting edging forward again.

"Why don't you two go straight home?" her dad suggested. "Your mom and I will appease everyone's curiosity and run damage control."

Chloe gave him a quick hug. "Thanks. And thanks for letting Marcus stay with us."

"Karen would've done the same for you if the situation had been reversed," her mom said, teary-eyed.

Chloe's eyes prickled, remembering Abby and Marcus's mom. "Yeah."

"Go," her mom urged.

As soon as she and Marcus entered the woods, he Changed back to a wolf, a flowing, almost painless transition that took less than ten seconds.

Sharp words rose in her throat, but she swallowed them back. Yelling at Marcus would only make things worse. Better to praise him instead. "You did very well, staying a boy while talking to the Alphas. I know it put a strain on you." She ruffled his ears. "We'll work hard on increasing your time in human form tomorrow. Okay?"

As he trotted at her side, she gave herself a pep talk. They had a week. They could do this.

The wolf whined beseechingly at Chloe. Why wouldn't she let him in?

"No," Chloe said firmly. "It's bedtime. You have a perfectly nice room of your own—Mom showed it to you earlier. Go!" She pointed down the hall and closed the bedroom door in his face.

The wolf padded down the hall to the other room. He jumped up onto the bed and lay down on top of the navy blue coverlet. But the bed was too soft, the blanket too noisy and slick. It was made to sleep under, but he didn't want to Change. Fur was better for sleeping.

And he didn't want to be alone in a room. He'd been solitary too long in the forest, the endless days cycling through the seasons. Pack should be with Pack.

He slipped back down the hall and waited outside Chloe's door. She was in the bathroom, brushing her teeth.

When she came out, she looked at him and sighed. "Okay. I don't have the heart to kick you out. But if you're going to sleep in here you have to stay a wolf. I don't want any lectures from Mom. Okay?"

She was letting him in! Overjoyed, he bounced into her bedroom, but after a quick sniff around he settled himself down to sleep at the foot of her bed.

"Goodnight," she breathed, giving his head one last stroke.

He licked her fingers and closed his eyes, content. He belonged right here, curled at her feet, ready to protect her from any threats.

He didn't understand everything that had happened tonight—people spoke too fast, and he missed things—but there was nothing wrong with his nose.

The female Alpha had smelled wrong. Metallic, though she'd tried to cover it up with flower scent. And he'd caught a whiff from one of the assembled wolves of something worse: the Evil in the Forest.

CHAPTER

12

Chloe woke up full of determination. She'd already achieved the impossible: persuading a feral to Change back to human. How hard could it be to get Marcus talking and behaving like a boy again?

Her optimism took a hit when Marcus showed no interest in either breakfast or Changing back into a boy. He sat by the back door and stared hopefully at it. His behaviour was uncomfortably dog-like. Best not to reward it.

She sat down to her own breakfast across the table from her parents. "I can't go to school," Chloe said baldly.

"Agreed," her mother said. "I wish we could stay home, but your Dad has three surgeries today. We'll be gone all day. Get Judy to collect your homework for you."

As if. "I'll ask Kyle," Chloe said. "He'll probably want to visit Marcus anyway."

Her mother sighed, but didn't comment on her quarrel with Judy. "Try to coax Marcus into Changing. The more time he spends as a boy, the faster his adjustment."

Chloe nodded. "I plan to lure him with video games. But, uh, I was hoping to Change myself and go for a run this morning."

Her mom frowned. "Well ... "

"She just had her first Change, of course she wants to practise," her dad said indulgently. "I wore fur so often the first month I Changed, your grandma threatened to set out a dog bowl for me."

"All right," her mom said. "It can be easy to lose track of time in wolf form, but try to set a mental clock to Change back in two hours. Don't go too far into the Preserve."

Chloe dipped her head in acknowledgement.

"Oh, and I hope this goes without saying, but no sex."

"Mom!" Chloe's cheeks burned, and she cast an agonized glance at Marcus who, fortunately, didn't appear to be listening.

"It's a natural instinct," her mother said, amused. "But neither of you are ready for the complications it would bring."

"Mom, I'm not going to have sex with Abby's brother," Chloe hissed, trying to keep her voice down. Yes, she'd kissed him, during a moment of high emotion and joy, but— "*Mom.*"

Her mother raised an eyebrow. "Good. Keep thinking that way."

As soon as her parents drove out of sight, Chloe walked barefoot out onto the prickly lawn. She stripped down and closed her eyes, waiting for the magic to take hold.

Nothing.

Her heart gave a great lurch. Terror gripped her throat and the old panicky despair rose up. Why wasn't it working? She tried to recapture the moment of Change, but what had been instinctual before now seemed walled away, out of reach.

Then Marcus nudged her knee with his furry head. She crouched down, shivering in her underwear, and stared into his bisected face and crystal blue eyes. Wolf eyes. Wild eyes.

Her breath sighed out of her, and she fell into his eyes, into the Change. Her transformation took longer and hurt more than the desperate first time, but she forced herself to relax and not fight it. Five minutes later, she pawed off her remaining clothes and stood shoulder to shoulder with Marcus as a wolf.

Connection flowed between them. As one, they turned and trotted deeper into the forest, farther away from the noise and stink of the highway and the town.

Ah, the smells! So much richer and more complex than her poor human nose could appreciate: moss and leaf rot and the spoor of squirrels. The taste of coming rain on the wind.

Marcus nipped her, saying *Hurry up* without words. She gave chase, and they ran and played in the forest. Marcus showed her his special spots, places Chloe, despite all her rambling and hiking, had never seen.

A stump that looked like an old man's face.

A mossy fallen log.

A rill running over a jumble of stones, and the clear, cold taste of its water.

Chloe's wet muzzle came up sharply, her ears pricking at a sudden noise. Not natural. Human.

She and Marcus exchanged glances, then in perfect agreement went into hunting mode: keeping to the shadows between trees, timing their movements with the gusts of wind. Instinct made them steal up on their target from downwind, though humans wouldn't spook like deer did.

Humans had guns.

Chloe's wolf shrugged the thought away. They were clever and quiet, and the humans wouldn't see them unless they wanted to be seen. They were Pack.

Three men walked among the tall firs and pines of the Preserve. A sweaty, pot-bellied man made notations on a clipboard, while a second stranger with fur on his face talked and gestured expansively with his arms.

The third man was Nathan Frayne.

Why would the Alpha bring strangers into the Preserve? Curious, Chloe cocked her ears and made an effort to listen to the human speech.

"—prime bit of timber you got here," the furry-chinned man was saying. "Old growth, never been logged, DBH over 20 inches … If it's all like this, you'll make a pretty penny. We'll need to build a road in, of course, which will take a bite."

Loggers! A bolt of surprise transfixed Chloe. The men were from the logging company raising such a controversy in town. But what were they doing in the Preserve? And why was the Alpha listening to them instead of driving them away?

Chloe suppressed a whine. It didn't make sense. It felt wrong.

She'd always loved going for cross-country hikes in the Preserve, but it was different as a wolf. She needed the untamed wilderness like she needed breath and blood. Something in her would die without it.

It was the Pack's sacred trust to hold and defend the Preserve, to keep it safe from humans.

Her wolf couldn't read facial expressions well, but the Alpha's body language bothered her. His shoulders were tense, and the logger's words made him flinch. But most of all he smelled of … Chloe sniffed again. Could that be right? Could the Alpha smell of defeat?

Why?

Marcus nudged her, and they silently trotted away from the men. Her pleasure in the morning ruined, Chloe headed back to the house.

The Change from wolf back to girl proved easier, if still unpleasant. She gritted her teeth through the pain, then quickly looked up. Had Marcus—?

Good. He was a boy again.

A naked boy.

"Uh, your clothes are in the house." Chloe turned her back and dressed. The hoodie felt blissfully warm.

Marcus had pulled on the sweatpants, but not the vest, by the time she came into the house. He quivered when she automatically engaged the deadbolt. Most people in the country didn't bother, but after junkies broke into her dad's vet practice, her mom had insisted on having one installed and getting in the habit of using it.

"Does that bother you?" Chloe asked. "No exits?" She unlocked the deadbolt and opened the main door, leaving just the screen door in place. So what if the house got a bit cold? Marcus was more important.

A glance at the clock told her they'd exceeded her mother's two-hour rule, almost doubling it. Whoops.

"Lunchtime. What would you like to eat?" Chloe asked. "How about grilled cheese sandwiches?" They were her speciality.

Taking his silence as a yes, Chloe went to work. Eyeing his protruding ribs, she slapped some deli ham in between the slices, too. While her back was turned, frying them up, Marcus wolfed down the rest of the ham package. She caught him stuffing the last bit in his mouth and couldn't help but laugh. "I guess you're hungry, huh?"

And thirsty, apparently, because he turned on the kitchen faucet then stuck his head under and started gulping the water down.

"You know, usually we drink from glasses," Chloe said. Puzzled and dismayed, she poured them both a glass of milk. Had he forgotten how to behave properly? But he knew how to turn on the taps. Maybe he just didn't care about etiquette.

In a few moments she slid the grilled cheese sandwiches onto two plates. "Careful, they're hot," she warned him, before nibbling at her own.

Marcus imitated her, picking the sandwich up by the crust. He sniffed at it, took a cautious bite, then immediately spat it out.

"Too hot?" She clamped her lips together to hide her amusement—until he did the same thing to the milk. "Lactose intolerant?"

Marcus shook his head, nodded, then shrugged. Not helpful.

While she cleaned the mess with paper towels, he ran water from the sink again. He didn't seem to care that the water splashed down his neck and chest.

Chloe pulled out her phone and sent a quick text to Kyle. *Does M have allergies?* She'd eaten over at his place numerous times, visiting Abby, and didn't remember Marcus having any special dietary requirements, but maybe she just hadn't paid enough attention.

She offered him the sandwich again. "It's cool now, I promise." He curled his lip.

"Well, you must still be hungry. What do you want to eat?"

He ate two crackers, but refused the rest. He stared longingly at the hamburger defrosting on the counter.

"No," she said firmly. "That's for supper." Opening the fridge, she scrounged up another package of deli meat. That seemed to do the trick: he happily scarfed down the corned beef.

She texted her mom, asking her to pick up some cold cuts.

Kyle texted back: *No allergies.* She invited Kyle over after school and dutifully asked him to bring her homework.

When she finished, Marcus had Changed into a wolf again.

Chloe swore as Kyle, Dean and Judy all piled out of Dean's junker car at four-thirty in the afternoon. Only Brian was missing; he must have had to go home and babysit his siblings.

She shoved Marcus, who was dozing, off the living room couch. He yipped at her reproachfully, and she threw his sweatpants at him. "Change, right now! Judy is the Alphas' daughter. We need her to give a good report."

The screen door squeaked open, and Chloe hurried down the hall to intercept everybody, arriving in the entryway slightly breathless. "Hey!" She raised an eyebrow, pretending surprise. "Does it take three of you to carry my homework?"

"Ha. Ha. Ha," Judy said. From her resentful expression, the fact that Chloe wasn't a Dud didn't impress her.

She thinks I'm still at the bottom of the Pack hierarchy.
We'll see about that.

"We came to see Marcus. Obviously." Judy tossed her pony-tail and took a step forward.

Chloe blocked the way from the porch into the hall. Marcus needed more time—at least she hoped he was Changing and getting dressed. "Not so fast," she stalled. "This is my territory. Nobody comes inside until I get an apology."

An instinct to protect Marcus had spurred the words, but once they came out, they rang true. She wasn't going to let them get away with just pretending the last three months of snubbing hadn't happened.

"Really?" Temper fired Judy's eyes. "You're going to invoke that rule after you stomped all over it, barging into my house and stealing something?"

"Borrowing," Chloe corrected. "And I apologized for my actions and have been assigned a punishment for my transgression." She crossed her arms.

Kyle broke the deadlock. "I'm sorry for calling you a Dud. I should have known you'd break through your block. You're a werewolf through and through." His tone held rueful admiration.

Chloe granted him a regal nod and turned to the side. "You may come in."

"I'm not sorry." Dean flashed her a cheeky grin. "Coach told us to give you a hard time, that it would push you to Change, and he was right."

Chloe reeled. "Coach ordered you to give me a hard time?"

"Pretty much," Kyle confirmed.

Her teeth ground together on a surge of hatred. If Coach had been standing there, she would have slugged him.

"I am glad you Changed," Dean added more seriously. "Welcome to the Pack." He gave her shoulders a quick pat and moved past her into the kitchen, already reaching for the jar of cookies her mom kept stocked up.

That left Judy still in the porch. She glared at Chloe.

Chloe waited.

"You never once asked for help Changing," Judy said abruptly.

Chloe blinked, taken aback. "I wanted to do it on my own." For it to be her own accomplishment. And by the time she'd grown desperate enough to ask for help her so-called friends had turned nasty, and she wouldn't have asked them for a cup of water while dying in the desert.

"And that, right there, is why it took you so long to Change," Judy said. "It's not the Pack way to do it alone."

Was Judy right? Chloe's insides churned. She'd assumed that once she Changed everything would go back to normal, but what if it didn't? What if there was a deeper problem?

"So no, I'm not going to beg your pardon," Judy said. "Are you going to let me in or not?" she challenged.

Her question hung in the air. Chloe considered it. Resentment simmered inside her, an ugly stew. Her wolf didn't want to let it go, wanted to force Judy to grovel.

But if she did, they'd never be friends again.

Did she want to be friends with Judy? Chloe didn't know. It was easier to forgive the boys, because they hadn't been as close. On the one hand, Judy had been pretty nasty to her. On the other hand, they'd known each other since birth. Judy and the boys were part of her Pack. They smelled right. Pack squabbles were family squabbles, and a permanent quarrel with your family could mean moving far away.

She didn't want that.

"You're not forgiven," Chloe told Judy—which made Judy's eyes flash with anger as she hadn't asked for forgiveness, "but you're Pack. You can come in." She walked into the kitchen.

"So where's Marcus?" Dean asked impatiently.

The fine hairs stirred on the back of Chloe's neck as Marcus moved up behind her. Relief blew through her: he'd Changed into a boy. Turning, she caught his wrist and drew him forward.

"Good thing your parents don't have a no shirts, no shoes, no service policy," Dean said, snickering.

Had he always been so thick? Chloe glared at him.

"Hey, Marcus." Kyle approached with his gaze diffidently down, careful not to challenge. "It's good to see you, bro. I missed you."

Marcus tensed, pressing his arm closer to hers. He watched Kyle carefully. Surely, he recognized his best friend?

Kyle glanced at her. "Rumour is he can't talk?"

"No," Chloe said reluctantly. "At least not yet. But he can understand speech and nod yes or no. Though he doesn't pay as much attention to words as we do," she admitted. "And he gets upset if you ask about the crash. So that topic is off limits," she said with a stern warning glance.

"But—" Judy started.

Chloe understood the grief on her face, the longing for a second miracle. She shook her head. "He's the only survivor."

"So what can we talk about?" Judy demanded.

"I'm so glad you asked," Chloe said sweetly. She took pleasure in the wariness that furrowed Judy's brow. "We can talk about how we're going to help Marcus regain his human half."

"I'm in," Kyle said.

"Not sure what you think we can do," Dean said around a mouthful of cookie.

Kyle elbowed his big brother. "Ignore Mr. Negative Thinking here. He's sulking because he broke up with Ilona."

"Hey," Dean said defensively. "She's hot."

Kyle didn't back down, getting up into his brother's face. "Well, excuse me, but I think *my best friend's life* is a little more important than whether or not you get laid!"

Instead of getting angry, Dean patted Kyle's back. "Okay, you have my help. For what it's worth."

Two down, one to go. Chloe turned to Judy again. "No offense to your parents—I know they have to consider the big issues—but they only gave Marcus a week to improve. I'm not going to just let that time drift past and hope for the best. Everyone needs to help."

Judy bristled. "There you go, giving orders again. You're not the Alpha, Chloe. Just because you Changed doesn't make you boss. That would be my parents."

I know I'm not Alpha material, but you're not top wolf either. The words hovered on the tip of Chloe's tongue.

"Ooh, Dominance fight," Dean stage-whispered.

Chloe ignored him, gaze still locked with Judy. She was stronger. She could Dominate Judy and force compliance. She could do more than that—she could make Judy grovel but doing so would just make Judy hate her more.

She'd hated it when the others Dominated her. Bullied her. *I won't let them push me around, but I don't want to turn into a bully.*

At her side Marcus's lip lifted in a snarl. Worry spiked through her—what would Marcus do if she and Judy fought? She put a hand on his shoulder, and took a deep breath. She could compromise. "I didn't mean to boss you around. You said Pack asks for help. Well, I'm asking for yours now. All of you," she glanced at the room before facing Judy again.

Judy blinked, looking off-balance and a little relieved at this de-escalation.

"I don't know if we can be friends again," Chloe continued, "but we were both friends of Abby's. Marcus is Abby's brother. He's Pack, and he needs our help. Will you help him, for Abby's sake, if not for mine?"

Judy's eyes filled with tears. She gave a quick nod.

"What do you need?" Kyle asked.

Deep breath. "For starters, I'd like to know his favourite foods." She grimaced. "So far, he's shown a strong preference for meat."

Judy wrinkled her nose. "Raw meat?"

Surprised, Chloe laughed. "No! Deli ham and corned beef. Last night he ate Mom's stew, vegetables included. Maybe because they were in gravy? Anyhow, so far he's turned up his nose at cereal, grilled cheese sandwiches and crackers."

"Kyle, what were his favourite foods?"

"Pizza," Kyle said after a moment. "Potato chips." He shrugged. "You know, the usual."

"Abby loved taco chips with extra hot salsa," Judy said wistfully. "And Peanut Butter Cups."

"And Snickers bars," Chloe added. "Anything chocolate, really."

"You could have put chocolate on chicken, and she would have eaten it," Judy agreed.

Marcus whined.

Chloe squeezed his hand. "Sorry. Okay, let's plan a pizza and junk food party Sunday afternoon. Everyone, keep talking. What did Marcus like to do?"

"Hiking," Dean said.

"I think we can scratch that one," Chloe said. She doubted Marcus would hold to human form for more than a minute if they went into the forest. "Any hobbies?"

Kyle snapped his fingers. "Model planes. When we were younger, he'd make epic things out of Lego, not just following instructions, but doing his own thing. Oh, and he loved hockey."

Chloe glanced at Marcus to see how he felt about being referred to in the past tense, but he was staring at Dean. Not with hostility, just in the wolf way of keeping an eye on the biggest predator.

"He was really good at getting the puck out of corners," Dean said.

Unfortunately, Pine Hollow only had outdoor rinks, and it wouldn't be cold enough to skate for at least another month. Well past their time limit.

"Pizza party and hockey night," Chloe said. "Any other suggestions?"

Silence. Judy fidgeted. "I need to get going. I promised I'd be home by five to start making supper."

They said their goodbyes and trooped out. Kyle lingered a moment. He squeezed Marcus's arm. "Hang in there, bud. No going feral, okay?"

Marcus didn't nod, but allowed the touch.

Kyle suddenly grinned, making his resemblance to Dean much more pronounced. "Hey, I have an idea to help Marcus stay human. Offer him an incentive."

Chloe sensed a trap. "Like what?"

"Yourself. Tell him if he eats his vegetables, you'll give him a kiss. Staying human for a full day earns him a cuddle on the couch." Kyle winked at Marcus and sauntered off.

Boys. "Har de har har." Chloe glared after Kyle then shut the door.

Marcus stared at her with hopeful eyes.

"Forget it," Chloe told him. "You're Abby's little brother." She kept her voice firm, but she couldn't help but remember their exuberant kiss when they were both naked and freshly Changed. The tips of her ears heated.

What would Abby have said if she'd been alive? Would she have been outraged? Protective of Marcus? Grossed out? Amused?

If Marcus had still been a wolf, his ears would have drooped. He'd Changed to be with Chloe, but she didn't want him.

At least that's what her words said. Her body had said differently. She'd smelled eager when she kissed him.

It was a she-wolf's right to change her mind, but he didn't understand why she had. She didn't act interested in the other males, even though one of them—Dean—was bigger and stronger than Marcus. Was it just because he was Abby's brother or was it something he'd done?

Was it because he couldn't talk?

He grunted, trying to form words, but they died inside him. His chest locked tight like a metal box. Speaking meant answering questions, and questions brought pain.

He wasn't ready to talk about his family yet.

Thinking about Abby and his parents hurt, a deep ache, worse than a thousand cuts. He'd learned to shunt thoughts of them away. After the crash, grief had hobbled him, and in the woods where survival balanced on a razor's edge, he hadn't been able to afford the distraction, so he'd stayed wolf. He'd cut off the part of him that was Marcus Jennings.

He'd do almost anything to make Chloe choose him as her mate. Could he do that? Go back to the boy he'd once been? He didn't know if it was even possible. He feared that his wolf had saved his body at the expense of crippling his soul.

CHAPTER
13

"Marcus, I'd like to run a few tests," her dad announced that evening. "Just simple ones." He produced a pencil and paper.

Marcus balanced on the edge of a kitchen chair, as if poised to flee. Chloe put a hand on his shoulder. "You'll do fine," she said, projecting confidence.

Her mother had approved the pizza party on the condition that Chloe keep up with her homework, so Chloe resumed making notes on her assigned Social Studies chapter and tried not to betray her tension to Marcus as he underwent the testing.

He had trouble writing, holding his pencil like a toddler in his fist, but followed her dad's questions well enough. When asked him to write his name, he scribed a huge blocky M A R then ran out of room and had to continue on the line below. He whined in distress.

"No, that's fine," her dad soothed. "It looks like you remember your letters, but have lost some fine motor skills. Let's try a little math."

So much for Chloe's plan to ask Marcus to write out his answers to the Alphas' questions.

His numbers were also big and uneven, but he proved adept at addition, subtraction, multiplication and division. Her dad didn't go beyond that, but demonstrated the proper way to hold a pencil and set him practising his letters. If Marcus resented being treated like a six-year-old, he didn't indicate it.

"I'm going to do a bit more research and then tomorrow we'll see about setting up some throat exercises for you, too. Limber up those muscles." Her father moved to pat him on the shoulder, then thought better of it.

In addition to more deli meat, her mom had purchased new clothes for Marcus and a toothbrush. She handed him the toothbrush. "Go brush your teeth," she said firmly.

Five minutes later, Chloe spotted him still in the bathroom. He stared at a large glob of blue freshmint toothpaste on his brush.

Chloe removed half of it and handed him back the brush. His nose wrinkled.

"C'mon, brushing is important," Chloe coaxed. She remembered what Kyle had said. "Nobody's going to kiss someone with shreds of meat stuck in his teeth." She had meant the words to be teasing, but they came out flirtatious.

Perking up, Marcus started brushing. His eyes widened in horror. He spit and spit and spit into the sink, obviously trying to get rid of the mint taste. He gave Chloe such an intense look of betrayal that she snickered.

"Sorry, I promise you'll get used to it." Heartlessly, she left him alone.

Two minutes later he slunk out of the bathroom in wolf form. The bit of foam at the corner of his mouth set Chloe off again.

"It's not funny," her mom told her. "I shudder to think what damage he may have done to his teeth without dental care for a year."

"It's not like he ate a lot of sugar as a wolf," Chloe pointed out.

Her mother narrowed her eyes. "Weren't you doing homework?"

Chloe hastily lowered her head back over her textbook.

Marcus picked a slice of pepperoni off the top of the pizza and ate it, but pushed aside the melted cheese.

Chloe sighed. "Maybe you should be tested for lactose

intolerance." She couldn't imagine voluntarily giving up pizza. Or pop, which Marcus had also scorned.

She'd pinned a lot of hope on this party. In the three days since the Alphas' ultimatum Marcus still hadn't spoken. He hated the throat exercises and practising writing the alphabet. Every time she turned around he'd gone wolf again.

The only time he seemed happy was when he was bounding through the woods.

Whatever form he took, he glued himself to her side. He'd even come with her yesterday when she did her punishment detail of raking and garden work at the Alphas. She hadn't liked the way Nathan had watched him the entire time as if expecting him to suddenly turn violent.

She'd half-expected Nathan to refuse to let Judy come to the party, but she was here along with the other Pack kids. Pizza had been consumed, and the hockey game would start soon.

Trying to relax, Chloe moved into the living room. "Who's playing?" she asked, plopping down in the empty spot beside Kyle on the sofa.

"Oilers versus the Flames, grudge match," Kyle said with relish. He put his feet up beside hers on the coffee table.

Before Chloe could blink, Marcus shoved Kyle over and squished in between them. His lip curled in warning.

He couldn't have been more obvious if he'd hung a sign around her neck saying Mine.

Judy was staring, her pop can halfway to her lips. Chloe blushed. What should she do? Ignore it?

Marcus was more Dominant than Kyle. By Pack rules, he had a right to shove the other boy aside. If she interfered with that, she would confuse Marcus.

But the muscles in Marcus's leg pressed against hers, and, since he was once again not wearing a shirt, her arm also brushed against his bare chest.

She did not want to spend the whole hockey game like this: hyperaware and overheated. She affected casualness. "Hey, you're crowding me. Shove over you two."

Kyle and Marcus obligingly bumped over, giving her a couple of inches of breathing room.

Chloe only pretended to listen to the TV hosts' pre-game chatter. To her disappointment, Marcus's gaze roamed the room, not focusing on the TV. Was this going to fail, too?

But when the game finally did start, he leaned forward, following the play. When the Flames scored early on, he growled.

Chloe relaxed and got caught up in the game herself. Thankfully, it was an exciting one, with lots of end-to-end action.

Pine Hollow wasn't particularly close to either Edmonton or Calgary so loyalties were divided. Dean and Kyle cheered for the Flames, whereas everyone else leaned more toward the Oilers.

Chloe cheered for the Oilers, her mom's team, most of the time, but if they didn't make the playoffs she'd cheerfully switch loyalties to the Maple Leafs, her dad's team of choice.

After the first period, she did the hostess thing and put out a tray of cut vegetables, as well as chips and dip.

When she re-entered the living room, Kyle was trying to persuade Marcus to play a game on his phone.

Chloe had had zero luck interesting Marcus in video games, but she hung back and let Kyle try.

But Marcus noticed her standing there and stopped paying attention to Kyle. She set the last two bowls down on the coffee table. "Have some chips!"

He rejected the nacho-flavoured Doritos, but started scarfing down the plain potato chips. Good. He was too thin, still.

Muscled, but too thin.

The Flames won, but otherwise the evening went well. Chloe was feeling cautiously optimistic until Judy's dad arrived to pick her up.

"Chloe," Nathan said. "Why does your property stink of wolf urine?"

Chloe winced.

"It's the feral, isn't it?" Nathan said heavily. "It's marking your territory."

"Marcus," Chloe correctly him sharply.

The Alpha turned the full weight of his stare on her. "Is Marcus responsible?"

Compelled, she nodded. While Chloe was in wolf form herself, Marcus's behaviour had always seemed perfectly natural and unremarkable. Now it seemed weird. Had he used the toilet at all? She thought he had, but she couldn't say for sure.

"We've been working on other areas," she said.

Marcus slipped into place beside her, his muscles taut and corded.

Don't growl. Don't challenge the Alpha.

Nathan nodded. "Has he spoken?"

"Not yet. My dad has set him some voice exercises. We're trying to limber up the muscles." Chloe struggled not to sound defensive.

Nathan grunted. "Judy, you ready to go?"

"Yes, Dad." Judy slipped into the entrance way.

While Judy put on her shoes, Chloe desperately tried to think of some proof of humanity or improvement she could offer. *He eats with us, but prefers meat. He sleeps as a wolf at the foot of my bed. He can't talk and he writes like a kindergartner. He refuses to brush his teeth.*

She still hadn't thought of anything convincing when Judy and her dad left.

"We're in trouble," Chloe told Marcus later that evening. She was sitting up in bed, unable to sleep, and Marcus lay beside her in wolf form. She petted his head, trying to soothe herself more than him.

Her emotions were all in a jumble.

Anger burned inside her chest. Marcus had been a wolf for almost a year. Asking him to return to being a boy like flipping a switch in a week's time was ridiculous. He wasn't any more a danger to others than soldiers who'd come back from war with post-traumatic stress disorder, and nobody suggested killing them.

He wasn't feral. She'd caught glimpses of Marcus the boy: his fascination with hockey, the devoted way he shadowed her, the small smile on his lips when she agreed to go for a run. He might be part wolf, but he was also Marcus, Abby's brother.

He just needed more time. She clenched her fists. Time they didn't have.

Underneath the anger lay stomach-churning fear. She'd never been more terrified in her life.

More than ever she didn't trust the Alphas to make the right decision. Olivia had been absent or erratic for months because of her illness, and Nathan was so worried about her that he'd become impatient with other issues. He wanted them settled fast. And Marcus's recovery wasn't going to be a quick thing.

The one-week deadline was rushing up at them with the speed of a Nascar racer.

She feared Nathan had already made up his mind to judge Marcus feral.

Chloe's heart ached, and her entire being rebelled. She couldn't let them execute Marcus. She'd promised Abby's soul that she'd keep Marcus safe.

She'd fight, if it came down to that. But she was one small wolf against the rest of the Pack. She'd lose. They'd restrain her, and Marcus would die.

Marcus lifted his head, whining, and she swiped away the tears running down her cheeks. "Don't worry," she told him. "I won't let them touch you."

The Alphas could get away with murder because Marcus was already believed dead.

So it was time to show the townspeople he lived. Chloe took out her phone, intending to post a photo on social media, but would that be enough? Photos could be faked. What if the Alphas claimed she was lying? No, if she was going to go public, she was going to need multiple eyewitnesses, too many to be dismissed or intimidated. She nodded firmly. Tomorrow, they were going to school.

CHAPTER

14

"You're up early," her mom remarked between sips of coffee. "What are your plans for the day?"

Chloe had big plans. Phase One: get her parents out of the house. Her dad had already left on an emergency call, and her mom would soon follow. All Chloe had to do was keep her mom from getting suspicious.

Chloe shrugged. "I might make an appearance at school. I don't want to fall behind on my homework." She skirted the edge of a lie.

"Leave Marcus alone for a bit? Hmmm. I suppose we'll have to get back to a regular routine sometime," her mother said.

Chloe took a bite of toast and said nothing. As much as her parents wanted to save Marcus, they couldn't go against the Alphas' orders. Physically couldn't. But Chloe hadn't received the Bite yet. She could.

Her parents would be mad at her afterward, but any punishment would be worth it to save Marcus. And she'd make it clear to the Alphas that her parents had known nothing of her plan.

"I have to go now." Her mom stood up. "It's my turn to look in on Olivia and run errands for her. Then I have a full day at the clinic. Prep supper, but don't put it in the oven until your dad and I let you know when we'll be in." Her mom continued giving instructions as she put on her shoes and jacket. "Don't let Marcus cut short his vocal lessons. It's vital that he start talking again."

"I won't," Chloe promised.

The instant her mother drove away, she sprang into motion. Phase Two: transportation to school. She snatched her backpack from where she'd stashed it in the closet, then retrieved Marcus from his bedroom where he was waiting, already dressed. "Hurry or we'll miss the bus." She grabbed his hand and hurried him out the door—only to backtrack seconds later when she realized he was barefoot.

He'd let her pull a T-shirt over his head for the first time this morning, though he'd growled a little. Now she made him slip on the new Crocs her Mom had bought him.

Stomach tight with nerves, she lectured him the whole trip down the driveway. "We'll be riding the bus. You can sit with me. The bus is bigger than the SUV so you shouldn't feel crowded. Remember, no growling at people even if they do stupid things. And absolutely no Changing. We're not going to stay at school long. We should be in and out in twenty minutes. If you get desperate, just tell me and I'll make an excuse to leave immediately, but I need you to try your best."

Marcus's head turned. The bus approached.

She touched his jaw and looked into his blue eyes, impressing her fierceness on him. "Today is important. You don't have to be perfect, but you have to stay long enough to be *seen*, okay?"

He nodded.

The bus screeched to a stop. Showtime.

To her relief, Marcus boarded without prompting, though his nostrils flared at the stink of exhaust.

The driver, Mrs. Patil, was accustomed to the Pack kids getting on or off at each other's stops and never fussed about it. But today her mouth hung open. "Marcus Jennings?"

"Go sit down." Chloe gave Marcus a little push. She paused to whisper a few words to Mrs. Patil. "After the plane crashed, he was lost in the woods for a long time. He doesn't talk much. Please, don't say anything about the crash. The rest of his family died, and it was really traumatic."

Eyes as round as ping-pong balls, Mrs. Patil nodded. She put the bus back in gear, but her eyes watched Marcus in the rear-view mirror several times on the way to town.

Dean and Kyle weren't on the bus—they usually drove. Brian was already on board, but had his head down on the padded seat in front of him, sleeping.

The bus bounced down another mile of gravelled road then slowed in front of Judy's house. "Hunch down," Chloe told Marcus. They couldn't risk one of the Alphas spotting him through the bus windows.

Judy boarded and headed toward the back of the bus. She stopped in the aisle when she saw Marcus and almost fell when the bus lurched into motion. She sat kitty-corner from them.

"What are you doing?" she hissed. "My mom hasn't approved taking him out in public yet."

Chloe hesitated. Play innocent or try to get Judy's support? In the end she shrugged. "He needs to get used to other people sometime."

Inside, her muscles coiled, ready to throw Judy's phone out the window if she tried to text her mother.

"But he's still half wild!" Judy protested. "He could give us away."

Chloe met her gaze. "He'll be fine for half an hour. That's not the real reason your mom wants him kept out of public view and you know it. *I won't let anybody kill Abby's brother.*"

Judy just shook her head. "I hope you know what you're doing, Chloe."

She hoped so, too. "It's already too late. Mrs. Patil has seen him."

"True." Judy steadied.

The last stop before school was Ilona's ranch house. As usual a wave of horse scent preceded the blonde. Chloe wrinkled her nose. Marcus sniffed several times as if puzzled. She patted his arm. "Ilona's okay, just horse crazy."

Ilona plopped down in the seat in front of Chloe and across from Judy. She frowned. "Who's this?"

"Ilona, you remember Abby's brother, don't you? Marcus Jennings." Ilona had moved to town a few months prior to the plane crash.

Ilona blinked. "But Abby—"

Judy frantically shook her head.

Ilona cut herself off. "Uh, good to see you again, Marcus."

Marcus nodded solemnly.

"So, I've been out of school a few days." Chloe changed the subject. "Tell me the latest gossip. What's up with you and Dean?"

Ilona's expression grew stormy. "The coward dropped me like a hot potato as soon as his dad found out."

Chloe nodded thoughtfully. "Yeah, Dean isn't much of an original thinker, is he? He just follows along with whatever the most dominant personality says."

"Still, that body. And face." Ilona sighed. "What a waste. So who should I set my sights on next? What about him?" She pointed to Brian, who was still sleeping like the dead. "Is he good boyfriend material?"

As if on cue, Brian started snoring.

Judy snickered.

Chloe joined in. "Brian is more easy-going than Dean, but I'm afraid he still thinks fart jokes are the king of comedy. He is cute, though," she offered fairly. Brian had a nicely muscled chest, ink-black hair and a firm chin. She tensed in case Ilona said anything racist about Brian's epicanthic eye folds. His half-Chinese ethnicity was a rarity in the predominantly-white northern community and had caused scuffles between Pack and townies in the past.

Ilona sighed theatrically. "Fart jokes? Now I understand your interest in younger men," she nodded toward Marcus, who was staring out the window as they entered Pine Hollow. "They are still trainable."

Judy snorted with laughter.

Chloe started to say Marcus wasn't her boyfriend, then settled for raising one eyebrow. Let Ilona think what she wanted. It could cause complications if Ilona set her romantic sights on Marcus.

"Pine Hollow needs to import more boys," Ilona complained. She went on in that vein until they arrived at school.

Brian raised his head and blinked a few times, but all he said was, "Hey, Marcus."

Chloe tugged on Marcus's sleeve once they hit the sidewalk. Phase three involved getting Marcus seen by as many adults as possible. "We'll start in the office. I bet there's a bunch of paperwork to fill out."

The school secretary, Mrs. Hopkins, was firmly in the pro-logging camp, but her usual coldness to Preserve kids melted when she recognized Marcus. "Marcus Jennings?" Her gaze flicked behind him, looking for a second miracle.

Chloe shook her head in a quick negative. No Abby.

"Hi, Mrs. Hopkins," she said with fake cheer. "As you can see, Marcus survived the plane crash after all. My parents are his guardians, so he's staying at my house. He's not ready to go back to school yet, but if you could print off all the paperwork that needs to be filled out I'll collect it in a few minutes and give it to my parents. Thanks!" She backed out of the office before the woman could get her tongue back.

If Chloe was really lucky the secretary would follow her

suggestion. More likely, her mom would shortly receive a surprising phone call.

The bell rang. Marcus flinched.

"Come on, we need to make an appearance in class. We'll pop in for five minutes maximum. Just stand by me and try not to growl. Everyone will stare, but when you do return to school later they'll be over the worst of it." She was determined to think positive: Marcus was getting better and would go back to school eventually.

The teacher wasn't there yet, but one of the townies immediately spotted Marcus and elbowed a friend. A chain reaction soon had five pairs of eyes trained on him.

"Is that—?"

"It's Marcus Jennings."

"I thought he was dead."

After one glance at Marcus, Dean stared at her. "Are you insane?" he mouthed.

"Hi, Marcus," Kyle said, waving from his desk. "Come sit by me."

"We're not staying," Chloe said. "We just stopped by to say hello and get my homework assignments from Mr. Presley."

A knot of hard satisfaction formed in her chest. This story would make the rounds of the whole town by supper tonight. There was no chance Marcus could be quietly 'disappeared' after this. Mission accomplished.

Mr. Presley bustled in late, dumped an armload of paper on his desk and started taking attendance without looking up. "Judy Frayne."

"Here."

"Chloe Graham."

"Here."

"Ah, back with us are—" Mr. Presley broke off as he noticed

Marcus standing next to her. His eyes widened. "Marcus Jennings?"

Marcus raised his hand, as if saying Present.

The class laughed.

"But … but … " Mr. Presley shook his head, then cleared his throat. "Good to see you again, Marcus." He was more subtle about it, but he checked for Abby, too, and looked disappointed not to see her.

Chloe squeezed Marcus's hand on a wave of sadness. This had to be twice as bad for him.

"We're not staying," she told the teacher. "We just wanted to say hi. So, hi everyone. See you later." She waved and Marcus copied her, then she steered him into the hallway.

She'd hoped to get the admission forms from Mrs. Hopkins and then slip out, but they were waylaid by the principal, Ms. Kim. "Marcus, welcome back." She extended her hand, and when Marcus gingerly did the same she held it for a moment. "I am so very sorry about your family. You have my condolences and those of the entire staff."

Marcus's throat worked as if he were trying to saw something. Chloe held her breath, but he didn't speak. Instead, he pulled free and went outside.

Ms. Kim stared after him.

Chloe gave a quick recap of the official story she and her parents had discussed—only survivor of the plane crash, lost in the woods, recently found again, but traumatized.

"He doesn't speak?"

"There's a scar on his throat. My dad—and the doctor—" she added quickly, "aren't sure if his larynx is damaged or if it's psychological." She shrugged. "He went through a lot and then didn't speak to another human being for months… . It's not surprising he's having trouble communicating."

"Hmmm." The principal fixed her with a stern glare. "You shouldn't have just sprung Marcus on us this morning without any warning. Why aren't your parents here?"

"It was a spur of the moment decision. I needed to pick up some textbooks and Marcus wanted to come along."

"Tell your parents to make an appointment so we can put together a learning strategy," Ms. Kim said sternly. "Mrs. Hopkins has been trying to get ahold of them, but apparently your mother's cell phone is turned off, and your father's dealing with an emergency."

Huh. That was odd. Chloe's mom was usually fanatical about keeping her cell phone on and charged. Oh, well. When her parents eventually got their messages, she was going to be in deep trouble. For now she seemed to be off the hook.

Chloe hurried outside.

Her heart lurched. Marcus wasn't in sight.

It was a relief to be outside again.

In the woods, Marcus had learned to be silent and to listen for signs of danger—for birds that suddenly stopped singing, for stealthy movement behind, for thunder. It grated at his nerve endings to be shut inside a sterile environment.

Being outside expanded his senses. The kiss of air moving against his skin, the mixed scents of town and nearby field, traffic and birdsong, the vibrant green of growing things instead of white walls.... It all helped, but his collar still felt too constricting. He wanted to tear it off. He itched to Change.

But if he did so, he'd get in trouble, and Chloe would be sad.

To remind himself to stay a boy, he climbed a large, four-trunked poplar and sat on one of the branching limbs, legs dangling six feet off the ground.

A few minutes later, Chloe came outside. "Marcus?"

He gave a soft yip to attract her attention. She spotted him and came to stand at the foot of the tree.

He tensed, expecting a scolding, but she sighed and climbed up to join him on the branch. After a moment, she reached for his hand and they sat together in harmony, faces lifted to the breeze. Marcus sniffed the air blowing across the sports field: grass starting to turn yellow, dogs that had passed this way and stopped to urinate. A vee of honking Canada geese flew by overhead …

Chloe started speaking. Marcus concentrated. What she said was important; what others said less so.

"It's nice out here. Thank you for showing me this."

He gave her a small smile.

"You did really well today. Do you think you'll be ready to go back in a few weeks?"

He lost his smile.

Marcus didn't want to go back to school. The old Marcus had spent hours upon hours cooped up in the dusty building, learning things, but it all seemed so meaningless now.

The sun would go down in a few hours and the dark would come. It was autumn, and sunlight was precious, not to be squandered.

The things learned in school was stuff the old Marcus had understood. He dimly remembered that learning was like a squirrel saving nuts for the winter, something to be taken out and used later in life. But that future that the old Marcus had taken for granted — university and a career in engineering — was gone now. Burned up.

The wolf part of him no longer believed in a future. Had stopped believing when the plane went down. There was only the present, here, now, sitting in a tree with Chloe.

Chloe sighed. "Sorry, but there's no way my parents will let you drop out. But we don't have to think about that today. Let's go home." She turned onto her stomach, then dangled from her hands for a moment before dropping to the ground in a crouch . Marcus copied her.

She started to pick up her backpack, but Marcus grabbed it first. "I can carry that."

A whine slipped out of his throat. Didn't she understand? He wanted to carry things for her, to show his respect.

Chloe rolled her eyes. "Fine, but we're going to take turns."

They had just finished crossing the parking lot when a new vehicle turned in and he recognized the man inside.

"Crap! That's Coach!" Chloe grabbed his hand and tried to pull him into a run.

Marcus resisted, every instinct telling him not to turn his back on this particular werewolf.

"He's seen us," Chloe said. She pulled on his hand and he broke into a reluctant jog.

A car door slammed. "Chloe Graham!" the werewolf bellowed.

Chloe ignored him and ran across the field toward the woods.

"Come here and explain yourself!"

Marcus slowed, turning to see if the werewolf was pursuing, but the blond man still stood by his car, glowering at them.

Chloe yanked on his arm again and hustled him into the woods.

Once they were screened by spruce trees, Marcus tore off his shirt, preparing to Change and fight.

"No!" Chloe caught his chin and made him look at her. "We're still too close to town for that. There's not going to be a fight. Look, Coach isn't chasing us."

Marcus growled. Every instinct he had told him the other werewolf was an enemy.

"I know Coach shot you, but he thought you were a feral at the time. You have to get past this."

Marcus shook his head, vehement. No. No. No.

"Yes," Chloe insisted. "He's a member of the Pack. He's Dominant to both of us, and he works part-time at the school, teaching Phys. Ed. You're going to see him often and you can't challenge him."

No. No. No.

"Ugh. We've got to work harder on your voice exercises, this lack of communication is driving me crazy. Look, let's just go." She started walking.

Frustrated, Marcus followed her. More than ever he resented having to take this form.

If they were wolves, he would've been able to convey what he meant. That the other werewolf, Coach, was a danger to them both.

Coach didn't smell like Pack. He smelled almost right, but some elusive half-note was off.

More than that, a black shadow of memory stirred whenever they crossed paths. Something to do with Abby. Something bad.

CHAPTER 15

Chloe's heart thudded unpleasantly when she got close to the house. Her mother's car was in the driveway. It was only eleven o'clock. Her mom ought to still be at work.

"Stay outside," she ordered Marcus. He was in wolf form and had been since they left the town limits.

Her mother was waiting for her in the kitchen. "Mom?"

"Oh, Chloe," her mother said, her eyes hollow and sad. "What have you done?"

Chloe kept silent.

"What on earth possessed you to defy the Alpha so blatantly?" her mother asked, despair heavy in her voice. "She specifically said Marcus wasn't ready to be out in public. By taking him to school, you risked exposing our kind."

Chloe's chin came up. "Our secret's safe. We only stayed for a little while and Marcus did really good."

Her mother's lips flattened. "No remorse, Chloe? You're not five years old. The fact that nothing went wrong this time doesn't excuse taking the chance in the first place."

"Marcus's life was at stake!" Chloe defended herself, not only against her mother's word, but against the pinch of guilt. "You heard Olivia. She only gave Marcus one week to improve— which is up in two days. I couldn't allow her to rule him a feral."

Her mother sighed. "The Alpha said she'd reassess the

matter in a week, not that she'd kill Marcus if he didn't show improvement. And he has shown improvement. Your father and I can testify to that."

"But what if they said that wasn't enough? You didn't see Nathan's face when he found out Marcus was marking his territory." Chloe trembled. Tears started in her eyes, and her hands clenched into fists. "I couldn't take the risk that they'd execute him."

"You should have talked to me about your worries," her mother said. "I could have gone to Olivia and Nathan and asked for an extension. But this? Going behind the Alpha's back and disobeying her order? You've Challenged her authority, Chloe, for the second time in a month. She has no choice now but to smack you down hard, otherwise she'll look weak."

Chloe's stomach sank, but she didn't back down. "I'll gladly take whatever punishment she dishes out to save Marcus."

"But, darling, don't you see? Your actions may have jeopardized Marcus's chances."

The words hit like a body blow. Panic bloomed like a bruise. "But all the teachers have seen Marcus now. They know he's alive. She can't disappear him."

Her mother shook her head as if mortally tired. "It will be more difficult, but if they tell everyone Marcus had to move to live with a relative, do you really think anyone will question it?"

"You'd do that?" Chloe whispered. "You'd let her murder Marcus and lie?"

Her mom's eyes widened, and her hand clutched her throat. A new necklace rested there: a purple crystal on a silver chain. "I—Your father and I will do everything in our power to protect Marcus."

But if the Alphas overruled them, she'd swallow it. For the

good of the Pack. Because she wouldn't have a choice. The Alpha must be obeyed.

"Your hands might be tied," Chloe said, "but I'll go to the cops if she tries it. I'll make sure there's an investigation."

Her mother gasped, hand still at her throat. "Chloe, please. Whatever you do: don't tell her that tonight. Don't threaten the Alpha."

Because threats got put down, ruthlessly.

"If she orders Marcus killed, she'll have to kill me, too," Chloe said baldly. Turning on her heel, she fled to her room.

The tension at supper was oppressive.

Her dad got home just in time to eat. Apparently, her mom had already filled him in on Chloe's misbehaviour, because he shot her a black look and barely spoke a word all through the meal.

Chloe doggedly chewed and swallowed, alternating bites of rice with bites of pork chop to remind Marcus the proper way to eat. He ate neatly, using his utensils correctly, but scorned the salad.

"What time do we need to be at the Alphas' house?" her dad asked.

"Ten minutes from now." Her mother served dessert to her dad and Marcus, pointedly leaving Chloe out. The punishment, which her mom hadn't used since she was a little girl, stung.

Marcus silently offered her his cookie, but she just shook her head.

Her dad touched her mom's new crystal necklace. "What's this? You don't believe that crystal therapy nonsense, do you? Olivia got better because she's a werewolf, not because of any mumbo-jumbo celestial harmonies crap."

Her mother studied her cookie. "It's a gift from the Alpha,

a thank you. Considering how much trouble Chloe's in, I think it would be a mistake not to wear it."

Chloe's lips parted. "You're not sick, are you?"

"No, sweetie," her mom said, "I'm not. I promise." She touched the necklace and grimaced.

"Why do you keep touching that? Is the metal giving you a rash?" her dad asked.

"No. The chain is silver. We need to go now if we're not going to be late." Her mother rushed to put away the leftovers, then herded them out the door.

This time they drove. "So they can see Marcus has made progress," her father said.

Gratitude thickened Chloe's throat. Her parents might be angry at what she'd done, but they were firmly on Marcus's side.

All too soon, they arrived. Instead of the full Pack, only the other teens and Dean's dad were present. Were the other kids in trouble, too?

Nathan stood in front of the house, arms folded. Judy huddled against the wall, looking sick. Chloe didn't see Olivia.

"Marcus, stay with us. Chloe, approach the Alpha and beg forgiveness," her mom said.

Dead silence reigned as Chloe walked across the lawn.

She braced herself to be raked over the coals again, but a white-and-grey she-wolf came out of the house and confronted her. Olivia.

The Alpha snarled at her, and Chloe's knees weakened. Her heart hammered. She'd expected to grovel, but also to have a chance to justify her actions. The she-wolf sent a very different message. Had she gone too far? Was she going to be driven from the Pack?

Behind her, her mom gasped.

"Marcus, no!" Her dad growled.

Chloe glanced back. Her dad and Dean had a firm hold on Marcus. He growled and snapped at them, but retained his human form.

Good. She didn't want him getting hurt. This was her trial. Her sin.

A rumbling growl snapped Chloe's gaze forward. She locked eyes with the Alpha's wolf eyes. The healing crystal still swung around her thickened ruff.

Nathan stepped forward. "Chloe Graham. Submit to the Bite or leave the Pack." His voice was heavy with portent.

Fear formed a cold lump in Chloe's throat. Once Olivia bit her, Chloe would have to obey her. Her instinct screamed that it was a bad idea to submit without knowing what her punishment would be or what the Alpha intended for Marcus.

But a glance at Nathan's closed face told her he wouldn't negotiate.

Chloe swallowed. She had to make a choice now. Bend to the will of the Alpha and possibly lose Marcus. Or lose the rest of the Pack. Her family.

One glance at her parents' strained faces, and her defiance crumpled.

"I submit to the Alpha!" Chloe dropped to her knees on the damp grass and fumbled to pull the collar of her shirt aside. She inclined her head, symbolically offering her life.

Jaws wide, the white and grey wolf lunged toward her. Fangs bit deep—into her shoulder, not her neck. Chloe would live through this.

Her mouth opened on a soundless gasp, and tears of pain ran from her eyes, but she bit back her scream. The hardest part was keeping her body still as the Alpha mauled her when her instinct urged her to Change and fight back.

The Alpha released her, like a dog discarding a chew toy.

Tail up, the Alpha trotted into the house, not even glancing back at the vanquished enemy. Chloe was left kneeling and bleeding in the grass.

Nathan came over to her and made a pronouncement. "Since Chloe has seen fit to tell the humans Marcus is alive, he shall continue going to school and he will be her responsibility."

Chloe gaped at him. She had no problem taking responsibility for Marcus, but did Nathan really mean for Marcus to go to school full-time tomorrow? He wasn't ready.

Nathan glared at her and she snapped her mouth shut and bowed her head. Now wasn't the time to argue.

Nathan gave a grunt of satisfaction, then went into the house. Judy followed. Dean's dad, Rick, jerked his head and Dean, Brian and Kyle and all walked away in silence. Only Kyle glanced back, his face white with shock. At a guess his Bite had been gentler.

This had been an object lesson for all the teens: disobey and be punished.

Finally, her family came forward.

Her mother helped her up. Tears stood in her eyes.

With a little cry, Chloe embraced her. She clung to her mother because for a moment, just a moment, she'd considering *not* belonging to the Pack.

"Let's get you home," her father said gruffly, patting her back. "You did very well not to make a sound. Your friend Judy squeaked like a mouse. Her dad almost died of embarrassment."

Marcus had Changed to a wolf. He pressed close to her legs, guarding her. She bent and petted him, almost falling over as a rush of dizziness hit her. "It's okay," she told him. "I survived." Then, whispering, "I'd take twice the punishment to save you."

He whined, not liking her words.

There had been no mention of judging Marcus tonight. She tried to take heart from that, but it was difficult not to think of Nathan's command as setting him up to fail.

She walked to the SUV under her own power, careful to choose the right-hand seat so the seatbelt didn't touch her fresh Bite. Marcus wedged his heavy body between her knees and the front seat.

Once at home, she studied her Bite in the mirror. She prodded the half-circle imprint of wolf teeth gingerly. The places where the incisors had punctured the skin were torn-looking. Savaged. They still bled slightly.

Her dad's face tightened and flushed red when he saw her shredded skin, but his hands were gentle as he washed the wounds clean. "I normally wouldn't bother with antibiotic cream, but … "

The cream stung, but only a little. Chloe moved her shirt to cover the Bite mark up; it made her sick to remember how she'd been forced to submit.

She spent the rest of her evening in her room. Her parents left her alone, but Marcus nosed open the door and kept her company.

She craved the comfort of her bedroom, but she couldn't settle down. She tried reading a book, but threw it down after a few pages. She went online, played a game of solitaire, then closed her laptop and gave up.

She hugged her knees and addressed Marcus. "Why am I so upset? I've been looking forward to getting my Bite and officially joining the Pack forever."

He rested his muzzle on her foot and regarded her with mournful eyes.

"Oh, yeah? Well, your turn is coming, buddy. You're going to have to join the Pack too." Once his feral status was cleared up.

To her astonishment, Marcus Changed into a boy. He crouched, naked, at the foot of her bed.

"No," he said, his voice raspy.

Chloe sat up, electrified with joy and relief. He could talk!

She opened her mouth to congratulate him, but he was still speaking, each word an effort. His blue eyes burned into hers.

"Sick One is not my Alpha. You are."

Did she understand? Marcus held his breath. He didn't have the words to explain the wrongness he sensed in the female Alpha, the sickness. And the male Alpha would act to protect his mate, rather than the Pack. The need to warn Chloe was so strong it had broken the silence inside his head.

Chloe's eyes widened. She put a finger to his lips. "Not a good idea to go around saying you won't obey the Alpha. Promise me you won't repeat that part?"

Marcus nodded, struck dumb by her touch.

"I'm so glad you can talk again! This is fantastic." She pretzelled forward over the foot of the bed and hugged him.

He hugged her back enthusiastically. Usually when she showed affection, he sniffed her neck, taking pleasure in her special scent, but the Bite smelled of the Bad Alpha so he turned his head. Their lips grazed. Marcus stilled.

He waited for her to spring back, to let go, but she didn't. Her breathing sped up, and her hands moved up to his shoulders. She closed her eyes, tilted her head, and kissed him.

Marcus kept his eyes open so he didn't miss a moment.

Her lips were petal-soft, and her chest pressed to his felt amazing.

His wolf howled at him to kiss her harder, to claim her, but she was his Alpha. She led, and he followed. He trembled with the strain of holding back.

After a moment, she broke the kiss. She smiled, but her cheeks glowed pink. "Um, better put on some clothes, and then we can go share the good news."

He donned a pair of sweatpants, then Chloe took him by the hand and pulled him into the living room. "Mom! Dad! Marcus spoke."

CHAPTER

16

To Chloe's relief, her parents didn't immediately interrogate Marcus about the plane crash. As much as Chloe needed to know how and why Abby had died, she did not want to risk Marcus clamming up again.

Instead her father asked about Marcus's time in the woods while her mother smiled through happy tears. "Wolves are pack hunters. How did you survive on your own?"

"Killed small things." Marcus's voice rasped. "Mice. Squirrels. Rabbits."

"And that gave you enough protein?" her dad asked, keenly interested.

He shrugged. "I scavenged some. Ate beavers."

Chloe blinked in surprise. "Beavers?"

He nodded. "Beavers are good eating."

"Any fish?" her dad asked.

"Tried." Another shrug. "Not a good fisher."

"Any trouble with predators?"

"Wolf pack chased me away once. I avoided bears. Moose almost killed me." He shivered. "Gored with antlers, then trampled."

Chloe nodded, unsurprised. Moose could damage cars.

Her dad leaned forward in his chair. "Now, this is very important. Your answer needs to be added to the Pack Lore to help others. Did you spend the entire time you were missing as a wolf?"

Marcus inclined his head. "Three times I Changed to boy. Twice in first moon after crash while I slept. But too cold. Changed back again right away. Once in summer to pick berries. But skin too vulnerable." He paused. "Too lonely."

"Amazing," her dad said. "Thank you. This is very important information." He patted Marcus's shoulder. Then paused. "Are you ready to talk about the accident? I know it's a painful subject."

Marcus shook his head. "I don't remember the crash."

Her dad nodded wisely. "That's not surprising. The memory may return in time, or not. But Marcus, know this: whatever happened, your parents and sister would be very happy that you survived."

Marcus stilled, neither agreeing nor disagreeing.

Chloe's heart squeezed. It had never occurred to her that Marcus might feel guilty that he'd survived the crash when the rest of his family hadn't. Was that why he'd stayed a wolf so long? To punish himself? Her throat tightened.

Her father stood. "Well, it's late, and it's been a long day. We should all head to bed."

"Dad, will you tell the Alphas that Marcus can talk now?" And that he isn't feral?

"Yes, of course. I'll call them first thing tomorrow morning." He paused. "If you want, I will also ask Nathan to rescind his order for Marcus to attend school until his control is better."

Chloe clenched her teeth in resentment at the need to beg permission, like a kindergartener asking to go to the toilet.

"Unless you feel ready to return, Marcus," her dad added.

"I will follow Chloe."

"More time would be better," Chloe said. She just didn't think they were going to get it. Marcus returning to school early was part of her punishment.

She got ready for bed, then dithered. Should she leave the door ajar for Marcus as usual? She squirmed inside, remembering their kiss. But he always slept as a wolf, and he'd be hurt if she shut him out.

Marcus didn't come. Chloe couldn't relax, listening for the tick of claws on the hardwood floor. After twenty minutes, she got up for a glass of water. Marcus lay on the bed in the room across the hall, wolf eyes gleaming in the shadows. Voices in the kitchen clued her in: her parents were awake.

"—worried about their relationship," her mom said.

Chloe paused.

Her dad sounded doubtful. "Marcus is younger than her. Isn't that the kiss of death in high school?"

Her mom snorted. "He Changed for her. Do you know how powerful and flattering that is? He looks at her like she hung the moon. That has an effect."

Oh, geez. Chloe's ears started to burn.

"Chloe's an Alpha in the making," her dad said. "She may just accept it as her due."

An Alpha? Anxiety seized Chloe's lungs, making it hard to breathe. Her dad had it wrong. There was no way she could be an Alpha. An Alpha was the best at everything. The only thing she excelled at lately was getting into trouble.

"A year ago, maybe," her mom said, doubt in her voice. "Now? It's different."

Yes, her mom understood. The vise around Chloe's chest eased.

"Chloe has had a hard time of it these last few months," her dad agreed. "She's not making it any easier on herself now that she's Changed either. I'm worried what will happen if she keeps pushing Olivia."

"It's her nature to protect. Everything Chloe has done has

been to defend Marcus." Her mom sighed. "I'm just worried she'll break his heart."

Chloe retreated silently, biting her lip. She wanted to protest that she would never ever hurt Marcus. Nor was she some femme fatale, breaking hearts left and right. But Marcus did have feelings for her, and she'd impulsively gone and kissed him again tonight.

And, to be truthful, she'd liked it.

Her wolf had wanted more, but her human side was wiser. Marcus was still a year younger than her, and Abby's brother. More than that, he didn't need a girlfriend, he needed friends. People to stand with him against the Alphas. He did not need her confusing him about their relationship by sending out mixed signals.

She would take more care with his heart.

Marcus nosed her awake at the ungodly hour of 5:30 a.m. She pried open one eyelid and peered at his wolf face. "Let me guess, you want to go for a run."

He licked her chin.

She recoiled. "Stop that! Okay, thanks for letting me know. See you later." She rolled over and closed her eyes again.

A moment later the quilt slipped down to her waist. She grabbed at the hem and a tug of war ensued.

Sighing, Chloe sat up. "Really?" The idea of leaving her warm nest and going out into the frosty morning didn't appeal, but in the end she couldn't resist Marcus. Marcus the boy was so solemn, but his wolf showed signs of the mischievous personality she remembered. "Fine. You win. We'll go for a run."

The ground outside froze her bare feet, and crisp, cold air chilled her lungs. Shivering, Chloe stripped off her pajamas and threw herself into the Change with new fervor.

Becoming a wolf was as good as donning a winter coat and boots. The weather changed from unpleasant to invigorating.

Marcus sat on his haunches, waiting for her.

Feeling playful, she darted past him, racing for the trees. He joined the game, running alongside her. Joy bubbled up inside her along with a feeling of rightness. Of belonging. Of Pack.

Of being courted by a potential mate.

The last thought troubled Chloe the girl. The she-wolf vaguely remembered resolving the night before to protect Marcus by pushing him away. How silly.

Dismissing the whole matter, the she-wolf charged under a conifer's sheltering branches and startled a brownish-white rabbit into flight. Marcus yipped, and the chase was on.

"Chloe!"

The faint call made the she-wolf cock one ear. Someone was calling her human name. For a moment, that seemed unimportant. Chloe had just scented something interesting on the wind: chicken, maybe? She sniffed again and wrinkled her muzzle in distaste. Foulness. If that was a chicken, it was a dead one. Maybe many dead chickens. Chloe took a step toward the rank smell, but the black and cream wolf nipped her flanks.

"Chloooo-eeeee!"

Memory returned. She abandoned the strange smell and bounded in the direction of her house. Marcus kept pace at her side.

She Changed as soon as she reached the pile of clothes she'd left in the yard. Marcus beat her, his transformation so smooth and flowing it looked almost painless. Naked, he entered the house. She gritted her teeth until the Change released her.

Chloe panted, crouching on all fours in the yard. Would that ever get any easier? Or less painful? It freaking hurt.

Both her parents' vehicles were gone. Odd. She'd thought

they were going to talk to the principal this morning. An emergency must have come up at the clinic.

How late was it? Chloe hastily redressed in her pajamas then hustled inside. She'd missed the phone call to the Alphas.

Instead of a note, her mom had left packed lunches for them both: hers in her usual insulated carrier and Marcus's in a brown paper bag. So the Alphas hadn't changed their minds.

Fine. They would do this. She would prove that Marcus wasn't a danger.

A glance at the clock told her they had ten minutes until the bus came. "We're going to be late!" she called to Marcus, hitting his doorjamb on the way to her own room.

Off with the pajamas. On with clothes. Bathroom next. She ran a quick comb through her short hair and sped into the kitchen.

She gobbled down some bran muffins for breakfast—not her favourite, but much faster than cereal or toast. Marcus just shook his head when she offered him one. She chugged chocolate milk and then strolled out the door as the bus pulled up.

Despite the challenges ahead, she was in good spirits. She was officially part of the Pack, a Dud no longer, and Marcus had made so much progress. She couldn't wait to see the expression on the other kids' faces when Marcus spoke.

Dean wasn't on the bus. Kyle was, which surprised her, but both he and Brian were dozing. Should she blurt out the news? Nah, more fun if she sat back and let it happen. Marcus was silent, absorbed in staring out the window at the passing trees.

"Is it true?" Judy asked as soon as she got on. "Can he talk now?"

Oh, right. She'd asked her dad to tell the Alphas.

Chloe smirked. "Why don't you ask him?"

Judy cleared her throat. "Hey, Marcus."

He kept staring out the window.

Judy tapped his shoulder, and he startled, whipping his head around. Judy shrank back, then tried again. "Hi, Marcus."

Chloe was afraid he wasn't going to respond, but after a few seconds he said, "Hi, Judy."

Judy started to cry. Marcus looked at Chloe in bewilderment. "It's okay." She slipped over into Judy's seat and gave the other girl a quick hug. Chloe teared up a little, too. "It really is going to be okay. Marcus, me, your mom. Everybody's good."

Judy offered her a watery smile. "Yeah."

Ilona boarded the bus and frowned at them. "What's up? Did someone die?"

"Yes," Marcus said, startling both Ilona and Kyle, who had woken up. "My sister."

Abby. Chloe's heart hurt, but less than it used to. Abby would be happy that Marcus had survived.

Ilona's mouth hung open. "You can talk?"

He nodded.

"That's great!" Kyle said. He pounded Brian on the back. "Marcus can talk!"

"So how did you survive the plane crash?" Ilona asked, being her usual forthright self.

Before Chloe could hush her, Marcus answered, "I don't remember." Ghosts haunted his eyes, and Chloe moved back across the aisle to hug him. He leaned his head against hers in a wolf nuzzle.

Ilona's eyebrows shot up, but Chloe didn't care.

"Shouldn't Marcus be in the other classroom with the nines and tens?" Mr. Presley frowned.

Chloe felt blindsided. Marcus had been in the same grade as Kyle and Judy, but he'd missed a year of school. Which would put him in grade ten. But there weren't any Pack in the split grade nine/ten classroom. Judy's sister Gail was the next oldest and she was in grade eight.

Beside her, Marcus became as tense as a bowstring. Taking him away from Pack was a bad idea.

"We're not sure," she said. "My parents were supposed to come in to discuss it with Ms. Kim this morning, but they got an emergency vet call. Please, can he sit with me until they arrive?"

"I suppose so," Mr. Presley said.

"I'll be quiet," Marcus said.

Mr. Presley startled, but quickly recovered. "Good."

True to his word, Marcus sat through English quietly, watching out the window with predatory intentness. Math, which was also taught by Mr. Presley, came and went in similar fashion.

All morning Chloe expected Marcus to be called to the office for his conference, but by noon her parents still hadn't arrived. Maybe the appointment had been rescheduled?

They ate lunch outdoors, the Pack closing shoulders against the townies. Dean sat on top of the table and cast longing glances at Ilona, who ignored him but did a lot of hair-flipping and posing.

Marcus looked around carefully at lunch. No one was watching so he let his bun fall on the ground where the gulls or rodents would soon find it and feast. He just ate the meat: corned beef with a thin film of mustard. He did not see the point of mustard, but at least there were several ounces of meat.

Mrs. Graham had also packed him apple juice—sticky sweet, but drinkable—and two cookies, which he traded for Kyle's potato chips. He ate all the chips and licked the salty grease off his fingers afterward. So good.

Lunch done, he resumed watching Chloe.

She smiled and laughed with her friends. Maybe once she finished eating they could sneak off and run as wolves.

But Chloe suggested playing soccer, so they all chased after a white ball that wasn't even edible until the bell rang and they had to go back inside.

Marcus couldn't focus on the teacher for more than a few moments at a time. He stared longingly out the window. Even chasing a stupid white ball was better than being cooped up indoors.

A cramp suddenly seized his belly. Marcus remembered this feeling from eating rotten meat, leftovers from a road kill. He had food poisoning.

He stood up.

The teacher and Chloe both said his name so he paused at the door. "Sick," he said.

Chloe got to her feet. "He looks pale. I better go with him."

The teacher said something more, and Chloe paused to reply. Marcus's belly cramped again, and he couldn't wait. He rushed down the hall and outdoors.

Fresh air. The sweat on his forehead chilled. He kept going, crossing the parking lot to the woods that fringed the sports field.

Sweat dripped from his forehead. More spasms hit his belly, sending him to his knees. His head spun, lightheaded. Instinct prodded him: danger! He obeyed the urge to Change into a wolf, shucking his clothes and crouching on his hands and knees in the litter of conifer needles.

Fur swept over him, but the pain in his belly didn't ease.

Wolf instinct took over, and he swallowed two mouthfuls of grass, which induced vomiting.

He ought to have felt better with the bad food out, but his blood burned in his veins. He vomited a second time, but brought up little.

This was more than just indigestion. He'd been poisoned.

He needed to find Chloe. She would help.

He stumbled out of the woods, whining, and headed back to the school.

The burning in his blood engulfed his entire body. His mind clouded over. A memory came to him:

Hanging upside-down in a tree, tight bands across his lap and chest. Blood ran down his neck and arms. Fur prickled under his skin, his Change coming at the worst possible time.

Heat bloomed against his face as a fireball exploded a hundred yards away. The plane.

The tree branch broke. He fell, screaming.

No. Someone else was screaming. A child's high-pitched shriek yanked him out of the memory. "Wolf!" a little boy yelled.

CHAPTER 17

"Marcus, are you in there?" Chloe rapped on the door to the boy's washroom. By the time she'd convinced Mr. Presley that Marcus needed help, he'd disappeared on her.

No reply.

She knocked again. "Is anyone in there?"

She listened hard. A drift of voices came from the office. "Jefferson ... on my way north on a hunting trip ... thought I'd stop by and thank you for hosting our informational meeting ... "

Visions of Marcus passed out on the floor had her easing the washroom door open. She'd just called his name again when screams blasted from the playground. Not I'm-having-fun-on-the-swings or Jimmy-took-my-toy screams, but real, terror-filled shrieks.

Chloe sprinted down the hall and stiff-armed through the school's double doors. The screaming child, a red-haired boy of kindergarten age, was pointing at an animal twenty feet away at the edge of the field.

A wolf with a bisected face. Marcus.

Oh, crap. Her blood ran cold.

Coach had drilled them on what to do if someone's hormones took over and he or she Changed in public. Step one: damage control.

Six little kids dotted the playground, but only the screaming kid looked frightened. The kindergarten teacher was headed for the boy at a run. Had anybody seen Marcus Change? Chloe couldn't see his clothes, which gave her hope that he'd Changed elsewhere. Even if the red-headed kid had seen, he was young enough to be disbelieved.

Step two: get the wolf out of sight.

Chloe cut across the gravel parking lot toward Marcus. "Shoo! Go away, wolf." She waved her hands. "Go back to the woods."

Marcus didn't listen, didn't even seem to see her. His path wove back and forth erratically, and he was panting. She moved to intercept him, and he veered again, now trotting parallel to the school.

"Everybody inside!" the teacher yelled.

A second kid spotted the wolf and started howling. Four of the six kids ran for the school doors, but the red-haired boy stood still, paralyzed by fear, and a dark-haired girl refused to leave the monkey bars. The teacher grabbed one under each arm and staggered toward the door.

The hullabaloo had attracted attention, and adults spilled outside.

The principal, Ms. Kim, hurried outside and took the second child from the teacher's arms. "Is that everyone? What's Chloe doing out there?"

"I'll take care of it." Coach pushed past Ms. Kim.

"Get everyone inside. I'll call Forestry Services." The principal vanished inside. The doors closed on the upset children.

Coach strode toward Chloe and the wolf. Chloe was torn between relief that an adult was there and worry for Marcus. Coach muttered under his breath in another language. "What's going on?" he demanded as he came closer.

"Marcus is sick," Chloe said quickly. "I don't know why he Changed, but there's something wrong with him."

"What's wrong is that he's a crazy feral and he has no control," Coach said, his expression harsh.

"I'm telling you: he's sick. Look at how he's walking in circles." Chloe's voice sharpened, worry for Marcus's health blending with fear of what Coach might do.

"He's broken Pack Law," Coach said implacably.

"He's sick!"

"And none of your Packmates have been sick at school? Did they Change? Marcus should have more control."

Chloe glared at him, to cover the sick fear trembling in her stomach. Because Coach was right. If she'd gotten sick she would have called her mom, not slunk off into the woods to Change. "We can argue about it later. Right now, we need to get him out of sight."

The two of them approached Marcus, fanning out to keep him from bolting. "Marcus?" Chloe said gently.

The wolf bared his fangs at Coach and growled.

Right. Chloe had forgotten about that wrinkle. "Stay back. He won't bite me," she said.

"Are you sure?" Coach asked.

Doubt nipped Chloe's confidence—how out of it was Marcus?—but she didn't let it show on her face. "I'm sure." She crouched down five feet away from the wolf. "Marcus, it's me." She waited for him to catch her scent.

Time was playing tricks on Marcus, leaping forward, then circling back around.

Again and again he found himself in the fire caused by the burning plane:

The flames were everywhere, burning through the underbrush, in the trees. A fir toppled in his path, the crown on fire. He veered left, running on four legs. Smoke scraped at his lungs as he raced to keep ahead of the blaze. Rabbits and deer ran beside him, all fleeing the hungry monster behind—

The vanilla and soap scent of Chloe … suddenly, he found himself in a field of grass next to a building. Chloe held her hand out to him. He quivered. Chloe meant safety from the memories that hurt him.

Movement caught his eye. Behind Chloe loomed a man. Blond, muscular, frowning. Conrad Wharton!

Marcus lunged at his enemy and snapped his teeth.

Coach jumped back out of reach. Marcus growled at him, teeth bared. He tried to move between Chloe and Coach, but Chloe grabbed him around the neck. She didn't understand the danger.

She thought he disliked Coach for shooting him, but that wasn't it at all. There was something else, something to do with Abby… .

The flames beckoned in his peripheral vision. Marcus shuddered. He didn't want to go into the flames, didn't want to remember—but the secret lay in the past. The reason why he didn't trust Conrad Wharton.

Without a reason, Chloe wouldn't believe him. She'd let Coach too close.

Whining, Marcus walked into the scorching flames of memory and let them burn him.

Smoke lingered in the air, but the fire had passed.

Marcus sniffed at the pieces of burnt fuselage and the skull in the pilot seat. He tipped back his head and howled, telling his grief to the moon.

No. Marcus pushed back the terrible, debilitating loss. This was the end. He needed to remember the beginning.

The flames beckoned again, and he walked through them like a ghost, through the forest fire and out the other side. Smoke morphed into grey clouds:

The plane spiralled steeply down, rushing toward the tree-tops below. His heart swelled in his throat, and he bit his lip to keep from screaming. His mom fought to control the plane. His dad was out of his seat, bending over a slumped Abby. Marcus's hands clutched the arm rests. Suddenly his fingers sprouted claws—

No. He knew what happened from here. Not far enough. Marcus trotted farther into the gray mists of memory. He needed to go back to before it had all started to go wrong.

Sitting beside Abby in the six-seater Piper Seneca, in the row behind his parents, listening to round five of Abby's argument with their mother.

"He shouldn't be giving gifts to young girls," their mom said from the pilot's seat.

"But Mom, it wasn't like that! It was just a thank you for helping him." Abby's voice crackled over the headsets they all wore to allow them to talk over the engine noise.

Marcus peered out his window, hoping for a glimpse of forest, but they were flying above a layer of light grey clouds. Except for occasional ripples, the clouds were as boring as an endless lake.

"It was inappropriate, and I don't want you to be alone with him ever again."

Abby crossed her arms. "What do you want me to do, Mom? Quit track and field? Stop going to school where he teaches? Stop going to Pack meetings? How's that going to work?"

"I'm going to talk to the Alphas about getting rid of him," their mom said.

"You can't do that!"

"Oh, yes, I can. It's my job as Beta to inspect his background. I know I initially recommended that he be allowed to join the Pack, but since then I've received some disturbing indications that Conrad Wharton is an assumed name. He's hiding something,

and he's ambitious. I think he means to take over the Pack or gain some followers and split off on his own."

"You don't know him!" Abby stormed. "He wouldn't do that!"

Marcus leaned forward, pressing his forehead against the cold glass. His heartbeat picked up. He'd glimpsed something about thirty metres away from the wing. Something crazy. A woman.

"Neither do you," their father said. "He's very close-mouthed about his past—"

"His Pack was killed. Of course, he doesn't talk about it," Abby said shrilly.

Marcus tuned her out, staring out the window. A chill crawled up his spine. They were thousands of feet in the air. How could he have seen a woman? There were no mountains out here. Was she hang-gliding? Parasailing? But he hadn't seen a glider.

"Hey, Dad," he said. "Look out the window."

Nobody heard him, because Abby was yelling now. And crying. "You can't keep me away from him!"

Marcus craned his neck. There she was: the flying woman. She sat in a giant cup, her grey hair streaming behind her in the wind. She had a hooked nose, and her skin stretched tight over her bones.

While he gaped, the woman made a throwing gesture and the left engine cut out. The plane immediately swung hard to the left. Abby shut up.

The plane dropped down out of the clouds, emerging several thousand feet over forest while their mom fought to steady out their flight with just the right engine. "It's okay," their mom said over the headphones when they'd levelled out. "Give me a minute. I should be able to restart it." Her fingers danced over the console, but the other engine didn't turn over.

"Karen," his father said, gripping the dash.

"I can still land it with one engine," his mom insisted.

The second engine cut out. His dad swore, shockingly loud in the suddenly silent cockpit. His mom pushed down the nose of the plane, once again fighting to level them out.

"What's happening?" Abby cried.

"You kids keep quiet and let your mom concentrate," their dad snapped.

"I'm going to do a glide landing," their mom said.

Marcus could barely breathe. The flying woman—the witch, for what else could she be?—had done this.

"Winston, get on the radio," his mom said with an eerie calm. "Give them our position. Kids, start looking out the window for a place to land. A road or a clearing or even a body of water. We can belly down onto the treetops if we have to, but I'd rather not."

His dad swore again. "The radio's out."

Marcus understood instantly: the witch had hexed their radio too.

And then time flickered, stuttered forward, flinging him back into the grassy field with Chloe.

"Stay back," Chloe warned Coach, struggling to hold onto the wolf in her arms. "He thinks he's protecting me."

Just then a woman's hysterical voice intruded. "Wolf! It has rabies! Shoot it!"

What now?

While she was distracted, Marcus pulled free of her hold. He kept growling but didn't attack, and she spared a glance toward the newcomers.

A dark-haired bearded man wearing a puffy orange hunter's vest stood beside a pickup truck with Jefferson & McIntosh Logging printed on the side. The conversation she'd overheard in the hallway came back to her. This must be the logging executive, Jefferson. After a moment Chloe recognized the thirtyish blonde clutching his arm as Basia Novaskaya, Ilona's mother/

aunt. Instead of her usual New Age funky clothes, she wore a skirt suit and had twisted her blonde hair up in a chignon. She'd restricted her crystals to a couple of rings that flashed in the sunlight. What was she doing here? Oh, right. Kyle had said Ilona's mother was pro-logging.

Jefferson shrugged off Basia's grip and removed a rifle from the rack on the back of his pickup. "Everyone get away from the wolf! Let me get a clean shot!" he yelled.

"No!" Chloe shouted.

"Get back!" Jefferson finished loading the rifle. Basia cowered behind the pickup truck.

Coach swore again. "Chloe, back away."

Chloe didn't move. She stared at Coach. "You can't just let him shoot one of the Pack."

"Marcus has broken Pack Law," Coach said in a harsh undertone. "There are consequences."

Chloe glared at him, her eyes so hot they ought to have shot out laser beams. "He's Pack. We don't abandon Pack. Ever."

Marcus lunged at Coach again; Coach skipped back. To Chloe it was clear that Marcus was just trying to scare him off. The wolf could easily have sprung twice that distance and taken Coach down by the throat if he'd truly gone feral.

"I said, out of the way!" Jefferson yelled. The hunter had moved out into the center of the parking lot where he'd have a better shot. He sighted down his rifle barrel—and fired.

Bang!

A hole cratered the parking lot. Marcus growled and shifted his focus to the hunter.

Even though Jefferson had obviously missed on purpose, trying to scare the wolf away with the noise, fury roared through Chloe. "Stop it, you idiot! That's not a wolf, it's a wolf-dog hybrid. Someone's pet. My dad's the vet. He's treated him before." The lies spilled out.

Jefferson didn't put down his rifle. "I don't care if its name is Fluffy. It's clearly sick, probably rabid. Move away before it bites you."

"I've had my rabies shot," Chloe shouted back. "Why don't *you* move away?" It couldn't be rabies, could it? Her dad had given all the Pack kids their shots. After a few initial doses, the rabies vaccine was long-lasting and rarely needed a booster.

"I'm not going to tell you again. Move away from the wolf."

Chloe's blood ignited. "Or what?" she yelled back. "Are you going to shoot me?"

Arms grabbed her from behind and yanked her off her feet. Coach. He'd sneaked up on her while she was distracted. Bastard.

"No!" Chloe struggled, but couldn't break his grip. She hammered her heels back, kicking him in the shin, then smashed her skull into his face—

Bang!

Another rifle report cracked the air. Coach's grip loosened, and Chloe broke free, darting forward. Terror seized her lungs. Blood. Blood on Marcus's white chest. He collapsed onto the ground.

He's not dead. He's a werewolf; he'll heal. Except Jefferson was advancing forward, lining up another shot, this time to the head.

Snarling, Chloe grabbed the muzzle of the rifle—singeing her hands in the process—and twisted it away. She threw it behind her while Jefferson gaped in astonishment. "Leave the dog alone!"

He swore and ran after the rifle.

Protectively, Chloe threw her arms around the wolf. Her heart pounded. Jefferson wouldn't shoot her, but if he shot Marcus in the head …

"He's dead!" She let tears come to her eyes while simultaneously leaning her full weight on Marcus. "Play dead," she whispered in his furry ears.

His eyes stayed closed though his chest still rose and fell. Blood soaked her shirt. Too much blood.

"Move away," Coach ordered. His voice sounded thick.

Chloe bared her teeth in vicious satisfaction: she'd given him a bloody nose.

Unexpectedly, Basia saved the day. She came forward, not tottering at all despite her high heels and the parking lot's uneven surface, and laid her head on Jefferson's shoulder. "Please, may we go? It's dead, and the sight of blood makes me ill. They'll know who to call to dispose of the mess." She shuddered again.

Instantly solicitous, Jefferson lowered the rifle and helped her back to his pickup truck. He turned to Coach. "Tell the police to call me, Ed Jefferson, if they need an incident report or anything." He held out a business card.

"I will." Coach nodded and pocketed the card. "Thank you for protecting our students, Mr. Jefferson."

The logging executive swelled up. "I'm just glad I got it before it infected some kid."

Chloe bit her lip to keep from shouting that the wolf didn't have rabies.

"Thank you again." Coach held out his hand.

Mollified, Jefferson shook hands, reracked his gun and climbed into the pickup beside Ilona's aunt.

Chloe waited tensely until the pickup drove off, then turned to Coach. "Help me get Marcus into the trees." Forestry Services would be on their way by now. Dean's dad worked for them, but there was a fifty percent chance that his human partner would respond to the call. Chloe wouldn't be able to bluff a trained forest ranger into believing Marcus was dead. Anxiety roughened her breathing. Time was running out.

Coach looked at her sharply. "He lives?"

"He's still bleeding. We need to call my dad," Chloe said urgently.

Coach growled at her. "You need to get back into the school."

Marcus lifted his furry head and growled back.

"Yeah, I don't think so," Chloe said. "Marcus doesn't like you. Leaving you two alone strikes me as a bad idea. Just call my dad, okay?"

"I'm ordering you to go back into the school. Now." Coach tried to intimidate her.

Chloe fought not to drop her eyes, not to admit his Dominance. Not with Marcus's life at stake. Desperation gave her the strength to push to her feet. She locked her legs, though Coach still had almost a foot of height on her. She would not give in.

Coach growled deep in his throat, baring his teeth.

Chloe's gaze flickered down for a second, but she forced it back up. She bared her own teeth. "Back off."

"He's too much of a risk. He'll expose us all," Coach said.

The hairs rose on the back of her neck. *Coach meant to break Marcus's neck.*

"I'll fight you." Tears stung the back of her throat.

"You'll lose."

The simple, brutal truth made her sway. Coach might not be able to Dominate her, but she couldn't Dominate him either, and he was physically bigger and stronger than her. She couldn't stop him from killing Marcus.

Chloe lifted her chin. "I'll still fight." Inspiration hit. "Unless you want to explain to the principal why you attacked a female student, back off!"

Coach and Chloe were fighting. She didn't understand how dangerous Coach was. Marcus had to stand with her.

The bullet was still lodged inside him, a hot ball of agony, and fever continued to rage through him. He wasn't healing as fast as he should.

Old advice from his father came back to him. "If you're grievously injured, Change forms. Sometimes that will put right whatever's wrong."

It hadn't helped with the sickness, but it might help with the bullet. Marcus concentrated on being a boy for Chloe.

CHAPTER

18

Coach took a sudden step backward. "He's Changing!"

"Marcus, stop! Change back!" Chloe pleaded, but Marcus's fur melted into skin, his muzzle shrinking.

So. Bad.

She moved to shield Marcus from view, and Coach did the same, swearing viciously.

They were still on the grass at the edge of the parking lot, right out in public. The parking lot and street were deserted, but there were houses across the street, and one of the classroom windows faced this way.

Was that Ilona's face by the window? Crap!

And then a naked, bleeding boy lay at her feet. Pieces of metal began to extrude from the open wound in his upper chest, pushed out by his amped up werewolf healing. The bullet had deformed into something more mushroom-like. Ew.

Once the bullet was out, the bleeding stopped, though the wound remained raw and angry looking. They needed to cover it up before someone non-Pack saw it.

"Give him your shirt," Chloe said.

"No. I could get fired," Coach said sanctimoniously.

"Don't want anything from him," Marcus said, glaring balefully. He sat up.

"Where did you leave your clothes?" Chloe threw his arm over her shoulder and helped him to his feet.

"Back in the trees." He waved a hand toward the far side of the playground. They walked in that direction.

"He's proven himself a menace. I'll be telling the Alphas," Coach called after them.

"He had a fever!" Chloe yelled back, but bile scoured her throat. How had things gone so wrong? Her mind worked frantically. Should she call her parents and ask them to pick her and Marcus up from school? Or was this one straw too many? Should she urge Marcus to flee into the woods for a while? Maybe go stay with Lady Sasquatch in her log cabin?

The possibility calmed her. The werewolf Pack carefully avoided Lady Sasquatch's area of the Preserve, but Chloe's father had gone out a few times on health matters, and he'd taken Chloe with him. Lady Sasquatch had the best blueberry muffins.

Chloe's nose twitched. She narrowly avoided stepping into a pile of vomit. *He had been sick.* A few feet away, Marcus's clothes lay strewn about.

Marcus got dressed. He winced as he pulled his shirt on, but his face no longer looked flushed, and he was already steadier on his feet.

"What happened?" Chloe asked.

"Got sick. Poison then fever."

Poison? Did he mean food poisoning? Before she could ask what he meant, Marcus grabbed her arm. "Chloe, I remember the crash now. Coach is trying to take over the Pack!"

Chloe rocked back on her heels. Marcus's story did cast a suspicious light on Coach's motives, but other than the argument distracting his mom, Coach hadn't had anything to do with the plane crash that she could see. The bit about the witch was just plain weird. It didn't fit. Why would a witch want to hex the Jennings' plane?

Witches were mentioned in the Lore—there was even a Law forbidding werewolves from having dealings with witches—but Chloe had never met one. She'd figured they were just stories.

"We can't go to the Alphas with this yet," she told Marcus. "All we have are your mom's suspicions. We need proof."

He growled. "Coach had something to do with the plane crash—I know it. I won't let him get away with it!"

Her gaze snapped up. "Of course not! We need to talk to my parents and find out what Pack Coach came from before he joined ours. See if we can find out what made your mom think Conrad Wharton was an assumed name. Maybe contact Scout," she added.

"Why?"

"He called Coach by another name, but Coach denied it. I can't remember the name he used." Chloe shook her head. "But in the meantime, you need to go into hiding. You broke Pack Law by Changing in public. Even if no one saw, the Alphas may still banish you for it." Or condemn him to death. *I promised Abby I'd keep you safe.*

Marcus shook his head, expression stubborn. "I won't leave you."

She blew out an exasperated breath. "I'm not in any danger."

"Are you sure?" Marcus grasped her shoulders. "You're an Alpha, and Coach is your enemy. He can't take over the Pack and leave you standing."

"Please." She rolled her eyes. "I'm not an Alpha."

"You're my Alpha." Marcus gazed at her worshipfully.

Chloe twisted her fingers together, flustered. He only looked up to her because she'd been the one to save him. It didn't mean anything. "Even if I have the potential to be an Alpha in the future"—a big if—"I'm not one now. Judy's mom gave me the Bite, remember?"

"I remember," Marcus growled. "But you don't bear her Bite." He tugged the neckline of her shirt off her shoulder, then stroked the skin. "No scar."

Chloe's eyes widened. Bites weren't supposed to heal. She went cross-eyed trying to take a look. Her fingertips couldn't find any raised scars. Her head spun like a carousel. "How?"

Marcus shrugged, unconcerned. "She isn't your Alpha."

For him it was that simple. Not so for Chloe. Mind. Blown. "Does that mean I don't belong to the Pack?" Panic tugged at her. She didn't want to be outcast and alone.

"You're my Alpha," Marcus said. "I belong to you."

She blinked back sudden tears at the certainty in his voice, her mind blown in an entirely different way.

"You should Bite me," he said.

Yes. Chloe's wolf reacted enthusiastically to the idea. *Bite him.*

"What?" Chloe took a step back. Why would Marcus suggest such a huge break in tradition? Logic kicked in. "Oh. You mean so that Olivia won't have authority over you?" And be able to condemn him. "That's a thought, but it might backfire on us." Chloe did not want to end up banished. She'd just avoided that fate, the fate of a Dud. And only an Alpha could make a Bite.

Marcus didn't argue, but he didn't agree either. His crystal blue eyes met hers. "I want everyone to know I belong to you."

Her wolf thrilled to the statement. *Yes. We belong together.*

Chloe struggled to ignore the wolf instinct urging her to do it, to Bite him. *This is a bad idea.*

The bell rang, breaking the spell. Time for last period. Go in or go home?

With a lurch Chloe remembered Ilona's face at the window. That settled it: they had to go in and do damage control if needed.

"Marcus is feeling better now," Chloe said, sliding into her seat. She watched Ilona carefully, but the girl only paid them cursory attention, busy getting out her binder. Good. Maybe she hadn't seen anything.

But then it struck Chloe that Ilona would normally have wanted to know all the details of why Marcus had left class. Was her silence now a sign that she had seen the wolf Change into Marcus? Chloe wouldn't have thought Ilona had enough self-control to keep quiet, but the possibility worried her. She chewed her lip.

After school she quietly pulled Dean aside. "Do me a favour? Make up with Ilona. She might have seen Marcus Change. If she did, I want her to confide in you, not somebody else."

Dean brightened. "On it." Moving like a predator, he cut Ilona from the herd of other students. He leaned his arm on the wall, half-trapping her. Whatever he said, it made Ilona's face light up.

Dean shoved Kyle toward the bus, and he drove Ilona home.

"So what happened?" Kyle whispered once the bus lurched into motion. Judy crowded closer, too.

The more allies the better. Chloe laid it out for them: Marcus getting sick and Changing in public view *and* his restored memory of the crash and what his mother had said about Coach.

"Judy, do you remember Coach giving Abby a gift?" Chloe asked.

"Nooo," Judy said. "But she definitely had a crush on him." She bit her lip. "Should I tell my parents he might be planning a coup?"

Chloe considered, then shook her head. "Not just yet, please. Could you get me Scout's phone number? I'd like a little more proof before we go to the Alphas."

Judy promised to do so, and then it was her turn to get off.

Ten minutes later, Marcus and Chloe jogged down their driveway. Her steps slowed; two vehicles were parked near the house. Her parents were home early again.

Apparently, Coach had been busy on the phone. Not good.

Fearing an ambush, Chloe motioned Marcus to stay outside

while she crept inside. She tiptoed toward the kitchen where her parents were talking.

"What're we going to do?" her father asked, voice heavy with despair. "It will take us months to pay off the credit card as it is."

Chloe paused in confusion. Were they having money problems? Was the town's stupid pro-logging boycott actually having an effect? She couldn't imagine anyone being foolish enough to drive a sick animal an extra hour and a half to the next nearest town with a vet.

"I don't give a damn about the money," her mother said. "It's Chloe I'm terrified for. Marcus, too." Shockingly, her mom began to sob.

"It's not your fault," her dad said. "They did it, not you."

"I should have fought harder," her mom said passionately.

"It's a wolf's nature to submit to the Alpha," her dad soothed. "We didn't know she'd been corrupted."

The hairs stood up on the back of Chloe's neck. What was going on? Suddenly the problem of Marcus Changing in public shrank. *There's something wrong with the Pack. Something wrong with Olivia besides the cancer.* Was that why Chloe's Bite had healed?

She shifted and the board under her foot creaked. Her parents stopped talking. Chloe walked into the kitchen.

"Chloe," her mom said.

"We're home from school," Chloe said inanely. *Act normal.* She went to the fridge to pour a glass of milk, but paused, shocked by her mother's ravaged face. Puffy eyes. Streaky mascara. She looked haggard and old. Beaten down.

Her father looked grey. He stood close by her mom, touching her.

The milk was hard to swallow. What was going on? Chloe didn't dare ask.

Her father cleared his throat. "We received a phone call about what happened at school. Is Marcus all right?"

"He got food poisoning and puked it up. Ran a bit of a fever. That's why he went outside. He Changed to his wolf hoping it would make him better, but it didn't help. He was feverish when he wandered onto the field. It could have happened to any one of us. It was just bad luck the kindergarten class was outside. Then after he got shot, he didn't have any choice but to Change in order to get the bullet out. I don't think anyone saw." Chloe didn't mention Ilona. "He's fine now."

"Good," her father said. "Good."

Chloe stared at him. Where was the lecture? Her parents lack of response to the near-catastrophe weirded her out.

"Call Marcus in," her dad continued. "We're having early supper. There's a Pack meeting tonight."

Her throat tightened. "Is it about Marcus? Coach threatened to invoke Pack Law."

"Olivia may think it is," her dad said, oddly. "But I spoke to Nathan, and I think he has something different in mind."

"Should we go?" Chloe asked. "Marcus and I could run off into the woods for a few days. Wait for things to cool down." She didn't mention Lady Sasquatch. It made her sick, but she didn't fully trust her parents right now.

"That might not be a bad idea," her mom said.

But her dad shook his head. "I don't think we're at that point yet."

But we may get there?

"Better to face the charge head on and let Marcus tell his side of the story than be condemned *in absentia*." He put his hands on Chloe's shoulders. "Marcus broke Pack Law. There will be consequences, possibly banishment, but I swear to you, I won't stand by and let them execute him, no matter what the cost."

"But—" Her mother stopped and bit her lip.

Chloe took a deep breath. "There's more. Marcus got part of his memory back. The plane crash wasn't an accident."

She called Marcus in while her parents were still gaping, and had him tell the story all over again.

Her parents' reaction confused her. They shrugged off the stuff about Coach and focussed on the witch. "Conrad has always been ambitious. That doesn't mean he had anything to do with the plane crash. Marcus, can you describe the witch again in more detail?"

"Long grey hair. Ugly nose." He shrugged. "Dunno. She was flying a cup."

Her parents exchanged disappointed looks.

"Are witches real?" Chloe asked.

"Oh, yes," her mother said grimly. "Very real." She touched the crystal hanging at her neck.

Are the crystals magic? The question died on her tongue when her dad caught her gaze and deliberately made the exact same gesture. She glimpsed a silver chain with a crystal hanging around his neck, too.

Her dad, who never wore jewelry, not even a wedding ring because of his profession. Her dad who scoffed at New Age holistic healing or anything without hard science backing it up. Her dad who had suddenly changed his stance on the existence of witches.

The hairs rose on the back of Chloe's neck, and a growl rose in her throat.

Danger. Danger to the Pack.

Yet another meeting in the Alphas' backyard. It got colder and scarier every time.

Olivia's eyes narrowed. "Marcus Jennings," she said in a carrying voice. "You broke Pack Law. Explain yourself."

Marcus's chest vibrated with a growl.

Chloe put a hand on his arm. "He was sick," she said loudly.

"Feverish. He tried to burn out the illness by Changing and made a mistake. No one saw." Crossed fingers. She hadn't had time to speak to Dean about Ilona.

"This cannot be allowed to happen again," Olivia said.

Chloe tensed, ready to launch counter-accusations against Coach, if the Alpha handed down too harsh a punishment.

And then things went sideways.

Nathan stood up. "I have an announcement to make!"

Olivia goggled at her husband. "What—?"

He didn't pause. "I'm resigning as Alpha."

Surprise punched Chloe's stomach. Is this what her dad had meant? A startled murmur burst from the other Pack members.

"No. You can't," Olivia said.

He never even looked at her. "I can no longer be a good leader, so someone else must step forward." He moved off the wooden deck.

"Oh, good," Chloe's mother said under her breath. "We have a chance to untangle this."

"God, he's brave," her father said, low-voiced. "She'll have his balls for this."

She, who? Olivia? The Alpha looked more hurt than furious, her face white and her lips pinched together. She had obviously had no idea her husband had planned this—another sign of something grievously wrong with the Pack. Judy's parents had always acted as a team, with Olivia more policy and Nathan more discipline.

Dean's dad shouldered his way forward and mounted the wooden deck. "I'm Beta, so I'll be Alpha now." Anticipation lit his eyes.

Chloe didn't know Rick Stravinsky that well, only that he was conservative, taciturn, worked as a forest ranger and when his marriage had failed he'd kept the boys. He'd always just been

Dean and Kyle's dad. She frowned. What kind of Alpha would he make? He was physically strong, but could he lead?

She wished her father could be Alpha, but he was a healer and a thinker. Sad to say it, but Rick would take him out in under a minute in a straight-up fight.

Her parents were whispering together. "... don't think he has one. Can't help but be better ... "

"Any other contenders?" Rick asked. "Right, then—"

"I Challenge." Coach Wharton stepped forward.

Chloe's stomach turned to ice: the man who wanted to execute Marcus, Alpha of the Pack? Marcus growled. She gripped his arm. "Dean's dad has forty pounds on Coach. He'll wipe the floor with him." She hoped.

Olivia cleared her throat. "Do you both agree to the traditional Challenge, a fight in wolf form until one of you surrenders?"

"Yes." Rick growled. From the way his eyes narrowed, he didn't appreciate being Challenged and intended to take his annoyance out on Coach's hide.

"Agreed." Coach stripped off his shirt.

Rick jumped down from the deck and cast off his red plaid shirt, exposing an impressively wide and hairy chest.

"No chains on either," her mother murmured.

"What?" Chloe asked.

Her parents didn't answer.

As the jeans came off the rest of the Pack silently cleared a space for the fighters, a ring of grass about fifteen feet in diameter.

"At the count of three!" Nathan bellowed. "One, two, three!"

Both men's forms furred over. Rick had the bigger wolf, but Coach finished his Change faster. His white wolf lunged forward and sank his teeth into his opponent's throat mid-Change.

Chloe smelled blood. Dean swore.

"C'mon, Dad!" Kyle called.

The big grey wolf finished Changing and shook hard. The white wolf clung tight to his throat, teeth gripping. Rick tried to bite back. He tore Coach's ear, but the white wolf ignored the injury and held on.

Blood spotted the grass.

"Yield," Chloe's dad whispered. "It's over. Yield before he does you serious injury."

Chloe clenched her fists, helpless to do anything but watch.

Apparently, Rick took stubbornness to the max, because he never did yield. Instead he collapsed from blood loss.

Her dad entered the circle.

The white wolf snarled a warning at him.

Her dad dipped his head subserviently. "You are the Alpha. May I tend to your opponent?"

The white wolf hesitated. A jolt went through Chloe— would Coach really kill Dean's dad? Dominance fights seldom ended in death, but she shouldn't have been surprised. If Marcus was right and Coach had been responsible for the death of the Jennings family, it followed that he was ruthless enough. The Pack held its breath. The white wolf gave the limp grey wolf one last contemptuous shake, then released him and backed away, jaws bloody.

Kyle and Dean rushed forward to help as Chloe's dad tried to stanch the wound with the discarded red shirt. Chloe bet the wound would scar as it healed, becoming a Pack Bite.

Coach Changed back to a man and calmly dressed. No one spoke as he ascended the deck beside Olivia. "I am Alpha." His gaze met the other males' eyes in a direct Challenge. One by one, they dipped their heads, though judging by Dean's red face, he was furious.

Worried, Chloe reached for Marcus and discovered him gone. Probably just as well. They were so screwed.

Marcus waited in the shadowy pines until Chloe and her family came home. He started to trot forward, but Chloe's dad signaled for him to wait.

Once Chloe and her mom went inside, Dr. Graham approached Marcus. The older man stopped at a respectful distance and tossed him some sweatpants. "Marcus, I'd like a word with you, please."

Marcus Changed back into a boy and dressed. He cocked his head to show that he was listening.

"It's about Chloe."

Marcus's heart began to beat faster. Was something wrong? Had Coach done something after he'd left? Chloe had looked okay when she got out of the SUV.

Dr. Graham shoved his hands into his pockets and studied his boots for a moment before bringing his gaze back up. "From the way you look at my daughter, I suspect you have feelings for her. Deep feelings, probably love. Am I wrong?"

Marcus shook his head. He loved her. Denial was not only pointless, it would have felt like a repudiation of Chloe, which he would never do.

"Good," her dad said. His muscles relaxed.

Marcus rocked back in surprise. The older male wasn't going to warn him off? Marcus wouldn't be forced to choose between either asserting his Dominance or disrespecting an elder? "You're ... glad?" His throat felt rusty.

"Yes. I think Chloe's going to need you. You're a good boy, Marcus. Your parents would have been proud of you." Moisture sheened Dr. Graham's eyes.

A keen rose in Marcus's throat, but he bit it back. *Live in the now.* He waited.

Dr. Graham raised his hand, cautioning Marcus. "Now, Chloe knows her own mind and will make her own choices. What I have to say is in the nature of advice."

Marcus waited. He had a feeling he wasn't going to like what the older man had to say.

"Chloe doesn't need a worshipper," Dr. Graham said bluntly. "She needs a lieutenant on whom she can rely absolutely. Do you understand the difference? An Alpha faces a lot of tough decisions. She needs someone she can talk things over with, who will tell her the straight truth—and who will support her decision, even if she goes against his advice."

Marcus's anxiety increased. Dr. Graham was describing a Beta, the second-most powerful position in the Pack. Some Betas nipped at their Alphas heels, pushing for the day when they would be Alpha. He would never do that to Chloe. But other Betas, good Betas, worked in harmony with their Alpha, exactly as Chloe's dad had described. Marcus wanted to do that for Chloe, but what her father was asking would be hard. He was comfortable being a follower. Could he be more?

Worse, it would mean interacting with the rest of the Pack, as a boy. Marcus was a wolf. He might take this form sometimes for convenience and to please Chloe, but in his heart he was a wolf. Dr. Graham was asking him to be something he wasn't anymore, something he couldn't be.

And yet the thought of letting Chloe down, or of her turning to another male like Dean to be what Marcus couldn't, was exquisitely painful, a dagger to the heart.

"I'll try."

CHAPTER

19

Judy gave Chloe Scout's phone number without making eye contact, like a spy passing secret messages, as she boarded the bus, then sat two seats behind Chloe and Marcus.

Chloe took the folded note in silence. She was a little surprised Judy had acted against the Alpha. Then again, Coach Wharton had replaced Judy's dad. Maybe Judy resented that—though Nathan had stepped down voluntarily. Chloe bet Judy's parents had had a huge argument after the meeting. She was dying to ask about it, but didn't dare.

Ilona got on next. Chloe made an effort to talk to her, wanting to see if the townie girl was now leery of Marcus. "Hi, Ilona." She searched for a safe topic. "So are you and Dean back together?"

Ilona rolled her eyes. "That boy! He doesn't know what he wants. On again, off again, on again, off again. He better watch it, or I'll get tired of waiting." She heaved a dramatic sigh. "Even if he does have the best butt in Pine Hollow."

"What did he do now?" Chloe asked, both entertained and relieved by the drama. She found herself relaxing. Ilona always said the first thing that came into her head. If Ilona had seen Marcus Change, she would've asked him by now.

Ilona leaned forward. "I am such a fool. Yesterday, I let Dean sweet-talk me into giving him another chance. He drove me home. There was much kissing. Very steamy." She fanned herself.

"He promised to pick me this morning—and look where I am: on the bus! He stood me up." She scowled.

Chloe lost her smile. "I'm not sure Dean and Kyle are coming to school today. My parents said their dad was in an accident and lost some blood."

Nearly all of it.

"Oh? Well, that is a good excuse. Maybe I will forgive him. Though Dean should still have called." Ilona nodded firmly.

Dean and Kyle were absent in the morning, but attended school in the afternoon.

At noon, Chloe tried calling Scout but had to settle for voicemail. Mentioning Coach's new Alpha status over the phone felt like gossiping, so she just left her name and cell number.

Dean spent most of Phys. Ed. class glaring at Coach. It was a relief when Coach cancelled track and field practice.

The cancellation also gave her an opportunity—none of the Pack kids would be expected home yet. Chloe was desperately worried: about her parents' strange behaviour, about Marcus's future in the Pack, about Coach's possible involvement in the plane crash. She needed more information.

More than that, she needed allies.

"Hey, guys, why don't you stick around? We'll have our own practice," Chloe said.

Judy declined, and Chloe let her go without argument. Judy's loyalties were divided at best.

"Sure, I can stay," Kyle said. "But just for a bit." He grimaced. "It's my turn to cook supper."

"If there's no practice, I'd rather catch up with Ilona," Dean said.

Brian snorted. "Yeah, no thanks, Chloe. I plan to enjoy my time off. Got better things to do."

Time to gamble. Chloe talked fast. "Better? I doubt it. Coach won the Challenge because of his fast Change."

"He cheated!" Dean burst out.

Chloe shook her head. "It wasn't cheating; it just wasn't very nice. A fast Change is a big advantage. You guys think Coach was quick?"

Reluctant nods.

"Marcus is faster. Like, twice as fast. I don't know about you, but I want to learn how to Change that quickly so I'm not the one left bleeding on the ground."

Dean growled agreement.

Chloe glanced at Marcus, but he didn't object to being volunteered.

"Where should we practice?" Brian asked, bouncing on the toes of his feet. "Not my place. My mom would want to serve lemonade."

"Not our place either," Kyle said. "Dad's in a pretty bad mood."

Chloe normally would have volunteered her place, but with her parents acting so weird … "Let's just find a spot in the woods."

Ilona came out as they were leaving and gave Dean a long kiss. "Ready to go?"

"Uh, sorry, babe, I have practice."

She frowned. "I thought that was cancelled."

He shrugged. "We're having a practice without Coach."

"Well, can I stay and watch?"

Knowing where this was heading, Chloe started a stupid conversation with Marcus about his shoes so she wouldn't have to witness Ilona's humiliation when Dean invented some lame reason for why they needed privacy.

Sure enough, two minutes later, Ilona stormed off.

The five of them headed off into the bush, stopping in a small clearing about five minutes' walk from the school, far from any beaten paths though not technically inside the Preserve.

"Okay," Dean said, hands on hips. "Let's see this superfast Change."

"Wait!" Chloe held up a hand. "I'll be timekeeper." She

opened her phone's stopwatch app. "Strip—just down to your underwear," she told Marcus sternly. He was totally unembarrassed by nudity. "Then wait for my signal."

He happily shucked his clothes, rolling his shoulders and taking deep breaths as if he'd been unable to move or breathe freely with them on.

"Whoa, check out his scars," Brian said.

Dean and Kyle both elbowed him, one from each side.

"Ow! What was that for?" Brian looked wounded.

Marcus stood in his underwear and gave Chloe a nod.

"Go!" She tapped Start.

As always, the sheer speed of his Change amazed her. It looked less like a painful, physical transformation and more like magic. As if he shed his boy skin like a snake.

Seconds later, his black-and-cream wolf stood before them, underwear tangled on his hind legs.

Tap. "Fourteen seconds."

Kyle whistled.

"Wow," Brian said, eyes wide with awe. "It took Coach at least thirty seconds."

Dean unzipped his hoodie. "My turn."

Chloe timed him at forty-three seconds, Kyle at thirty-eight and Brian at fifty-six.

Then the wolves Changed back into boys. She didn't time them, but it seemed to her that Marcus, although still the fastest, was slower than his boy-to-wolf time, while the other boys were significantly faster.

A chill tiptoed down her spine. *Marcus could Change to wolf faster because the wolf felt like his natural form. For the others it was the opposite.*

"What about you?" Brian demanded.

Chloe handed him the cell phone. She'd had the least practice of any of them and would almost certainly be last, but she wasn't about to make excuses. "I need practice, too."

She stripped down to her sports bra and panties. Kyle politely didn't look, but Brian outright ogled her. Marcus growled and stepped between them.

"Sorry, dude, but I like boobs and hers are *right there*," Brian said.

"Give me that." Kyle grabbed the phone. "Go!"

Chloe crouched down and closed her eyes, filling her nose with the smell of the forest floor: damp earth and rotting leaves and life. The things a wolf smelled. She threw herself into the Change like diving off a cliff, without letting herself think about the pain of twisting bone and sliding muscle and shrinking skull.

Panting, she finished and howled in triumph. *I am Pack!* This was the first time all of the boys had witnessed her ability to Change. Pride filled her.

She wanted to stay a wolf and run and frisk and play, but that wasn't what this was about. A fast Change was just the lure to get the boys here. She needed to enlist their aid and for that she needed human words.

She Changed back. It hurt more, for having been so recently done the other way, and she stifled a whine. Finally, she was a girl again. She adjusted her underwear, which had gone askew, then stood. "Time?" she asked.

"A minute five," Brian said.

Not bad. Chloe nodded, satisfied.

"So how does Marcus do it?" Dean asked, scowling. "He was feral for months, so it's not like he's been practising Changing into a wolf."

Good point. Chloe raised her eyebrows at Marcus.

He frowned, his head tilted to one side. "I feel it, then I do it."

"You feel it? Big help he is." Dean scowled again.

Kyle stared at her, but not at her boobs. At her neck.

Crap. She'd forgotten. She clapped her hands over the smooth skin.

Before she could shake her head and warn him to be silent, Kyle blurted, "Where did your Bite go?"

Dean and Brian stared, too.

Sighing, she removed her hand. "It healed," Chloe said simply. "There's something wrong with the Pack."

"What?" Brian screwed up his face in a frown.

Dean tugged on one ear, also confused, but Kyle just nodded as if she'd confirmed something he'd suspected. "Last night was weird. I mean, the way Nathan resigned out of the blue, and Olivia obviously had no idea it was going to happen. Just weird."

"I wish your dad had won. I don't like Coach," Brian said unexpectedly.

Chloe blinked. He didn't? "Why?"

"He went out with my mom for a few months on the down-low, but all he wanted was ... you know." Brian clenched his fists. "He wanted nothing to do with us kids at all. Could barely bother to learn our names. I'm glad Mom dumped him."

Chloe's respect for Kristen rose. She bumped Brian's shoulder. "He's a jerk." Something she could have told them all months ago.

She cleared her throat. "My parents have been behaving oddly, talking about money problems, and touching those crystal necklaces that Olivia gave them. I overheard them say the Alpha was 'contaminated'. Anyone else notice anything?"

"My mom has a crystal necklace," Brian volunteered. "The Alpha gave it to her as a thank you. It's supposed to harmonize her energies or something." He shrugged. "I didn't pay much attention."

Dean swore. "After we got dad home last night, Olivia came in and gave him a supposed healing crystal. He didn't want it, but she ordered him to wear it and not to take it off without her permission. What do they do?"

"I think they give the Alpha control over Pack members," Chloe said.

Dean blinked. "That doesn't make sense. She's the Alpha. She can already Dominate us."

Chloe brushed at her unmarked neck. "Can she? Maybe she's losing control." And Domination only worked when the Alpha was there to enforce it. What if this was something more?

"Our Bites are still there," Kyle said. "So is my dad's."

"Nathan made your Bites," Chloe pointed out. "Has anyone seen Judy's Bite lately?"

They exchanged looks. "Not since you got yours."

Silence, then Marcus said, "The Alpha smells wrong. Metallic."

"The only weird smell I noticed was the cancer smell," Brian said. He made a face. "That horrible sweet rot. Ugh."

"That was the first weird thing," Chloe said. "Olivia getting sick. Werewolves aren't supposed to get sick, much less almost die." Though hadn't she read somewhere else about a werewolf getting cancer? The memory tugged at Chloe, but she couldn't pin it down. "Olivia was at death's door two weeks ago, and now it's like she was never sick at all."

"Not the first," Marcus growled. "The plane crash came first."

"Tell them what happened." Chloe touched his arm. "What you saw."

While he spoke, she pulled her clothes back on. She was cold, and they weren't going to be practising any time soon.

A patch of deep blue in among the bushes stood out from the forest colours.

It was probably just a piece of trash stuck down there, but just in case, Chloe let her gaze drift past. She dug out her phone and walked a short distance away from the boys and, coincidentally, a little closer to the bush as if seeking privacy.

She hit redial and got Scout's voicemail again. "Hi, Scout, this is Chloe from the Pine Hollow Pack." She took another step closer, pretending to be absorbed in the call. Her pulse picked up when she spotted more blue patches. It looked like fabric. "I wanted to ask you about Conrad Wharton," she continued. "Call me. Bye."

She pocketed the phone, started to turn back to the boys, then dived into the bushes. Branches scratched her face, drawing blood. The owner of the blue shirt squeaked and tried to run, but Chloe caught an ankle. She hung on despite a vicious kick to the jaw, and then the boys jumped in and it was all over.

They dragged Ilona Novaskaya, kicking but not screaming, into the clearing. But this was a different Ilona than Chloe had seen before. Her clothes and face were smudged with dirt, her blonde hair leaf-strewn, and her eyes were wild.

Dean stood behind her, arms wrapped around her middle, anchoring her.

Brian began to swear, a tedious litany of all his favourites.

"Shut up!" Chloe pegged his shoulder.

"But she saw us!" Brian hissed. "She saw us Change!"

"We don't know that," Chloe said sharply. "Quiet or you'll end up telling her our secret yourself!"

"I didn't see anything!" Ilona said, still struggling.

Dean gave her a shake. "What were you doing out here? Why'd you follow us?" His expression was grim, almost haunted. *He thinks we're going to have to kill his girlfriend.*

Not if Chloe could help it. She liked Ilona. But Pack Law was clear.

"I just wanted to know what you were doing," Ilona cried. "I didn't see anything!" She wrenched herself sideways again, almost breaking free, but Kyle grabbed her other arm.

"Everybody calm down," Chloe said forcefully. "This is fixable. Ilona, just answer one question, and we'll let you go."

Well, they would if she gave the right answer. "Okay, Ilona. Just breathe for a moment."

Ilona stopped struggling, inhaled twice and nodded.

"Now then, you wanted to know what your boyfriend was up to. That's perfectly natural human curiosity. So you followed us into the woods. Then what happened?"

Ilona shrugged. "I saw you standing around. You mentioned crystals. I thought it might have something to do with my mom."

You said she was your aunt. Which is it?

Another shrug. "I was curious, so I hid behind a bush to listen. Then Marcus started talking about the plane crash and you jumped me. That's it."

Hope blazed across Dean's face.

Oh, how Chloe wished she could believe Ilona, but— "You're lying. There's no way you walked close enough to overhear what we were saying. We would have seen you. There's dirt ground into your clothes. You crawled at least the last twenty feet then hid in the bushes to spy on us. Now what did you see?"

Tears welled in Ilona's blue eyes. "Please let me go." Her voice emerged as a broken whisper.

Dean grunted as if he'd been hit in the solar plexus. "She saw us. What are we going to do, Chloe?" Misery etched lines onto his forehead, but he never slackened his grip on Ilona's waist. "She's a threat to the Pack."

Why was he asking her? A surge of anger shook Chloe. Fourteen months of being shunned as a Dud, but now that she'd Changed they were all looking to her for the answers. She opened her mouth to say it wasn't her decision—but that smacked of cowardice. They all knew what needed to be done.

As a kid she'd secretly dreamed of becoming Alpha, but a terrible weight of responsibility came with the title. She was glad she wouldn't be Alpha.

"I don't know what you're talking about!" Ilona howled, throwing her weight backward and almost overbalancing Dean. "I didn't see anything!"

Chloe's stomach churned. The Alphas would order death.

No. There had to be another way. Maybe they could scare Ilona into silence. But they'd have to truly frighten her, otherwise it wouldn't take and somewhere down the line Ilona would tell someone, and if that someone also lived in Pine Hollow and had seen something strange once themselves then the Pack could easily find itself facing a witch hunt. Just as the Pack scorned the townies, Pine Hollow residents had never warmed to the Pack. Especially now with tensions running high over the proposed logging deal.

"You didn't see anything?" Chloe asked coolly. "Then maybe we should *show* you. Marcus, Change, please."

Ilona's eyes widened with horror, then slammed shut. "No! I won't look."

She had seen, then. Why else would she be so alarmed? "Dean, make her open her eyes. Marcus, wait until she's looking, then Change."

Marcus didn't understand why Chloe wanted him to Change in front of the blonde girl, but he obeyed his Alpha. He was already stripped down to his underwear. Dean threatened to poke out the girl's eyes unless she opened them. Once she was watching, he Changed.

Taking wolf form was a pleasure. He looked to his Alpha for instructions.

"Show her what we are," Chloe said. She smelled sad.

Marcus growled and raised his hackles, advancing forward on the shrinking girl who always smelled of horses. Except today she was terrified and sweating, all the horse smell melting away. He stuck his nose in the sweat stain under her arm. She squealed, but all he did was take a good long sniff.

Marcus Changed back.

Chloe snarled at the horse girl. "That is what we are, all of us. And if you tell, we'll tear you to pieces. Understand?"

"She won't tell," Marcus said with absolute certainty.

Dean looked at him with naked hope. "How can you be sure?"

Marcus answered matter-of-factly. "She won't tell because she's a werewolf, too."

CHAPTER

20

Ilona, a werewolf? Chloe tried to conceal her shock. Not that she doubted Marcus. If he said Ilona was a werewolf, then she was one.

"What?" Dean's jaw went slack in surprise, then his eyes brightened with hope. He hugged Ilona and sniffed her neck. Ilona bit her lip, looking dismayed, but didn't object. "She's one of us!" Dean pronounced triumphantly.

Everyone breathed a sigh of relief. They hadn't exposed their secret to a townie. They wouldn't have to kill Ilona.

But they were forgetting something. "She's not Pack," Chloe pointed out.

"Nobody's going to hurt her," Dean said fiercely. "Nobody's going to touch her." He growled a warning.

"Nobody's going to hurt her," Chloe agreed. "But she does owe us an explanation." She met Ilona's gaze. "Are you spying for another Pack?" Like the Quesnel Pack? She tried to remember when Ilona had moved to Pine Hollow—about two years ago? Did that predate Quesnel's resettlement troubles or not?

"I don't have a Pack." Ilona's gaze darted around nervously.

"Why didn't you tell me?" Dean asked. His arms still encircled her waist, and he sniffed her neck again in obvious satisfaction. "Now my dad can't forbid us to date."

"Yes, Ilona, why didn't you tell us?" Chloe put her hands on her hips. "And why the horse perfume?"

Ilona pressed a little deeper into Dean's embrace. "Some Packs drive out lone wolves."

"So what? You wanted to be in tight with us before you asked to join our Pack?" Chloe asked.

Ilona's chin lifted. "Basically, yes."

But there must be more to it than that. Ilona had lived in Pine Hollow too long and—Chloe's heart jolted—Basia, Ilona's mother/aunt, had made the crystal necklaces.

"So, how did you become a lone wolf in the first place?" Chloe kept her tone friendly and interested. "What Pack were you born into?"

Ilona's lips twisted. "I never had a Pack. My mom's Pack was wiped out by a mudslide while she was pregnant with me. She took refuge with another Russian Pack, but they never really accepted her or me. We were tolerated, but that's it. We were permanently bottom of the Pack hierarchy, always hungry. And then—then my mom died, and I left the Pack with Basia." The corners of her lips turned down. "I want to belong, but not if it means being low-rank forever."

Dean hugged her again. "That won't happen."

"So Basia is a werewolf, too?" Chloe asked.

A slight hesitation. "Yes."

"Then why is she on the loggers' side?"

Ilona shrugged. "You would have to ask her."

"What about the crystals? Did she really heal Olivia?"

"Basia thinks so."

"What do the crystals do?"

Another shrug. "Different types have different effects sup-posedly. Ask Basia, not me."

Ilona was being evasive. She knew more than she was telling. Chloe knew it, but she didn't know how to get Ilona to tell the truth.

Already Dean was giving her stink eye, apparently not liking the hard tone of her voice. "Well, I think it's really amazing how you fooled all of us with the horse scent. How'd you pull that off?" he asked. "Most horses hate us."

While Ilona answered, Chloe's phone rang. She glanced at the screen: Scout returning her call.

"Excuse me." She took a few steps away before answering. "Hello?"

"Hey, Chloe," Scout said breezily. "Congrats on your first Change."

Wow. He really was a gossip. "Thank you."

"So what's up?"

"Just a quick question. The day we met, you called Conrad Wharton by a different name. What was it?"

He took a moment to respond. "Did I? Must have been mistaken."

Chloe started to pace. "I don't think you were. I think he changed his name."

"Listen, Chloe, we received word that Conrad Wharton is your new Alpha. I don't want to damage relations with him by spreading rumours."

Crap. He was going to hang up.

She lowered her voice. "He may have been involved in my friend's murder. Please."

Scout paused again, then sighed. "Okay, kid, but you didn't hear any of this from me. I first met him as Bill Josephs. He was with an American Pack, I don't remember which one, but I do remember one of the European delegates pointing him out and saying he'd been kicked out of a Russian Pack and gone by a different name there, too. And don't ask me the other name, I really don't remember."

Russian. Chloe played a hunch. "Was it Novaskaya?"

Scout paused in surprise. "Actually, I think it was. Josef Novaskaya. Huh."

Marcus gravitated to her side as soon as she rejoined the

group. Ilona was describing how she'd spent hours and hours accustoming one particular horse to her scent, then gone for a ride every morning and kept a sweaty horse blanket in her locker for emergencies.

"Very clever," Chloe said truthfully. "But when you were telling us about your old Pack you skipped part of your story."

"Like what?" Ilona's nostrils flared. "Like how my mother had to sleep around to keep us from being kicked out? Like how the male wolves were starting to eye *me* and the female Alpha turned a blind eye?"

The pain in her voice set hooks in Chloe's heart. Chloe growled. "I promise that won't happen to you here. That's not the way a proper Pack is run. Feel free to break up with Dean anytime you want to."

"Hey!" Dean protested. "I'm standing right here."

Ilona nodded, thoughtful, but stayed in his embrace.

Chloe hardened her heart. She couldn't let pity blind her to the lies Ilona had told and was still telling. "What was your uncle doing while you and your mom were treated so badly?"

"He ignored us. Pretended we weren't even related—" Ilona stopped, eyes widening at what she'd let slip.

"But you all left the Pack together: you, your aunt and your Uncle Josef," Chloe guessed.

"Yes." Ilona pressed her lips together.

"So why didn't your uncle—Josef Conrad Wharton—bring you and Basia in with him when he joined our Pack?"

"Wait. Coach is your uncle?" Dean asked.

Chloe continued to stare at Ilona. "Answer the question."

A shrug. "He wanted to wait until he was established before bringing me—I mean, us—in."

"He's been part of the Pack for over two years. He became Alpha last night. Seems pretty well established to me. And yet here you are, still spying on us." Chloe circled around. Ilona's gaze followed her warily, even as she nestled deeper against Dean. Chloe wasn't buying her helpless act. "What's his plan? Is he going to have Basia step in as Alpha after Judy's mother has a convenient relapse?"

Ilona sneered, but bitterness and helplessness showed through her expression. Her fists were clenched. "Why should I tell you?"

Chloe got right up in her face, consciously trying to Dominate the other girl. "Because something is endangering my Pack, something to do with your uncle and aunt and those stupid harmonic crystal necklaces. And if you don't tell me what's going on *I will hurt you.*"

Ilona looked down, losing the Dominance contest. "I can't tell you."

"My mom has a purple crystal. What does it do?"

Ilona barked out a harsh laugh. "The *crystals* don't do anything."

Liar. Chloe opened her mouth, but then her brain twigged to the emphasis Ilona had put on it. The *crystals* didn't do anything; they were just for show. It was the other part of the necklace that was important: the chain. She inhaled sharply. "The silver. In the stories werewolves are always killed with silver bullets. Silver doesn't poison us on contact, but maybe it does something else, makes us vulnerable to witches."

From Ilona's expression she'd got it right. "Silver collars for all the little wolves," Ilona said, mockingly.

"Your aunt is controlling the Pack with the silver." Another guess framed as a statement.

Rage flushed Ilona's face. "She's not—" Her words choked off. Ilona clawed at her neck.

Too late Chloe realized the danger. "She's wearing a silver

necklace! Get it off her!" She yanked open the collar of Ilona's western-style shirt. A silver chain writhed around her neck, choking off her air.

Ilona fell back against Dean, gasping. Her face quickly turned red.

"Do something!" Dean yelled.

Chloe tried to pull the chain away, but it burned her fingers. Worse, the chain had sunk into Ilona's flesh. Her nails were too short to grab it.

Ilona's body went limp. Dread seized Chloe as he lowered her to the ground. Had Ilona passed out or was she dead?

The chain loosened, and Ilona's chest rose in a deep breath.

Chloe backed off, afraid to touch the chain, afraid any attempt to take it off would make it tighten up again. Chills raced up and down her arms, and her hands shook in reaction. Ilona had almost died right there in front of everybody.

Chloe flashed on the way her mom's hand had gone to her own necklace when Chloe had asked too many questions. Had her chain started to choke her?

"I'm confused," Brian complained. "Is anyone else confused?"

Chloe ignored him.

Marcus stood rigid beside her. "I remember." His voice rasped. "The necklace Coach gave Abby—it was silver like that. While Mom was trying to do a dead-stick landing, Abby started to choke. Dad tried to help her. Maybe he hit something getting out of his seat, or maybe he just distracted Mom at the wrong moment, but that's why the plane crashed."

Chloe slipped an arm around his waist, wordlessly offering what comfort she could. Poor doomed Abby.

It began to sink in that they were in serious trouble. Olivia wore a collar and had forced collars on most of the adult Pack members. Maybe even Judy and Nathan. Chloe and the boys were free, but Dean, Kyle and Brian all bore the Pack Bite and would have to submit to the Alpha, if given a direct command. Or did the fact that Nathan gave them their Bite mean they could resist? Nah. If that were true, Coach would no doubt have insisted on Biting them all last night. So only she and Marcus were rogue agents—and the Alphas thought Chloe was under control.

Which was why the Novaskayas had attempted to get Marcus shot yesterday. It was no coincidence that Basia had been on the spot with her hunter friend.

What did Basia and Coach want? Just to take over? Chloe remembered the conversation her parents had had about their credit cards. Money, then. Maybe power.

Ilona would know, but Ilona couldn't tell them.

As soon as Ilona went home, Coach and Basia would know that Chloe knew. Worse, they would know that Chloe's Bite had healed.

Chloe started to pace in tight circles, growling under her breath. Her heart beat under her breastbone like a bird trapped in a cage. They were so screwed.

"What's wrong?" Marcus asked her when they were a little distance away from the others.

"I don't know what to do," Chloe said in a low voice. "We have to save the Pack, but I don't want to throw Ilona under a bus either." Ilona was a victim, too, and another werewolf. And somewhere along the way, when Chloe wasn't looking, she'd also become a friend.

"You want to protect both," Marcus said quietly.

"Yes."

"Then make Ilona Pack. Bite her."

Chloe stared at him, open-mouthed. He said it so simply, as if the solution were obvious.

Maybe it was.

Chloe was no Alpha, but she was more Dominant than Ilona. It might work. And it was better than the alternative: keeping Ilona prisoner. Besides, they desperately needed the insider knowledge Ilona had.

Chloe took a deep breath. "Okay. I'll do it."

She didn't want to waste time arguing with Dean, so she swiftly undressed and threw herself into the Change.

Ow, ow. Not her most graceful or fastest Change. Chloe gritted her teeth and waited until the transformation was complete. She rose on four legs and approached Ilona. The horse smell had faded, washed away by sweat. No wonder Ilona always sat out of Phys. Ed.

Ilona was sitting up. Her eyes widened when Chloe the wolf approached. "What's she doing?"

"I don't know. Chloe?" Dean asked.

Chloe growled a warning as Ilona scrambled backwards. Ilona stilled. Chloe caught her gaze and words gave way to instinct. Face-to-face they engaged in a staring contest until Ilona submitted. As soon as her gaze dropped, Chloe sprang forward and bit her shoulder. She sank teeth in skin and growled. Ilona went limp.

Chloe released her and backed off.

"What the hell did she just do?" Dean asked in a strangled whisper.

Chloe concentrated on Changing back. Double ow.

"Okay, Ilona," she said, coolly getting dressed. "You wanted to be part of a Pack. Now you are." *Sort of.*

Ilona shook her head in disbelief. Her whole body trembled. "What have you done? *She'll kill me.*"

Chloe rolled her eyes. "Would you rather we killed you and buried your body in the woods?"

"If she finds the Bite, I'll wish I was dead." Ilona shuddered convulsively.

Chloe shrugged. "So don't let her see it."

"Easy for you to say," Ilona said resentfully. "You don't live in the same house as her. What do you think is going to happen the next time she drinks my blood?"

Blood? What the heck? Chloe boggled. So Ilona's anemia was real and not an excuse to avoid sweating in gym? "Is Basia a vampire?"

"She—" Ilona stopped as her silver chain twitched in warning. "I can't tell you what she is."

"Understood," Chloe said soothingly. Basia must be a witch—though she didn't match Marcus's description of the one who'd hexed his family's airplane. Did Ilona have a grandmother hanging around, too? She refrained from asking, concentrating on more relevant matters. "As your Alpha, I command you not to tell your aunt or uncle about what has happened today." She paused, thinking. "If I command you to remove the chain, will Basia know?"

"Yes." Ilona's lips were pale and bloodless. "Please don't. Trying to escape never works."

"Okay," Chloe said reluctantly. "I won't give the command until I'm sure I can protect you." She bit her lip. "The chain enforces Basia's commands, but surely there are some loopholes she's missed. You can't tell us what she is, but can you show us?" Chloe needed to confirm her suspicions.

Ilona hesitated.

"You're on borrowed time until Basia finds the Bite," Chloe reminded her. "I'm your best bet for getting that chain off."

Ilona laughed bitterly. "Then I'm doomed."

If Ilona was doomed, then so were Chloe's parents and the entire Pack. "I don't accept that." She met Ilona's gaze, asserting Dominance. "Show us."

Ilona hung her head and closed her eyes. "Okay, but we have to be careful that we're not seen. Please listen if I say 'stop.'"

"Agreed."

A half-hour tromp through the woods brought them to the Novaskaya horse ranch. No Mazda sat in the driveway; Basia wasn't home. Ilona halted when the barn came into view. "This is as far as I can take you."

Marcus bared his teeth and whined in his throat. "The Evil in the Forest. I can smell it."

"Ugh. What is that?" Kyle and the other teens grimaced.

Chloe inhaled and caught a half-remembered scent floating beneath the horse manure smell. Chicken or poultry, but foul and rotting. She'd smelled something like it as a wolf once, and Marcus had herded her away.

"Dean, you and Ilona fade back. In fact, why don't you go into town and go on a date so she has an alibi? I'll text you when it's over. Keep her safe."

Dean nodded tightly. Once they were out of earshot Chloe continued her instructions. "Kyle, Brian, you play lookout. Marcus, Change and come with me." In case she needed his keener wolf senses.

Chloe walked forward in a crouch, keeping her profile low, using every bit of cover she could. She could tell they were getting closer from the smell: the foul scent coated her throat and made her want to spit.

Finally, she edged around the barn and found the cause of the horrid odour. A grey hut with a thatched roof squatted on the forest floor, blending into the trees. Literally squatted. The house had two giant chicken legs with yellow talons folded up underneath it. They were the source of the reek.

Something about a hut on chicken legs rang a bell. In a second she had it: there had been a picture of it in the Pack Lore. The hut was the home of Baba Yaga, the witch of Slavic folklore. Not only did Baba Yaga live in a hut that could walk on chicken legs, she was ugly and flew around in a giant mortar and used a pestle as a rudder—the mortar looked like a cup. That fit with what Marcus had seen out the plane window.

So witches did exist. Her dad was wrong—as he'd probably already found out.

She shivered. Baba Yaga wasn't just a witch, but a legendary, very old and powerful witch. Great.

The hut would be where Baba Yaga did her magic. Chloe eyed it speculatively. Could they burn it down? The thatch looked rotten, and the wood dry, but no. She couldn't risk a forest fire.

Marcus pressed his furry body against her legs, silently asking what she wanted to do next.

Chloe bit her lip. "I want to look in the windows if we can. See if the witch has anything we should steal." A black charm causing Olivia's cancer or a master bracelet controlling all the collars or who knew what? Not Chloe. Last week she'd thought witches didn't exist and that silver had no effect on werewolves.

Too bad she didn't have binoculars. Chloe crept up on the hut. She stayed human so she would be tall enough to peek in, but it left her vulnerable. She was glad Marcus accompanied her.

Twenty feet away, then ten … still no sign of movement from within or without, but her heart pounded like a steel drum, and she had to breathe through her mouth so as to not choke on the terrible odour.

Ah, crap. The windows were dark because they had curtains or shutters on them. If she wanted to see, she'd have to open the door. But that would mean actually going up the steps between the chicken legs.

Fear dried her mouth. She really didn't want to go within reach of those talons.

Apparently, Marcus didn't like the idea either. He grabbed her jacket in his teeth and held her back.

"I know," she told him. "But I need to find out what's in there, what we're up against, if there's something I can use to free my parents. Besides, the witch isn't here. It's just a bird. We are wolves!"

Her pep talk convinced Marcus, if not herself. He released her.

Moving as silently as possible, Chloe ghosted up the steps. At the last second she changed her mind and put her eye to the crack between the window and the shutter instead of opening the door. She didn't want to risk being trapped inside.

Benches lined the three walls of the hut. Against the far side was a huge stone oven, big enough to fit Hansel and Gretel both. The other wall was lined with shelves.

At first glance, it looked like an old-fashioned pantry with rows of glass bottles full of canned things sitting on shelves, bunches of dried herbs hanging from the ceiling, and a mortar and pestle sitting on a plain wooden table. The breath she'd been holding escaped on a sigh of relief only to stutter to stop a moment later.

A line of rats hung by their braided tails, some dead, some wriggling and biting their fellows. And many of the jars contained eyeballs and beaks and blood and viscera instead of vegetables. Okey-dokey, witch's hut confirmed. But was there anything in there she could use to defeat Baba Yaga or break the hold of the silver collars?

Of course, since she didn't know what she was looking for she could be staring right at it and miss it. Nevertheless, Chloe pressed her nose close to the glass, her breath fogging the pane.

The shutter jumped up. Chloe stumbled back. Was someone inside?

But both shutters had lifted at the same moment. Her hackles rose. Those weren't windows, they were eyes. *Baba Yaga's hut was alive.*

Chloe jumped off the porch and dropped five feet to the ground. She landed in a crouch. Marcus rushed to her side, growling.

The hut raised itself up on its huge chicken legs and lurched towards them. Chloe sprinted deeper into the woods, Marcus at her side.

The house was big and clumsy; it ought to have quickly fallen behind, unable to get through the places she did. Instead, it crashed through smaller saplings, or raised its tall legs to a horrifying height and stepped over grown trees. And each long stride ate up a dozen of Chloe's.

Marcus howled, calling for help.

Should she Change? She could run faster as a wolf, but in the minute it took her to Change from girl to wolf, the hut would catch her. She gasped for breath, put her head down and powered on. If she could just make it between that line of firs—

A giant claw snagged the back of her shirt, tripping her before the cloth tore in half. Before she could scramble back up, the chicken foot came down over top of her, three toes in front and a shorter one in back, trapping her in place.

Adrenaline compelled her Change without her calling it. Fur sprouted on her arms and legs, her skull crunched and flattened, her muzzle pushing out. She kicked her legs, trying to free herself from her jeans.

She was vaguely aware of Marcus dashing forward to nip and tear at the chicken foot. In her wolf form, she tried to squeeze out from under the yellow talon holding her in place, but it put more weight on her. She yelped.

It would either squash her or trap her until Baba Yaga arrived.

Two more howls split the air. Her ears flicked, recognizing the voices of her Pack brothers: Kyle and Brian.

Each toe was tipped with a foot-long curved claw, impossible to damage. Chloe jumped up and sank her teeth into a toe, then spat the foul taste out of her mouth.

Three other wolves rushed in, snapping and tearing off strips of flesh, then retreating. The chicken feet didn't bleed, but oozed yellow pus. The smell was rank.

The second foot snaked out, trying to grab Marcus. Chloe howled a warning. The talon stabbed the earth where his body had stood only moments before.

Kyle darted in on the other side and tore off a scaly chunk of skin.

The hut shot up, the chicken legs unfolding to their full height of eight metres, as tall as a two-storey house. The talons curled tighter around Chloe, lifted her up into the air, too, then slammed her back down, as the chicken legs took long, lurching strides toward the edge of the forest.

The force of the impact robbed her of breath, and one of her ribs cracked.

Marcus howled and attacked with a renewed vigor. Kyle and Brian joined him. Whenever the claw imprisoning Chloe touched down, they stripped off more and more of the foul meat. White bone shone greasily through.

The floor of the house above crashed down, clipping Brian. He yelped and fell back. Crap! How did you kill a house?

Marcus leapt for the back of the foot. Snarling, he tore at the exposed muscle and severed the tendon. The claw holding Chloe suddenly released. She rolled on the ground and out of the way as the hut whomped down again, reducing a Christmas-tree-size conifer to matchsticks.

Marcus nudged her side, urging her to her feet. Ribs still sore, but healing, she trotted after him into the underbrush. Kyle and Brian made two more howling runs at the chicken feet, distracting it. The hut reached for Brian with its still-working foot, tugged the tip of his tail, then lost its grip and over-balanced, the bad leg giving way under it. The house crashed over on its side.

As one, the Pack howled in triumph.

Chloe lifted her voice in unison.

Only after she'd turned human again did she realize what they'd really done was announce to Baba Yaga that they knew about her.

From here on, the witch would be on her guard.

CHAPTER
21

Her dad cleared his throat, face grim. "Another Pack meeting has been called for tonight."

Chloe's supper became unsettled in her stomach. What would the witch's move be this time? Marcus's punishment for breaking Pack Law and Changing in public, that Nathan's announcement had delayed last time? An accusation of destruction of property levelled at Chloe? Would Olivia step down and Basia Challenge for Alpha?

Chloe had chosen not to tell her parents about Baba Yaga and the Novaskayas. Like it or not, her parents were compromised. The advantage gained in telling them didn't outweigh the risk to Ilona.

"Chloe, do you feel well enough to attend?" her father asked. Since up until now she'd been packing away her food with a healthy appetite, the out-of-the-blue question felt like a strong hint.

"I think I should stay home," Chloe said.

Instead of giving her a lecture on Pack responsibilities her mother said, "What excuse should I give the Alphas for your absence?"

"Tell them I'm having my period," Chloe said, skirting the edges of a lie. 'Tell them' wasn't the same as 'I am.'

In humans, menstruation was a time of infertility. In wolves, it was the opposite. Menstruating females were forbidden to Change lest the scent cause 'unfortunate incidents.' Not that there was any real reason why Chloe couldn't attend in human form.

Both her parents nodded. Her mother's face relaxed in relief. "Marcus, would you prefer to stay with Chloe?" her dad asked. Marcus nodded.

Her parents left in the SUV. As soon as they drove out of sight, Marcus lifted his eyebrows.

"We sneak over through the woods, keeping downwind," Chloe said. If Kyle and Brian got in trouble for their part in this afternoon's adventure, she would have to intervene.

Other than that, she needed to tally who amongst the Pack adults wore a silver chain and if any still walked free. Aside from Coach, who was Baba Yaga's partner and didn't need one. She clenched her fists remembering his duplicity. Pine Hollow had taken mercy on a lone wolf, welcoming him into their Pack, instead of shunning him as had been their right, and he'd repaid them with treachery and black magic.

Chloe would *never* acknowledge him as Alpha. Olivia had likely been tricked into taking her chain, promised a cure for the cancer eating away her life. Coach had no excuse.

Marcus started to take off his shirt.

"No, stay in human form," Chloe said. "If we're discovered, we don't want them to accuse you of being feral."

Marcus grimaced, but left his shirt on.

The sun was setting as they slipped into the woods, keeping parallel to the path. Chloe followed Marcus's lead, walking carefully to keep noise to a minimum. Fortunately, the rising wind would cover their footfalls.

The usual fire pit burned in the Frayne's backyard. Chloe used the deep shadows it cast to sneak herself and Marcus into hearing range, to the left of the deck where Olivia stood between Nathan and Coach.

Olivia stepped forward. "I hereby banish Marcus Jennings for breaking Pack Law. He has one hour to leave the Preserve."

Chloe winced, but better banishment than an order of execution. Banishment could be lifted—once the rot at the heart of the Pack was carved out.

"Some of you may think my judgement is harsh, but Pack Law is enforced for a reason. Marcus broke it, and now we must all pay the price."

What was she talking about?

"I have terrible news," Olivia continued. "Someone saw Marcus Change in the school parking lot—and recorded it."

No. Chloe didn't believe it. If any of the kids at school had a video of Marcus Changing, they wouldn't have been able to resist showing their friends. She would have noticed that kind of suppressed excitement and secrets circulating among the townies.

"We're being blackmailed," Olivia continued. "They've demanded that we open up the Preserve to logging or they'll go public."

The Pack ought to have erupted into anger and outrage. Instead everyone merely looked sick. Chloe's mom turned into her husband's arms, openly crying, but only Dean protested. "No! We can't do that. We have to protect the forest."

Coach glared him down. "Enough! The decision has already been made. The Pack is more important than trees. We won't allow clear-cutting. The trees will grow back. But if who we really are becomes public, it will ruin lives. Not just our lives, but the lives of every werewolf in the world."

Chloe's lip lifted in a snarl. She still thought the video was a bluff. The witch had tried to kill Marcus to shut him up about the plane crash, first by poisoning him, then by her backup plan of having Jefferson shoot him. Otherwise it was too big of a coincidence that Basia would happen to be on school property at the time. But—Chloe frowned—that meant the witch had to have arranged for the poison. How? Had Ilona slipped something into Marcus's lunch?

Never mind. She was getting sidetracked. The point was that the witch had been trying to kill Marcus. This so-called video was just a way to discredit him and get money from the logging deal.

"The papers are being drawn up," Olivia said. "We will sign them two days from now. The decision is final. Go home." She lifted a hand and casually dismissed the Pack.

No. This couldn't happen.

Chloe imagined loggers cutting roads in the Preserve for their heavy trucks, wounding and scarring the earth and making the animals flee from their machines' terrible noise, leaving behind only stumps of once proud trees. The wolf in her keened.

"No!" Chloe didn't remember making the decision to step forward; her body did it for her. Marcus stayed glued to her side.

Olivia turned towards her, unsurprised. "Chloe. Not at home after all."

"There is no video!" Chloe shouted. "No one who isn't a werewolf saw Marcus Change—and he wouldn't have Changed if he hadn't been poisoned. There is no blackmailer! The witch just wants the money she'll get from the logging deal."

Her Packmates' faces showed anger and shame, but little surprise. Her aunt and Dean's dad touched their throats, no doubt warned to silence by their constricting collars. Her heart quailed; Aunt Laurie had been her last hope.

Olivia's face held no regret, only impatience.

That seemed wrong somehow, but Chloe didn't have time to pursue it. She had to stop this right here, right now.

"I Challenge you!" Her voice rang out, high and frantic. "I Challenge you for Alpha!" Even as the words came out, she knew it was madness. *I'm not Alpha material.*

Anger pushed back her doubt. No matter how unfit Chloe was, she was still a better choice than anyone wearing a collar. Only Chloe was still free to do this.

Olivia laughed—and that struck another chord of wrongness. Shouldn't she be angry?

"Oh, little puppy," Olivia said. "Challenge not accepted. You are too young. You had your first Change only days ago and likely cannot even Change under your own control."

"Oh, yes, I can! And it doesn't matter if I'm too young, because someone has to stop you!" Olivia had to know the video was a setup, but she was still going along with both banishing Marcus and the logging deal.

"Then prove it." Olivia raised her brows. "Change into a wolf. I will wait."

"Chloe, be careful," Marcus whispered in her ear. "She smells smug and wrong. This is a trap."

Her scalp prickled, but she couldn't back down now. "Fine," she told Olivia. "I'll Change and then we'll fight for Alpha position."

Olivia crossed her arms. "Proof first, little puppy."

Angrily, Chloe stripped off her clothes, then closed her eyes and summoned the Change.

Except it didn't come.

The wind picked up, raising gooseflesh, making her very aware that she stood there before the Pack half-naked. It brought back painful memories of her humiliation during the obstacle course.

No, curse it. She'd broken through the barrier. She'd Changed just this afternoon for heaven's sake!

Was that it? Was she too tired? Chloe gritted her teeth and strained harder, gathering all her rage and determination and throwing them at the barrier. She tried to ignore the sick fear bubbling underneath.

Nothing happened.

Judy huffed in disgust. The small sound brought back all her other failures and made this one real.

Devastation crashed over Chloe with the force of a tidal wave. How could this be happening to her again? What had she done wrong to deserve being punished like this? Her throat swelled, and tears burned in her eyes.

Olivia sniffed. "It is as I said. Go home, little puppy." She turned her back and walked into the house, leaving her foe vanquished behind her.

The Pack all dispersed in silence. Kyle shot her a sympathetic look, but Dean and Brian avoided her gaze.

Chloe's mother handed Chloe her shirt. "Get dressed, darling. It was very brave of you to Challenge her."

The words were supportive, but her mother couldn't meet her eyes, and her father's expression almost drove her to her knees: it was one of shame.

She'd shamed her family.

Sobbing, Chloe broke and ran blindly into the woods.

Marcus followed her, but he must have sensed she couldn't bear words of commiseration right now because he ran at her side as wolf. He kept her company in silence and protected her.

She ran and ran until her muscles burned and her lungs couldn't draw in enough air, until she collapsed to the ground in sheer misery, first crying, then beating her fists against the hard-packed ground in rage.

The wolf licked tears from her cheek. She threw an arm around his neck and bawled out all her anger and frustration and heartbreak into his soft fur.

She might have stayed there all night, but the cold needled her bare skin—she'd run off in only her underwear. As she climbed to her feet, she suddenly remembered the one-hour deadline Olivia had given Marcus. "Crap. I forgot. You're banished."

Marcus didn't react, indifferent, but Chloe pushed herself to jog faster. "We have to go back to my house. We need clothes, food … money." The challenge threatened to overwhelm her again.

Marcus nudged her thigh with his nose.

She rubbed his head affectionately, despite her sorrow. "Yes, I said we. If you're banished, I'm coming with you." She couldn't stay here anymore. It was impossible.

The SUV was parked in the driveway. Their clothes were folded on the porch. Chloe dressed quickly and hurried inside while Marcus was still Changing.

She'd expected her parents to be waiting for her in the kitchen, but instead the house was eerily silent as if they'd gone to bed. At 8 p.m.?

She grabbed her backpack, set it on the table and emptied it of schoolwork. Marcus joined her in the kitchen, still bare-chested. "Can you get out the granola bars?" she asked him. "And any unopened boxes of crackers?" Sealed food, that didn't smell too enticing or need to be refrigerated, would be best.

They worked together in silence for a few moments. Chloe rummaged in the junk drawer and found the barbecue lighter. What else? Tissues for kindling—

Marcus interrupted her chain of thought. "Chloe, look." He pointed to the hand-bound leather book sitting on the table instead of on its usual shelf. The Pack Lore. A number of pages were bookmarked. With $100 bills. They stuck halfway out, practically waving for her attention.

Heart beating faster, she opened the handwritten journal to the bookmark closest to the end. On it were inked the phone numbers and addresses of the nearest other Packs and their Alphas. La Ronge, Quesnel, and even Churchill.

Chloe huffed out a bitter laugh. "As if any of the other Packs will want a former feral and a Dud."

"You're not a Dud!" Marcus said angrily. "Don't call yourself that!"

"I can't Change. What else would you call it?" Maybe she was exaggerating—she had Changed successfully a few times—but there was clearly something defective about her if the ability could just vanish for no reason.

Marcus growled, the sound shockingly hostile. He grabbed her shoulders. "You are not a Dud. You're my Alpha. Is this why you've been crying?"

She blinked. "Yes, of course."

"That's the stupidest thing I've ever heard." He gave her a shake. "You can't Change for the same reason I got sick. Poisoned food."

Chloe stopped crying, her mouth opening in shock. "What? That's impossible."

"He's right," her mother said behind her. Her parents entered the kitchen. They both looked a decade older than usual, hunched and grey. Her mother's eyelids were puffy from crying. "It was a small quantity of silver nitrate."

What was she saying? A gulf yawned between Chloe and her parents. Bile rose in her throat. "The only thing I had to eat was the supper you cooked ... "

Her mother covered her face, obviously guilty.

And still Chloe couldn't believe it. "Mom?" she pleaded. "You—you didn't, did you?" Her mom knew how hard she'd worked to Change. How much it had hurt her to be called a Dud. Betrayal stabbed Chloe, brutal as a knife to the chest. She stumbled back a step. "*No.*"

Her mom wept helplessly.

Her dad put his arm around his wife. "Your mother didn't do it," he said. "She refused after what happened to Marcus."

Which was an admission that her mother had poisoned Marcus.

"Her collar choked her into unconsciousness four times." Her dad's voice broke. "I was worried about brain damage, and about what would happen to you if we disobeyed. I did it."

His shame hadn't been for Chloe, but for himself.

"You should have warned me," Chloe said harshly.

"She ordered us not to speak of it. We planned to discourage you from attending the meeting, but then you said you were going to stay home." Her dad sighed and rubbed a hand over his head. "We should have found some way to tell you. I'm so very sorry, Chloe."

Heartsore, Chloe backed away. Marcus stepped between her and her parents, lips drawn back, feral.

"Are you going to go with Marcus?" her dad asked.

She nodded, unable to speak.

"I think that's best," he said softly. "Safest. Pine Hollow Pack isn't a good place to be right now."

"No," Chloe agreed, her voice brittle. "Not as long as it's under the witch's control."

"Come on," her dad said. "I'll drive you to the bus depot. A bus leaves at 2 a.m. for parts south."

Chloe wasn't certain where she wanted to go, if she was ready to leave, but she didn't say so. Anything she told her parents could be tortured out of them.

Her mother tucked the Pack Lore volume into her backpack and handed it to her. Somehow that solidified the coming break even more. It felt as if her mother was entrusting her with the Lore because the Pine Hollow Pack was doomed.

Just then a vehicle crunched down the gravelled driveway.

Her mother paled. "The deadline! It's five minutes past." She went to the window. "It's Conrad's truck. He's alone, but he has a rifle."

Her dad swore. "That petty bastard. You kids hide. I can't stand against the witch, but I can hold off a bully."

Hiding under a bed or in a closet would put them at a

disadvantage. Chloe grabbed a kitchen chair and placed it in the hallway under the attic access.

The doorbell rang.

"Who's there?" her dad called, stalling.

Marcus stood on the chair and moved the hatch aside, then jumped up, caught the edge and pulled himself up into the air.

"Let me in! I know you're there!" Coach called.

Chloe stood on the chair and passed the backpack to Marcus, then raised her hands. While Marcus hauled her up, her mother whisked the chair back to the kitchen.

The unfinished attic was little more than a crawlspace. Chloe crouched on a rafter, careful not to trust her weight to the ceiling panels, while Marcus silently replaced the hatch. She picked out voices from down the hall.

"Move aside, Curtis." Coach sounded impatient.

"What's this about—oof!" Her father grunted.

Chloe tensed, outrage flaring inside her. Had Coach punched her dad?

"Where's the feral?" Coach sounded closer now, in the kitchen. "You were instructed not to help him."

"As you can see, he's not here," her mother said.

"No?" Coach sniffed. "Let's make certain, shall we?" A number of noises followed. Footsteps in the hall. Doors being thrown open. The creak of heavy furniture being shoved across the hardwood floor.

Chloe readied herself to jump down on Coach if he looked in the crawlspace.

"Where's your daughter?" Coach demanded.

"I'm her father. I have a right to send her off to visit my relatives in Churchill," her dad said carefully. "For her own safety."

"And the feral? Did you drive Marcus Jennings to the bus depot, too?"

A pause then, "I didn't notice any stowaways, but it was dark."

Coach swore. "You mean you didn't notice on purpose." The sound of flesh hitting flesh made Chloe flinch. "I won't forget this, Curtis." Coach stomped off.

"Neither will I," her father said softly.

The door slammed, and a pickup roared off.

"I'm fine, Rachel," her dad said. "It's just a bruised rib. I won't even feel it by morning. Let's go to bed, shall we?" He was speaking as much for her benefit as for her mother's.

Chloe stayed where she was. Best if her parents could deny seeing her after Coach left, if asked.

Only after her parents' bedroom door shut did she and Marcus creep out of their hiding spot.

Wordlessly, Chloe and Marcus slipped out the door. She feared Coach might lie in wait on the route to town so they headed deeper into the Preserve.

She didn't look back.

Worry gnawed at Marcus. As a wolf he couldn't be sure, but it felt like it was taking too long for the drug to wear off. It had been full dark for hours, and Chloe kept shivering in her inadequate denim jacket. She needed fur, either her own or cuddled up to his. He nosed her thigh, trying to steer her toward a suitable den.

"Not yet." She patted the top of his head, her fingers lingering for a moment before she jammed them back in her pocket. In an effort to keep warm, she broke into a jog again, the beam of her flashlight bobbing with each stride.

A scent reached his nose that lifted his hackles. It wasn't the foul scent of the witch's hut, but the earthy one of a predator. A big one. Marcus whined. When Chloe didn't take the hint, he blocked the way, growling a warning.

To his surprise she smiled. "You smell something, huh? I guess that means we're close enough. It would be rude to arrive this late anyhow. Tomorrow will be soon enough."

Marcus cocked an ear. She'd entered the predator's territory deliberately? His Alpha wasn't usually so foolish. They would need to be careful tomorrow, but now it was time to den.

He scraped out a hollow under a willow tree and crawled inside.

"One more try ... " Chloe put down her backpack, stripped off her clothes and stood shuddering in the cold for a moment before the Change suddenly gripped her in its painful vise.

Afterward, he greeted the she-wolf with a nose touch. The two of them curled up under the tree, fur to fur, and slept away the first night of their exile.

CHAPTER

22

Chloe woke to the smell of woodsmoke. Good, they were close to the log cabin.

She Changed, the cold air nipping at her bare skin, and all but dived into her clothes. She threw some sweats at Marcus. "You, too."

He chuffed, but obeyed, crawling out of their hollow a moment later to put on the jacket she'd packed for him.

He tilted his head. "I thought we were going to another Pack."

"We are." She'd come up with a plan the night before. While the Quesnel Pack was the nearest in terms of distance, its recent resettlement had already strained it to its limits. La Ronge, Saskatchewan where Scout was from or Churchill, Manitoba where she had some cousins were the better options.

However, before she left Pine Hollow, maybe forever, she was determined to do what she could to thwart the witch.

"We won't stay here long. This is a … courtesy call."

"It's a predator," Marcus said flatly. "It already knows we're here."

"Nonetheless, we need to be polite." She tipped back her head and howled as best she could with a human throat. Marcus joined in. Together they walked up to the snug log cabin in the woods.

The witch might think she had the logging deal sewn up, but the Preserve had another trustee, one Coach might not know about: Lady Sasquatch.

Chloe knocked, and the door opened at her push. Inside, Lady Sasquatch bustled about the stove. Three plates were already set at the table.

"Good morning," Chloe said. Always be courteous to a creature that can break your spine with one blow.

Lady Sasquatch grunted without looking up from the stove. "Werewolf children. Sit."

Lady Sasquatch stood over seven feet tall, and her chairs and table were commensurately higher, giving Chloe the weird sensation of having shrunken back to a child's size overnight.

Brown fur covered Lady Sasquatch from head to foot, and she didn't bother with clothes, except for a belt to carry tools. From the back she resembled Chewbacca, but Chewie had more of a dog's face. Sasquatches were more ape-like.

Chloe and Marcus sat quietly while Lady Sasquatch finished making breakfast. Sasquatches weren't shy, exactly, but they hated chitchat and considered it rude to talk while food was on the table.

Lady Sasquatch served them each two bannocks and sat down with a stack of four in front of herself. Chloe followed her host's example, spreading jam on the flatbread before rolling it up and eating it with her fingers. Marcus sniffed each jar then spooned up a big glob of raspberry jam. To drink, they had tea with green herbs and dried flower petals floating in it. Chloe didn't like the flavour, but bravely drank hers down. Lady Sasquatch didn't have running water on tap, so it was important to boil water before drinking.

By the time breakfast finally ended, Chloe was wild with impatience.

Lady Sasquatch signalled her willingness to talk business by asking bluntly, "Why are you here?"

Taking a deep breath, Chloe laid it all on the line. "The

Pack is in trouble. A witch has put silver collars around all the adults' necks and taken over." As succinctly as possible, she told the tale of Olivia's cancer and sudden cure, the crystal necklaces, Marcus's memory of the crash and Coach's ascendance to Alpha. She finished with Olivia's announcement that the logging deal would be put through.

Lady Sasquatch finally showed a reaction, baring two-inch long fangs in her mouth. Holy crap.

"You're a trustee," Chloe said. "Can you block the vote?"

But Lady Sasquatch shook her head. "On paper, I have the power. The vote must be unanimous. But in practice, they will call a public vote and record me as absent."

"What about a proxy vote?"

"That can buy us some time. But their lawyer will find a way around it eventually. I will start proceedings, but unless the true problem is dealt with, I will ultimately fail."

Chloe's hands clenched. She hadn't realized just how much hope she'd placed in Lady Sasquatch until it crumbled. "So the Pack is doomed."

"Probably. I will nonetheless try."

The bannocks turned to lead in Chloe's stomach.

Lady Sasquatch stood.

Chloe took that as a signal to leave and stood as well. "Thank you, Lady Sasquatch," she said formally. "You are a true friend to the Pack."

Lady Sasquatch graciously inclined her head. "I owe your father a debt. May I give you some advice?"

"I would be glad of any advice you can offer."

"I understand your reluctance to leave your parents and Packmates as the witch's prisoners," Lady Sasquatch said. "But do not pit yourself against her directly. You will lose. Do not burden your parents with this grief. Do as they wanted. Live."

She was right. Chloe's parents wanted her to be safe, and yet... "Thank you again." Chloe lifted her hand in farewell.

Lady Sasquatch nodded back. By the time they were out the door she'd already begun to clear the dishes.

Spirits low, Chloe trudged through the wood.

Do as her parents wanted ... Well, that was pretty clear from the list of addresses bookmarked in the Pack Lore. Which reminded her.

She unzipped her backpack and took out the leather book, turning her back so that it was sheltered from the wind, and began to collect the $100 bills.

When she opened the page to the middle she saw another bill taped to an entry partway down the page.

October 15, 1951. June showed her healed Bite to the Pack, as proof both of the Alpha's advancing age and her own ability to be Alpha. Alpha Henrietta stepped down peaceably.

Chloe blinked. A healed bite was a sign of a potential Alpha? Her mother, who'd made this bookmark, still thought she was an Alpha? No. Even with the bite she'd given Ilona, Chloe didn't buy it. Maybe sometimes a healed Bite was a sign of an emerging Alpha, but this time it must have more to do with Olivia's illness.

She turned to the first bookmark, unsurprised to see the illustration of Baba Yaga's hut. It hadn't looked nearly so charming in person.

She'd read the stories years before, but had forgotten many of the details. She read them again now, with a fresh eye.

Most of them were standard folktales, but one, in spiky handwriting was different. *I had this tale from my great-grandmother who had it from hers: Baba Yaga created the werewolves.*

Baba Yaga is a shapeshifter, able to take on the appearance of someone living by drinking their blood—

Chloe couldn't stifle a small exclamation. Was that why the witch had taken Ilona's blood?

Did that mean some of the time when she'd been talking to Ilona, it had really been the witch? How horrid.

—or the dead by wearing their skin. According to the tale, Baba Yaga fell in love with a young man and gave him one of her wolf skins so they could run and hunt together. But the man betrayed her with Baba Yaga's sister. As punishment, Baba Yaga turned both her lover and her sister permanently into wolves. The wolves had pups, as wolves do. When the pups grew to adulthood they discovered the ability to Change from wolf into human form. These were the first werewolves.

Chills crawled up Chloe's arms. There was one final line:

Great-grandmother says we fled Europe to escape from Baba Yaga's control and not to trust the Packs who stayed.

Chloe kept reading, looking for more useful information, like how to kill Baba Yaga, but had no such luck. In most of the tales she was very old and powerful. Sometimes immortal.

But something must have happened to drive her away from Russia. Hmmm. If the Russians could do it, maybe Pine Hollow could, too.

Of course, maybe Baba Yaga had left Russia of her own accord.

"I wish I knew what she wanted," Chloe said after telling Marcus what she'd read. "Why has she taken over our Pack in particular? Why make a deal with the loggers? What does an immortal want with a tiny insignificant Pack like ours?"

Marcus shrugged.

Her frustration mounted at this non-answer. "What do you think we should do? And *don't* just say you'll follow me," she added sharply. "If it were your choice, what would you do?"

"Go," he said simply. "But I am not Alpha. You need a Beta's advice."

She was tired of arguing that she wasn't an Alpha. "Okay. Play Beta for me then."

He pondered for a moment. "If you simply Challenge for Alpha again, Baba Yaga will kill you or chain you. I won't let you throw your life away for no purpose." He watched her with a determined expression.

Should she be touched or irritated? She ignored his delusion that he could stop her.

"So, you think we should flee then?" Tactically, it made sense, but something inside Chloe rebelled at the notion. Her instinct urged her to fight, but fighting without hope of victory was stupid.

"Survival comes first. Every living thing knows this. There is no shame in it."

"Live and fight another day?" Chloe asked thoughtfully.

Marcus shrugged. "Tomorrow will keep. Live today."

She blinked. That was wolf thinking, not human. She couldn't do that—live solely in the now. Marcus could. Marcus would be perfectly happy to run off with her into the woods right now, abandon their backpack, their humanity, and live as wolves

The prospect enticed her wolf: endless days of running through the forest. Unfortunately, Canadian winter loomed. Freezing in the snow sounded considerably less romantic. Nor did she want to risk losing who she was and going feral.

"Okay. No head-on attack. We retreat and regroup." Retreat implied return. "We can't defeat Baba Yaga alone. We need allies." She thought about that a moment longer. "The next bus doesn't leave until 2 a.m. So until then, let's see what we can do to harass Baba Yaga in small ways. Step one: get back within cell phone tower range."

A two-hour hike took them close enough to town to get three bars on her phone. Chloe took care to cross the highway so they weren't technically on the Preserve any more.

She phoned Ilona.

"Hello?" The other girl sounded subdued.

"Hi, Ilona, it's Patty," Chloe lied, just in case the witch could hear. "I'm doing my English homework, the creative writing assignment, and I'm a bit stuck."

"Oh?" Ilona asked cautiously.

"I'm getting close to the rescue part, and I can't decide if it's only the daughter who should be rescued or if her mom or aunt is still alive." Chloe crossed her fingers, hoping the story would keep Ilona's silver collar quiescent.

Pause. "Just the daughter. The mother is dead. There is no aunt."

Which meant Baba Yaga was wearing Ilona's dead mother's skin like a coat. Ugh. Chloe's skin crawled. No wonder Ilona had preferred to call her aunt.

"So how's the story going to end?" Ilona asked.

"Oh, the usual," Chloe said breezily. "An epic battle followed by victory. Anyhow, the other part I'm having trouble with is the villain's motivation. Why did she make a deal with outsiders? Does she need money?"

"Maybe she has an eBay addiction," Ilona said. "Maybe she orders exotic … things, and then gets angry when they're fakes or get confiscated in customs."

Magical items. That did what?

"Ooh, good idea," Chloe said. "But I need to dig deeper. What are the classic motives? Love, hate, revenge."

"Revenge and hate are kind of the same, aren't they?" Ilona asked carefully. "You hate someone, so you seek revenge. But in order to get revenge, you need money and power."

So the magical items were probably a means to an end.

"With enough money and power you can buy an army." Ilona inhaled sharply.

"Are you okay?" Chloe asked urgently. Oh, God, had they set off the collar's choking mechanism?

"I'm all right," Ilona said after a moment. "But I need to go now. Good luck with your story. Bye."

Chloe thumbed off her phone and sighed. "It's not looking good," she admitted to Marcus.

He nodded. He'd been standing close enough to hear the phone call with his enhanced werewolf hearing.

Her phone rang, startling her. The screen showed a familiar name. "It's Kyle." She accepted the call. "Hello?"

"Chloe, finally," Kyle said in relief. "Where are you? Things have gone bad, really bad." The story gushed out of him. "The Alphas came over last night. When they turned into the drive-way, Dad told Dean and me to escape out the window, but Dean circled around because he was worried that Coach might try to kill Dad. Dean didn't return. I'm pretty sure they collared him, too." Kyle's breathing was ragged. "I stayed out all night, but I'm cold and hungry. Can I run away with you and Marcus? Have you left town already? Where are you?"

Chloe was about give Kyle directions, but Marcus shook his head and touched his throat.

A chill ghosted down her spine. Marcus was right; Kyle could be compromised. He could have a silver collar and be phoning her on the witch's orders.

"Chloe?" Kyle sounded frantic.

"Before we meet, we need to set up a protocol," Chloe said firmly. "Send me a selfie of your neck. I'll do the same." She ended the call. She used the camera function to take a quick snap of her bare neck, then sent it to Kyle. A glance at the clock showed that it was noon recess so she sent the same pic to both Brian and Judy. Dean's dad was an obvious target, but Brian's mom was already collared so they might not have bothered with her kids. Judy, however … Chloe winced. She didn't hold out much hope for her frenemy's freedom.

Ping. A pic of Kyle's bare neck.

Ping. A text from Brian. "Dontcha know? selfie = ur face. LOL."

She texted back: "I'm starting a new game. Send a pic of your neck or you're out."

Ping. A pic of Judy's neck with a blue crystal on a silver chain.

Ping. Ping. Two texts from Judy, one word each: "not" and "mother".

Chloe shivered. Baba Yaga had control of Judy then—and the witch must be wearing Olivia's face. But was Olivia dead and skinned, or just suffering from some blood loss? Chloe remembered how Olivia's reactions had been off the night before. Maybe that hadn't been Olivia either. Brave of Judy to risk her wrath to warn them.

Ping. An upside-down pic of Brian with a face drawn on his chin, which, incidentally, also showed his bare neck.

Chloe breathed a sigh of relief and sent Brian and Kyle a new text. "Meet at the lightning-struck fir. Don't tell anyone."

Ping. Brian wrote: "Cut school? I'm in. 😌"

A third text came in from Judy. "Save her."

So she was still alive. Bitterness surged inside Chloe. How, exactly, was Chloe supposed to save Olivia from the witch? And why should she, when Olivia was the one who'd gotten them into this mess in the first place? Yet she hurt for Judy. Chloe would help if she could.

"So, basically, we're screwed," Kyle said, when Chloe had finished laying out everything she'd learned to him and Brian. The younger boy's freckles stood out on his pale face, and he'd already devoured three granola bars from their supply.

"Basically," Chloe agreed. Emotion tightened her throat.

A glum silence fell. "So are we moving to Saskatchewan or Manitoba?" Kyle asked eventually. "I'm guessing B.C. is out?"

She nodded. "We go to whichever of the other two is willing to take us."

"I can't." Brian scuffed a toe along the ground. He glanced up, his expression the most serious Chloe had ever seen it. "I can't leave Mom alone with the kids. She needs me to babysit or she'll lose her job. I have to stay, even if it means being collared."

"We understand." Chloe squeezed his arm, a gesture she wouldn't have dreamed of making two weeks ago, when Brian, Dean and Kyle had been the bane of her existence. They couldn't take his half-siblings with them—they didn't have the money. As it was, three teens would be a burden on any Pack—

A thought flitted across her mind. She stood there, mouth half-agape, thinking furiously.

"What is it?" Marcus asked.

"I have an idea," Chloe said. Hope warred with trepidation inside her, setting her pulse jumping. "I know how we can save the Pack, but it's going to cost us a heavy price."

"Heavier than losing our homes, our parents and seeing the Preserve logged?" Kyle asked bitterly.

She took a deep breath. "Almost."

"And why should I believe a word of this crazy story?" the Quesnel Alpha, Thomas Fedorchuk, asked, his voice crackling impatiently over the cell phone.

It had taken several hours and a hike to and from Lady Sasquatch's cabin to set up this call. Chloe could blow it with one wrong word.

Nervousness made her hands sweat, but she kept her voice steady. "Because of what we're offering. You have everything to gain, and if witches don't exist, very little to lose."

"And what would that be?" His voice dropped to a low basso rumble.

"Everyone knows your Pack needs more land. I'm offering one quarter of the Preserve. Pristine boreal forest, in exchange for you killing the witch." Since Thomas was already skeptical she didn't mention the witch's possible immortality. Even if Baba Yaga was immortal, it probably only meant she was immune to old age. Decapitation still ought to do the trick.

"Half," he said at once.

Good. She had him hooked. Now to reel him in.

They eventually compromised on one third. He tried to strong arm her into more, but she cited the deal with Lady Sasquatch that meant one third had already been set aside. "One third gives you equal territory with our Pack. I won't take less."

"How do I know you're even authorized to grant this much?" he asked suspiciously.

"Technically, I'm not," Chloe said, "but Lady Sasquatch has agreed to stand as guarantor that the deal will be honored. You know her species' reputation."

"That they'll tear the arms off anyone who impugns their honour, you mean?" Thomas's voice held a trace of humour. "So your story has sasquatches *and* witches."

Chloe went cold. She'd assumed all the Packs had contact with the small sasquatch community. Was she wrong? "I assure you, both are very real."

"I saw a sasquatch once as a child... . They're rare, but yes, I know they're real. Though you're lucky you called me with the offer and not—well, suffice it to say that there are werewolves who scoff at sasquatches. All right, Ms. Graham, you have a deal."

The relief was so intense, Chloe felt lightheaded, but the sick churn of nausea remained long after the phone call ended. *I just gave away a third of the Preserve, entrusted to Pine Hollow for future generations.*

No. Olivia gave all of it away when she allowed the witch a toehold on our Pack. I'm just trying to get some back.

But would the rest of the Pack see it that way? After she saved them, *if* she saved them, they might well kill her.

"What do you think?" she asked Marcus. "Am I crazy to even try?"

Marcus laid his cheek against her, nuzzling like wolves did. Chloe became hyper-aware of his lips only a breath apart, but he didn't kiss her.

"You are my Alpha," he said simply. "Running away isn't in your nature."

His faith in her brought forth a surge of gratitude. Words gone, she rocked up on her tiptoes and kissed him.

For a heartbeat, he didn't react. Then his arms closed around her as if she were the most precious thing in the world. Her eyes drifted closed, concentrating on the messages sent through touch. The world spun around her. She let feeling sweep away her fears.

She threaded her fingers through his shaggy hair and inhaled his scent. Marcus, feral and wild, quiet and watchful, quick and deadly. Marcus, who believed in her absolutely.

Who cared if he was a year younger than her? In many ways, his year of surviving alone in the woods had made him stronger and more mature. Abby's face intruded. Chloe silently apologized: *I wish you were here to tease me about my poor taste in guys, but you're not. And Marcus and I have both changed since you knew us.*

She tugged his hair until he stopped kissing her. She looked him straight in the eye so he would know how serious she was. "You're mine," she said, and they both dived back into the kiss.

Decision made.

CHAPTER

23

Lying prone on the forest floor, hidden in the shadow of a big pine, Chloe watched the Frayne's house through Lady Sasquatch's binoculars. The Alpha paced back and forth, raging and spouting off orders. Was this Olivia, or Baba Yaga wearing her face? Chloe suspected the latter. She'd never seen Olivia so angry, red-faced and slit-eyed, full of hate.

The last Pack family arrived. Brian and his mother sent the younger kids inside and joined the Friday night meeting on the lawn. From her body language the Alpha appeared to be lambasting Kristen for being late.

"Maybe we should go," Chloe whispered. "There's no chance of catching the witch alone tonight, and if anyone gets a whiff of our scent …"

The Quesnel Beta, a muscle-bound twenty-something with a military haircut, cast Chloe a scathing glance. "We didn't come all this way to cool our heels."

"Let me see." Thomas, the Quesnel Alpha, motioned for the binoculars. She handed them over without a word.

When the forty-five-year-old Alpha had first seen Chloe he'd sworn for two minutes straight. "You're just a kid." He probably would have walked right then and there if not for Lady Sasquatch. But he'd signed the legal papers that afternoon and silenced his Beta's objections with a Dominant stare. Still, his control over the four werewolves he'd brought—three men and one woman—seemed shaky. The rumours about the Quesnel Pack being on the verge of fracturing looked to be true.

Which was bad, because Chloe didn't trust his Beta. At all.

All five of the visiting Pack looked at the Preserve with greedy eyes that raised her hackles. She had to keep reminding herself that she needed this alliance to defeat the witch, and that the loss of land would be worth it to save the Pack.

Though how exactly were they going to co-exist afterward? Pine Hollow wasn't exactly brimming with job opportunities. Where and how were the Quesnel Pack going to live? Would they commute on weekends?

One problem at a time, she counselled herself.

"Are you sure that's the witch?" Thomas asked her in a barely audible whisper. "It looks like Olivia Frayne to me."

"I told you, Baba Yaga can impersonate someone else." Still, Chloe took out her phone and texted Judy. "Still not?" Meaning, *still not your mother?*

Chloe's phone vibrated with a text a minute later. "Not." Then mere seconds after that, a second text came in. "Save her. Skinning."

Chloe stared at the word in horror. Cold prickles broke out on the back of her neck.

"What is it?" Thomas snatched the phone from her, but frowned, baffled by Judy's message.

Chloe found her voice. "Baba Yaga is skinning Olivia alive. She must intend to permanently assume her identity. We have to find her and rescue her." Chloe tapped her chin. Where would Olivia be? Inside the Fraynes' house?

No. Baba Yaga's hut.

She turned to Marcus. He had the better nose. "Is Baba Yaga's hut around here?"

Before he could reply, Thomas raised his hand. They all fell silent, even his surly Beta.

"I've called you here because of a threat!" Baba Yaga yelled with Olivia's voice. "Lady Sasquatch has filed papers to prevent the logging deal! We need that contract to protect ourselves and our way of life! She is threatening our survival! We can't let her get away with endangering the Pack. The hairy beast must submit!" Baba Yaga/Olivia raged.

Beside Chloe, Lady Sasquatch bared her teeth.

So. Bad.

"I smell the hut," Marcus whispered in her ear. "It is nearby."

Baba Yaga was still insulting Lady Sasquatch and harping on her disrespect for the Pack.

"We're out of time," Thomas declared. "We need to act now to protect our ally." He nodded to Lady Sasquatch, then turned to his Beta. "Take the others and circle around in case anyone gets frisky. You know what to do."

Wait, what? This was just an intelligence-gathering mission. They didn't have a plan yet. Unless Thomas hadn't shared his plan with Chloe?

So much for being grateful to have a competent adult take over. Instead, she had to keep biting her tongue to stop herself from correcting him.

She moved in front of the Quesnel Alpha. "Please wait. We need to act on the information we've received. If we free Olivia, it will weaken the witch's hold."

"There's no time for side missions," Thomas said brusquely. "Your Pack has to be stopped before they attack Lady Sasquatch. Once I win the Challenge, we'll get things straightened out."

Challenge? She'd never said anything about an Alpha Challenge. God, the whole thing was spinning out of control. If Thomas beat out Coach as Alpha, then he would effectively control Pine Hollow. The Pack could lose a lot more than one-third of the Preserve.

Worse, Thomas was treating this like an ordinary fight. He didn't believe in Baba Yaga, not really. His Beta had openly scoffed at the idea of silver chains controlling werewolves. Thomas was counting on stopping everything with an Alpha-to-Alpha challenge, but Baba Yaga might not follow the rules.

Chloe grabbed his sleeve. "It's not a good idea to attack Baba Yaga head on. The collars give her complete control. She'll throw the other werewolves at you." And Chloe's parents and her Packmates could get hurt.

Thomas stubbornly shook his head. "She won't have a choice. Pack Law is very specific. Challengers must be answered. Quinn, you have three minutes to get into position. Go."

The Quesnel Beta cracked his neck. "Let's do this." He and his Packmates loped off.

Thomas turned to Lady Sasquatch, shutting Chloe out.

Her fists clenched. He was making a mistake. She knew it.

"We need to rescue Olivia," Chloe said to Marcus and Kyle. "Now, while Baba Yaga is distracted by the attack. But ... " She bit her lip, torn.

"But you need to stay here," Marcus said for her. "We will go."

Chloe stifled a protest. Even crippled, Baba Yaga's hut was likely to be dangerous. But if Kyle and Marcus could free Olivia, she could command the Pack to remove their silver collars. The risk was worth it.

Except it would be Marcus and Kyle taking the risk, not her. She needed to stay here, and protect the Pack if she could. She hesitated one painful moment more. She'd promised Abby's spirit to keep Marcus safe. How could she send him into danger?

Chloe gave him a fast, hard kiss that had Kyle gaping at them. She gripped a handful of his hair to ensure she had his attention. "Promise me you'll be careful, both of you. No risking your life. Olivia isn't worth it." She waited until they'd both nodded. "Go!"

They vanished into the dark woods.

Tears stinging her eyes, Chloe turned her attention back to the Pack meeting.

Baba Yaga had stopped ranting. Coach clapped his hands for attention. "I'm going to lead a punitive raid on old Bigfoot." He smiled nastily.

Lady Sasquatch bared her fangs. Sasquatches hated the term Bigfoot and considered it a slur.

"We won't kill her," Coach said, "just destroy some of her things and apply some pressure. Make her understand that she needs to change her vote."

The Pack was silent. No cheers—but no protests either. Chloe's cheeks reddened with embarrassment.

Coach sneered. "Curtis, you know her best. You can show us where her cabin is."

"No. I—" Her dad's face turned red, and he fell to his knees, choking.

Bastards. Chloe couldn't stand it. She dashed into the backyard, ahead of her two allies. "Stop!"

Marcus trotted on four paws at Kyle's side. He'd Changed back to wolf as soon as they parted company with the others. He was willing to tolerate boy-form to be with Chloe, but when she wasn't there he didn't see the point. Wolf-form was stronger, faster, more deadly. Sneakier too.

Baba Yaga's hut crouched malevolently in a grove of dark firs. Its window-eyes were shuttered, as if asleep, but its new location showed that it had healed from its laming. The chicken legs were tucked under the hut's bulk. The odour of rotting poultry assaulted Marcus's nose.

He approached cautiously, staying in the shadows of the trees.

"How are we going to get in?" Kyle whispered. His friend still walked on two legs and could thus speak. "The door is certain to be locked, maybe booby-trapped … "

People always wanted to talk-talk-talk as if they had all the time in the world. Marcus's wolf knew better.

Chloe had asked him to do this, to find Olivia. The faster he got this done, the faster he could get back to Chloe.

He threw his body into a run, moving on silent padded feet, faster and faster. Like a rocket, he launched himself up onto the porch, then through the window.

Glass shattered around him with a sound that made his ears flatten. Marcus landed hard on the wooden floor, shards spraying everywhere. Cuts stung his nose and one paw, but his fur protected him from most of it. His werewolf healing kicked in, slowing the flow of blood.

A potpourri of bad smells swirled inside the witch's hut: sickly-sweet rot, dust, astringent herbs, pungent garlic, pickled things, and, everywhere, the scent of blood, old and new, as if the walls had been painted with the substance.

Where was Olivia? His grey-shaded vision allowed him to make out minimal furnishings in the dimness: a table and benches lining two walls. Cleavers hung in graduated sizes on the wall. Jars of strange, dead things lined the shelves.

He sniffed cautiously and picked out the scent of Olivia's sickness. She was here. Where?

A fat drop of blood splashed into a wooden bucket. He tipped his head up.

Hanging from the ceiling, body bound head-to-foot in a sticky web, was the old Alpha. Her arm was red from elbow to wrist—the skin from it dangled down. Olivia's furious eyes met his, demanding that he take action.

A furry brown spider the size of a cat crouched on her chest.

CHAPTER

24

Thomas and Lady Sasquatch followed at Chloe's heels. The Pack turned as one and stared at them.

Coach focussed on Lady Sasquatch. "Come to negotiate? Good. We can make sure loggers don't touch your sector of the forest."

Lady Sasquatch hawked and spit on the ground at his feet. "If any loggers try, I will tear them limb from limb."

Coach's face pinkened, making his white-blond eyebrows stand out.

Before he could respond, Thomas intercepted him and roared, "I am the Quesnel Alpha! I Challenge you!" Without another word, he ripped open his shirt and began to Change.

The suddenness of it left Coach gaping for a moment, then he began to shuck his clothes, too.

Chloe grinned—Coach had just lost the advantage of his quick Change.

Baba Yaga threw her head back and laughed. Her eyes twinkled with amusement. "Why, Chloe, thank you for the unexpected gift. I need more wolves for my army. I intended to seduce the Quesnel Alpha next, but here you've brought him straight to me. Once Conrad kills him, I'll control both Packs."

Chloe's mouth gaped open in horror.

Thomas glared at Baba Yaga. "You'll never get my Pack."

Any more words were lost as his mouth turned into a muzzle with vicious sharp teeth.

Both Alphas completed their Change at the same instant. Thomas was salt-and-pepper grey with a white underbelly. And noticeably bigger than Coach's white wolf. The animals snarled at each other and met in a ferocious clash of jaws and teeth.

While they grappled, Baba Yaga studied Lady Sasquatch appraisingly. "They didn't have your kind in Europe. Hmmm. Powerful as a bear, but able to talk. Do you have true hands?"

Lady Sasquatch bared her fangs. "Come closer and I'll show you my claws."

"Yes, that looks like a thumb. I could use a form like yours." The witch turned to the Pack. "Take her! Hold her down, but do not kill her. The skin needs to be taken alive to work." She idly caressed the white fur belt at her waist. My god, was that Olivia's pelt? No, Olivia was a grey wolf. The belt must be made from Basia.

The Pack reluctantly started to advance. Only Chloe's father resisted the command—and was choked to unconsciousness again.

Lady Sasquatch bared her teeth and swung her cudgel threateningly.

"Everybody Change!" Rick yelled. "We'll need the protection of fur!"

He was right, but he was also giving Lady Sasquatch an opportunity to flee from their greater numbers.

"It's okay," Chloe said to her ally. "Go."

Lady Sasquatch faded back into the woods, cudgel in hand.

The white wolf and the salt-and-pepper wolf still circled each other. The scent of blood hung in the air. Coach's ear was bleeding, but neither wolf had the upper hand.

Chloe bit her lip. How had it all gone so wrong? Even if Thomas defeated Coach, the problem of Baba Yaga would remain. Lady Sasquatch would only have a couple of minutes head start and would be captured. The best Chloe could hope for now was that Marcus and Kyle would free Olivia. If the true Alpha commanded the Pack to throw off their silver chains, then maybe …

She needed a distraction. "I Challenge you!" she shouted at Baba Yaga, frantically stripping off her T-shirt. The witch was still impersonating Olivia, so Pack Law still applied.

Baba Yaga sneered. "This again? You can't Challenge me, little puppy." They locked gazes. Baba Yaga's had the full power of Olivia's Alpha behind it. She tried to Dominate Chloe.

Chloe's turn to laugh. "Olivia is not my Alpha." She touched her shoulder. "See? Her Bite has healed."

A murmur of interest from the gathered Pack, who were still dawdling about removing their clothes or Changing, instead of chasing Lady Sasquatch.

Chloe stripped off her jeans and threw herself into the Change. It was long and painful, but when she finished and stood there proudly as a wolf, Baba Yaga still wore human form.

"Foolish little puppy," she crooned. "I don't need a Bite to control you, for I control your parents. Rachel, come forward."

Chloe's mother slunk forward. The silver collar gleamed amongst her brown fur. A spike of dread impaled Chloe. The witch was right. She could subjugate Chloe by threatening her parents.

Chloe's mom growled at her, urging her to run.

Too late.

Baba Yaga held out a silver chain, her smile cruel. "Put this on, Chloe, or I'll skin your mother alive."

Marcus whined, uncertain what to do. He could kill the spider, crush it in his jaws, but it might poison him or the Old Alpha. Plus, it would taste really bad.

"Marcus isn't it?" the Old Alpha said. "Go get help. The spider will poison me if you get too close."

Marcus ignored her. If he Changed into a boy, he could pluck the spider off Olivia and fling it against the wall. But could he do it fast enough, before it stung him? Could he throw it hard enough? He wasn't sure. He'd be blind for a few seconds while he Changed, blind and vulnerable with all that unprotected bare skin. He shuddered. He wished he could make a hand but keep his fur, but that wasn't how the Change worked. It was all or nothing. Might as well stay wolf then.

"Why did they send the useless feral?" Olivia demanded of the ceiling. "Listen, Marcus. You must kill the witch disguised as me, then come back with the others and free me." She met his eyes and spoke with the authority of an Alpha.

Marcus growled, shaking off the urge to obey her. Olivia wasn't his Alpha. Chloe had sent him here—well, him and Kyle, but Kyle was still hesitating outside—to keep the Old Alpha from being skinned. To rescue her if they could.

But Chloe had commanded him to take care, to not risk his life. She wouldn't want him to bite the spider and swallow poison. He should report back to Chloe.

The wolf retreated to the window, picking a path through the glass, then hesitated.

"What are you waiting for? Get help! Stupid feral," Olivia cursed. Her face was the wrong colour, purplish-red from being dangled upside down.

Her hair hung down like Judy's ponytail. Which made him remember that this was not just the Old Alpha, but Judy's mother. Over the years Judy and Chloe had visited Abby at his house a hundred times. He'd never paid as much attention to pixie-sized Judy, fascinated as he was by Chloe, but she'd still been there. Abby would have wanted him to spare Judy the same grief he suffered for his dead family.

Why was he hesitating? The risk was too high—he should leave. The choice was clear to the wolf—but not to the boy.

He stilled. I am a wolf, not a boy!

But the words stank of lies, the worst kind of lies, ones to himself.

Oh, he would never be that unscarred teenage boy again. That Marcus was gone. But no longer was he a solitary wolf, living only in the now.

After the plane crash, a future without his family had been too painful to contemplate. Thinking of it had hurt too much so he'd shoved it away along with his grief. The future that Marcus had dreamed about, going to university and learning to be an engineer, was no longer appealing. But that didn't mean he couldn't have a different future: one with Chloe and Kyle and a new Pack.

The boy understood what the wolf didn't: that sometimes you had to risk the Now for the future you wanted.

Baba Yaga had the rest of the Pack under her control; Chloe needed Olivia to command the Pack to take off their silver collars or Baba Yaga would win.

He would not fail her.

Marcus turned away from the window and pretended to pounce. He snapped his jaws inches away from the spider. Olivia screamed as it ran up her body and into the webbed ceiling.

"What did you do?" Her bound body heaved, but stayed trapped in the web. "I told you to get help!"

Marcus ignored her. Eight more spiders, all unnaturally large with a freakish number of eyes, hung from the ceiling.

As one, they all sprang down.

The brown wolf whined. Chloe's mother silently urged Chloe to run.

Her mother skinned, dead, Baba Yaga walking around in her body. No. To protect her mother, Chloe lowered her head for the chain—

Snap. Snarl. The two Alpha males closed again, biting and clawing. They rolled across the lawn, coming between Baba Yaga and Chloe's mom. The white wolf ended up on top, but the salt-and-grey one had a chokehold on Coach's neck.

"Shake him off," the witch muttered.

Baba Yaga's distraction gave Chloe an opportunity. She darted forward and with her teeth grabbed the white belt that allowed the witch to shape-change. She yanked it off, ran over to the fire pit and threw it in.

A terrible smell filled the air, not just burning fur, but a foul stench of rot and death. For an instant, a ghostly blonde woman appeared in the smoke. Basia. The ghost smiled and vanished.

Olivia stopped screaming when one of the spiders fell on her head.

Marcus had his own problems. Three landed in his back and tried to bite through his thick fur.

He threw himself into a roll, crushing two. The third scampered across his belly. A fourth one landed on his head.

The door burst open. Kyle came in, took one look at the spiders, then slammed the door shut again. Good. No fool, his friend.

Marcus kept rolling, twisting his head, biting and snapping at spider legs or abdomens, anything he could reach. He regained his footing and banged the one digging into his scalp into the wall. He killed it, but staggered, suddenly dizzy. Fear clawed at him. At least one of them had injected him with poison.

If he Changed, it might burn out of his system, but exposing so much skin would lead to more bites. Better to fight through the poison, kill all the spiders, then Change.

Olivia had fallen unconscious. Two swollen bites marred her cheek and neck. She would not be helping him, and the two spiders who'd been occupied with her were now heading his way.

Marcus growled and lunged forward. He grabbed one in his jaws and threw the foul-tasting thing to splat against the wall.

The door to the hut opened again. Kyle barged in, armed with stout branch this time, but still human.

He was wrong. His best friend was a fool.

Kyle attacked a charging spider with the stick. He pulped it, but a second one ran nimbly up his arm. Kyle screamed.

The spider stilled to inject its venom, and Kyle whacked it with his stick. It thudded against the wall and lay still.

Three spiders remained. Marcus pounced on one, crunching it in his jaws. Bitter juices filled his mouth. Ugh. He spit them out, but not before his tongue went numb. Another spider jumped onto his head from the table, while the last one ran up Kyle's leg.

Marcus could do nothing about the one on his head without braining himself. He shouldered into Kyle's leg, trying to smash that spider, but misjudged the distance and knocked both himself and Kyle sprawling. Marcus bruised himself on the oven. The stick clattered across the floor.

The hut made too confined an area for a battle.

He yipped as the spider on his head stung him again. The room spun around him: oven, door, walls, all revolving like a washing machine. He lurched to the side. The spider fell off.

Kyle ripped apart his spider with his bare hands—squishy spider parts rained on the floor. Kyle slumped against the door, obviously succumbing to poison, too.

His mind urged him to Change, but his wolf didn't want to take on his more fragile human form. The wolf whined and resisted, lost to panic. The wolf was stronger than the boy; he could fight the poison off.

Yes, you are strong. You can fight off the poison, but not in time to save your friend and Chloe.

His mate. For Chloe, his wolf closed his eyes and surrendered to the Change. The process stretched out over a minute, but it worked. When he finished Changing the poison had burned off.

Naked, he hunted for the last remaining spider. "Change," he rasped at Kyle.

His friend nodded jerkily, screwing up his eyes and keening as his bones shifted.

Marcus kept his gaze alert and wary while he grabbed one of Baba Yaga's cleavers off the wall. He hefted the knife, watching for movement out of the corners of his eyes.

There. It had resumed its guard position on Olivia's chest. Sneaky spider probably thought it was safe there since skewering it would mean stabbing Olivia.

Why didn't she do something useful and Change?

Behind him, Kyle gave a final grunt, Changing into wolf form.

Marcus swung his arm down, using the pommel of the knife to hammer the spider. Brown blood burst out of its hairy abdomen.

He waited, half-expecting another surprise attack from above. When nothing came, he began cutting the sticky silk from Olivia's body.

He caught her body as it fell and lowered her to the floor. Was she dead? Had all this been for nothing? But no, she breathed. "Wake up!" Her eyes remained closed, so he slapped her face. "Change! Your Pack needs you."

A howl went up from all the wolves. Coach's white wolf lay broken and defeated. He'd yielded to Thomas. Victory!

Chloe's triumph melted away when Thomas began to Change forms. No! She howled a protest. Why was he Changing back to a man? They needed to attack the witch!

Baba Yaga pointed at Chloe. "Sit on her," she commanded Rick. The hate in her eyes promised punishment for the destruction of her belt. She walked over to Thomas. The silver chain dangled from her hand, glinting in the firelight.

Chloe didn't know how the witch intended to chain a Dominant werewolf, but suspected Baba Yaga had another trick up her sleeve.

Chloe rocketed forward, aiming for the back of Baba Yaga's legs. Instead of Olivia's usual jeans, the witch was wearing soft black yoga pants. Chloe's teeth would tear right through the fabric. Wolf instinct urged her to hamstring the witch—

A large grey wolf hit her in the side, knocking her off course. As ordered, Rick sat on her, his full weight holding her down. She tried to wiggle free, but another wolf, Dean, sat on her hind legs. They didn't bite her, and, knowing they were under compulsion to obey the witch, she didn't bite them either.

The wolf couldn't help her now. Giving up, Chloe began the slow, grinding Change back to a girl. Recognizing what she was doing, Rick and Dean gave her enough space to complete the Change.

When she emerged from the haze of pain, Thomas and the witch were having a stand-off. "I am now the Alpha male of Pine Hollow Pack. Ma'am, I will return tomorrow with sixty of my people. I strongly suggest you vacate by then or we will drive you out with only the clothes on your back."

Baba Yaga hissed like an outraged cat. "You do not want to make an enemy of me," she warned.

"You wormed your way into this Pack through witchcraft and deceit," Thomas said. "I'm wise to your tricks. Without your silver collar and potions what can you do?"

Fly. Make plane engines cut out. She absently petted Dean when he whimpered.

"Now!" the witch said.

Coach's white wolf, who'd been quietly healing, suddenly leaped at Thomas. The wolf tore out his throat in a gory flood. Shock kept Chloe still, and Rick put his weight back on her legs, warning her not to try to get up. She groaned as Thomas fell to his knees and bled out. His eyes accused her, then became glassy and unfocused. He collapsed, dead.

Numbness set in, along with despair. What now? Could things get worse?

Wolves howled in chorus, their voices speaking of treachery. The four Quesnel wolves that Thomas had kept in reserve swept in. As a Pack they fell upon the white wolf, mauling him. Chloe glimpsed red blood against white fur, and then Coach disappeared under the pile of snapping and snarling Quesnel wolves. They tore him to shreds.

Chloe swallowed thickly. Two people dead just like that.

She'd hated Coach, but she felt bad for Ilona, who'd just lost her last living relative. And Thomas had seemed like a good man.

The witch glared, hands on hips in an I'm-annoyed fashion, rather than grief for the loss of her ally.

For some reason her lack of loyalty angered Chloe. The witch had treated Coach like a tool. She didn't understand the first thing about Pack. "Aren't you even going to pretend to be sad that your helper's gone?"

"Minions can be replaced," Baba Yaga sneered.

Minions and bodies, too. Chloe had only inconvenienced her by burning Basia's wolfskin. Baba Yaga was already in the process of replacing her with Olivia, who, as Alpha, was more useful anyway.

Except in one area.

"Thomas's Beta, Quinn, will be Alpha. He's about twenty-three. Good luck seducing him in that body," Chloe told her nastily. During her illness, Olivia's body had softened like dough left to rise. She was still bald from the chemotherapy, and crow's feet wrinkled the corners of her eyes. "Better change back to Basia. Oh, whoops. I guess you can't," Chloe taunted her.

Dean's wolf cringed, obviously wondering if she'd gone crazy. Chloe's heartbeat sped up. Either she would be punished in the next moment or—

Baba Yaga reached into her pocket and took out a glass vial filled with red liquid. Blood. She drank it down in one gulp.

Chloe's mouth fell open as Olivia's mature face melted into a more youthful one and her body became slender and fit. The witch removed the black wig, revealing long blonde hair. Ilona now faced her.

Chloe had a moment of doubt. What if there never had been an Ilona, and Chloe had been sitting beside this thing on the bus?

Olivia's shirt sagged at the collar on Ilona's smaller frame, and Chloe's lips curved in a sudden triumphant smile. *Gotcha.*

The witch's clone body also bore her Bite.

Chloe wriggled free from the other wolves' hold and slapped Baba Yaga's face. "I am your Alpha! Submit to me and don't speak!"

Looking astonished, Baba Yaga/Ilona dropped to her knees.

CHAPTER
25

Chloe's heart pounded. She'd done it! She'd defeated Baba Yaga!

But the victory felt uncertain, like riding a rodeo bull, which might buck her off at any time. Baba Yaga was old and dangerous and powerful. Chloe had outwitted her for now, but she had to act fast to stay in control.

She glanced around, but only Dean and his dad remained. Everyone else had Changed into a wolf and was following Baba Yaga's orders to chase down Lady Sasquatch. "Dean, try taking off your silver chain."

She looked back at Baba Yaga in time to see her trace something in the dirt.

Chloe stamped on her hand. Bones snapped. "Don't move! I am your Alpha, and I command you not to speak or move!"

Dean made a choking noise and pawed at his neck. That was a no then.

Nerves jittering, Chloe trained all her attention on Baba Yaga. Mute and powerless, Baba Yaga glowered at her from out of Ilona's blue eyes and young face, but Chloe Dominated her until she looked away.

Chloe chewed her lip. She could kill the witch—or try to. The Lore had said she might be immortal, but Chloe was more worried about the possibility that attacking the witch might trigger the collars. Baba Yaga seemed like the type to enjoy booby traps.

They needed Olivia.

Before she could order someone to go help with the rescue, Marcus, Kyle and Olivia entered the yard, the boys supporting the pale older woman. The skin from her elbow down flapped like a coat.

"Olivia, order everyone to take off their necklaces," Chloe said urgently. Baba Yaga hadn't moved and still seemed bound to Chloe's will in this form, but Chloe didn't want to take chances. "Yell as loud as you can." Wolves crashed through the underbrush. Some should still be within earshot.

"What?" Olivia gasped. She knelt in the grass, too weak to stand.

Rick finished Changing to human. "Free us."

Olivia coughed weakly. "Take off the crystal necklaces," she croaked.

Shuddering, Dean pawed his off. It glittered in the dirt like a snake. His dad followed suit.

"Where's the witch?" Olivia asked.

Rick pointed to where Baba Yaga knelt in the dirt.

"That's not her, that's the niece," Olivia protested.

"It's her," Chloe said sharply.

"We all saw her change from your form to this girl's. There's no doubt," Rick assured her.

"Why is she just staring?"

"Because her body bears my Bite," Chloe said, without taking her eyes off the witch. "I'm her Alpha, and I command her to be quiet and not move." She reinforced the orders with a Dominant stare.

Olivia's eyebrows winged up. "Your Bite?"

"Yes, mine," Chloe retorted. Her hackles lifted. Despite Olivia's fragile appearance, Chloe was very, very angry at her. She raised her voice. "Wolves, this way!"

Lady Sasquatch stumbled into the yard, limping, pursued by four silent werewolves. More stragglers followed, including Nathan in human form.

"Order them to stop!" Chloe shouted.

"What's going on—?" Olivia started, one step behind the action again.

Lady Sasquatch stumbled to a halt near the fire pit. Her leg was bleeding, and she raised her cudgel high. Three of the werewolves arranged themselves in a triangle in front of her.

"Just do it!" Chloe snapped.

"Please, love," Nathan said. "We're being compelled to obey the witch's commands." As he spoke, he walked toward the sasquatch.

Olivia raised her voice. "Stop!"

Brian, who'd been sneaking up behind Lady Sasquatch, managed to twist his leap and miss both the sasquatch and the fire pit.

"Take off your necklaces!"

As the Pack complied, Chloe snapped her gaze back to Baba Yaga. The witch hadn't moved, but the suggestion of a smirk twisted her mouth. Ilona's blonde hair had turned grey. Baba Yaga was shapeshifting!

"Stop that!" Chloe snapped. She stared at the witch and didn't allow herself to blink.

Baba Yaga glanced down, but she wasn't cowed. Sure enough, wrinkles began to appear at the corners of Ilona's eyes.

Chloe scrambled backward. "I need some help here! She's getting free!"

Leisurely, Baba Yaga climbed to her feet. Now she was the big-nosed, grey-haired crone Marcus had described, except she didn't move like an old woman. She wasn't stiff or careful.

"Very well. You have unmasked me. The time for deception is past. I am Baba Yaga, Witch of the Russian Steppes. I Challenge Olivia for the Alpha position."

Olivia cringed. She tried to cover the motion, to meet the witch's eyes, but her gaze kept sliding away.

Chloe's throat tightened. Olivia was too hurt from her time as a captive and her earlier illness. More than that, Olivia feared the witch. She would lose.

Chloe stepped forward. "Under Pack Law you can't Challenge. You're not a werewolf!"

Baba Yaga snorted. "As if being able to turn into a wolf were some great skill. Who do you think taught your ancestors the trick?" She lifted a hand, bright with blood—probably Thomas's—and began to lick it up.

Everyone watched, paralyzed, as Baba Yaga grew three feet taller, muscled shoulders bursting out of Olivia's clothes like the half-wolf half-human all-monster form that Hollywood loved.

Olivia just stood there, mouth agape.

Baba Yaga was a monster: salt-and-pepper fur bristling beneath the remnant of Olivia's clothes. Wolf's head and fangs. Clawed hands. But no tail and standing on two feet. Hairy toes burst out of her boots.

Chloe quailed. How was she going to fight that?

But then Marcus brushed her side, offering silent support. She wasn't alone.

As long as there was Pack she need never be alone. That was the Pack's strength. That was how wolves took down elk and moose. Together.

This wasn't an Alpha Challenge; this was a battle for the survival of the Pack. Chloe yelled, "We are wolves! We fight and hunt as a Pack!" Then she dropped to her knees and let anger power her Change. It swept through her like fire, rearranging her bones with a snap.

Marcus beat her to wolf form. He jumped into the fray and tore a chunk out of the monster's calf before jumping back.

The monster roared and turned on him—which allowed Chloe to land a blow. Then the whole Pack was there, ringing the witch. Whenever Baba Yaga tried to hit one of them, she turned her back to three others who darted forward and bit.

Yes. This was how Pack fought its enemies. Together.

It took the unchained wolves only five minutes to tear Baba Yaga to pieces.

CHAPTER

26

Olivia took over so smoothly, directing the clean-up of the bodies and the disposal of the crystal necklaces, that Chloe almost didn't notice.

When she did, she hesitated. It was late. Chloe was exhausted, physically and mentally drained from the stresses of the past few days. She wanted to go home and sleep for a week. Her parents drooped, equally tired. Did she really want to provoke another confrontation?

But then Olivia asked Dean to bring Ilona forward.

The Russian werewolf had joined the Pack a few minutes ago, no doubt having been texted by Dean. She seemed in a daze and kept repeating, "She's dead? Really, really dead?" She'd kicked Baba Yaga's wolf head across the yard and done a little dance.

She had taken the news of her uncle's death calmly—maybe too calmly. Chloe suspected Ilona was in shock and had quietly asked Dean to make sure Ilona wasn't alone that night. "And keep your lips to yourself," she'd added with a glare. "She doesn't need that right now."

Dean had crossed his heart and promised. "No taking advantage of newly-made orphans, I swear. If she tries to ravish me, I will nobly resist."

Chloe had kicked him, and he'd laughed and danced away,

but he'd stuck close by Ilona's side, hugging her occasionally. Maybe his feelings did run deeper than attraction.

He stood with Ilona now.

"So you're a werewolf, too?" Olivia murmured, studying Ilona's face. "I should have guessed from your resemblance to Conrad."

Ilona shied away.

"Well, now that you're here, let's see about getting you properly inducted into the Pack," Olivia said.

Ilona's eyes widened like a deer caught in the headlights. "Uh … "

And Chloe broke.

"No, Olivia," she said harshly. "You will not Bite Ilona. You will not Bite me again either. You are not my Alpha."

Olivia met her angry stare with a calm one. "I admit, I haven't been the best Alpha these past few weeks, but the witch forced me to cooperate."

"No." Chloe wasn't buying it. "You failed the Pack. Your weakness gave the witch a toehold and almost cost us the Preserve."

"She took advantage of my illness," Olivia said. Her voice remained calm, but her fists were clenched. "I was dying."

Their argument drew attention. Pack members drifted closer, a silent audience.

Chloe held the former Alpha's gaze. "She took advantage of your weakness, your fear of death. You knew she was a witch when you went to her for the cure."

"I knew," Olivia admitted. "I believed her to be a white witch. She fooled me."

"Pack Law forbids contact with witches."

"I had no choice!" Olivia said sharply. "I would have died otherwise and left the Pack without an Alpha. That was unacceptable."

Chloe remembered visiting the dying Olivia in her bedroom, how Nathan had urged her to 'set Alpha's mind at ease'. He'd wanted her to lie about being a Dud so that Olivia would think the Pack had another potential Alpha and wouldn't choose black magic, but he hadn't been strong enough to keep his dying wife from her disastrous decision.

"You may not have known she was a black witch when she collared you. But you knew before you collared the others on her behalf," Chloe accused. Her eyes burned from the effort of not blinking, but she wouldn't look away. She refused to acknowledge Olivia as her Alpha. "You gave my mother and Kristen silver necklaces as gifts."

Olivia threw up her hands. "I had no choice! She would've killed me if I'd refused."

"You had a choice! You could have died!" Chloe roared back. "A true Alpha would have given her life to save the Pack. My mother refused to drug me even though the silver necklace choked her to unconsciousness four times! How many times did you get choked unconscious before you gave in and did a much larger evil?"

Olivia looked away. "I—I knew defiance to be futile, so I chose to survive to fight another day," she said. But it was too late. A murmur went through the Pack. They'd all seen her acknowledge Chloe as Dominant.

"You chose yourself over your Pack," Chloe said hoarsely. "And so did Nathan, though he at least had the decency to step down afterward. Neither one of you are my Alphas." The accusation hurt. She'd always admired Judy's parents and enjoyed going over to their house for supper, but Olivia wasn't the leader she'd respected.

Olivia shrank. Nathan put his arm around her, but she pushed him away. Ran into the house. Nathan nodded once to Chloe, then followed.

Judy bit her lip, but stayed. Her gaze darted around. "So what does this mean? Is Chloe our new Alpha?"

"She's my Alpha," Marcus said, but some of the other Pack members stirred uneasily.

Weariness rolled over Chloe in a wave. "It means our Pack doesn't have an Alpha right now. I suggest we meet again tomorrow and decide then. Everyone is tired now, and some of us need time to heal." She wanted to check Marcus for wounds, and Kyle's face was puffy as if he'd been bitten.

Her dad stepped forward. "I don't need time. Chloe is young for the job, but she proved today that she is an Alpha. She could have run away and left this problem for the adults. Instead she stayed and risked her own life to save us. That's what Alphas do, and I'm proud to call her both my daughter and my Alpha."

Chloe blinked back tears, overwhelmed. Her father's faith and pride in her meant a lot, even though he was wrong. She was far too young to be Alpha even if she had the right instincts, which she doubted.

Kyle stepped forward next. "Chloe's an Alpha. Us teens have followed her lead for years. Chloe, show them that the Bite Olivia gave you healed up," he urged.

"I already did." She moved her hand protectively to her shoulder.

"Not everyone was close enough to see," her father said. "Please, Chloe."

Grimacing, Chloe pulled the collar of her T-shirt aside, displaying the smooth skin. A collective Ah went through the gathering. The sound made her nervous.

"Chloe has my support, too," her mother said.

Chloe stared. What were her parents thinking? She couldn't be Alpha. She'd made so many mistakes and had barely avoided being exiled as a Dud!

"Well, I sure don't want the job," Brian's mom, Kristen, said, prompting laughs.

Her aunt Laurie stepped forward. Relief whispered through Chloe. Aunt Laurie was the most logical choice to replace Olivia as Alpha.

"I bear some of the guilt for this mess," her aunt said heavily. "I've been using the twins as an excuse to shirk my duty to the Pack. I should have stepped forward as Beta when Karen Jennings died. Chloe, I would be honoured to be your Beta."

Chloe's mouth fell open in shock.

"You're all insane!" Judy burst out. She said exactly what Chloe was thinking. "I know Chloe better than the rest of you, and I'm telling you, she won't be a good Alpha! When she was a Dud, she kept breaking the rules, going her own way. She never knew her place. Packmates lean on each other, but she thinks she's better than the rest of us."

Chloe winced, but Judy had only spoken the truth. Chloe wasn't fit to be an Alpha.

But, to Chloe's surprise, the adults laughed.

Judy flushed angrily.

"Judy," Aunt Laurie said gently, "what do you think being an Alpha means? The Alpha needs a high opinion of herself in order to lead. Of course, Chloe had trouble being at the bottom of the Pack hierarchy when all her instincts were urging her to dominate."

Chloe's breath caught in her chest. Was that true? Was that why she'd had such a hard time?

"Let me ask you this," her aunt continued. "When Chloe did finally get the ability to Change, how did she treat you? Did she snub you and bully you, the way you did her?"

Judy's mouth crimped, but she said nothing, looking down at her feet.

"No, she didn't," Kyle answered for her. "Chloe would've been perfectly justified in taking petty revenge on us all—ordering us to do push-ups and fetch and carry for her—but she didn't. She asked our help with Marcus instead."

"And that's what good Alphas do," Kristen said. "They protect the weak."

"She could have run away," Marcus said, standing by her shoulder. "Kyle and I would have happily gone with her. She stayed to fight instead. Because she couldn't abandon you—her Pack."

Chloe elbowed him in the ribs. "Shut up!" She didn't want to be Alpha. Did she?

Judy didn't give up yet. She jabbed a finger at the Quesnel werewolves, who'd been hovering on the fringes. "And what are they doing here? She brought the Quesnel Alpha onto our land! She let him see our weakness!"

Nausea hit, and Chloe tasted bile in the back of her throat. She'd done a lot more than that. Forget being Alpha: they could banish her for this. "Judy's right. A true leader would have been strong enough to avoid doing what I did." Tersely, she explained about the deal with Quesnel for one third of the Preserve.

"You had no right to do that!" Rick yelled.

"She had no choice!" Kyle yelled back. "Would you rather we lost it all to the logging company? At least this way we have something."

"As it happens," Lady Sasquatch said, "the Quesnel Alpha failed to fulfill his half of the bargain—"

"What?" Quinn, the Quesnel Beta, snarled in outrage. "Our Alpha died for you!"

"The contract reads, 'in return for ridding the Pine Hollow Pack of Baba Yaga," Lady Sasquatch quoted from memory. "Thomas Fedorchuk signed this agreement, but he did not kill the witch." She turned yellow eyes on Quinn. "And neither did you. You stood by and watched."

Quinn glared at her. "So we lose our Alpha and get nothing?"

"Thomas was a good man," Chloe said, tactfully leaving aside for now Thomas's plan to take over Pine Hollow Pack. "He knew the risks going in and thought the prize was worth it. He gambled, and he lost."

Quinn bared his teeth. "He beat your Alpha. That made him the Alpha of your Pack. I was his Beta, that makes me your new Alpha."

Rick growled. "You'll have to fight me for that."

The two men began to shuck their clothes, things getting out of hand fast. "Wait!" Chloe moved between them. "Mom, what does Pack Law say? Does Thomas's win over Coach give his Beta a claim on our Pack?"

The men paused.

"It's an unusual situation," her mom said. "I don't know if anything like this has ever happened before. If Quinn had killed Thomas or even killed Conrad single-handedly, then yes, he would have a claim. As it is, both Betas' claims are equal."

"So we fight." Rick seemed happy about the prospect.

Chloe turned to Quinn. "If you Challenge and lose, then Rick will be Alpha of Quesnel Pack as well as Pine Hollow. Are you sure you want to risk that?"

"Quinn," one of the other Quesnel werewolves said softly, "John's already texted the news of Thomas's death to the Pack. Colin and Ranger and maybe Kevin will all want to Challenge you. You need to stay rested and in top form."

Quinn growled and pulled his shirt back on. "Very well. No Challenge today. But this isn't over. You'll be hearing from our lawyer!"

She breathed a sigh of relief as the Quesnel werewolves left, burdened with the body of their dead Alpha.

She turned to face her Pack. "So now you know. I made the

deal with Quesnel to save us, and it may still cost us down the road. I'd do the same again." She trailed off. Instead of looking angry, everyone was exchanging smiles. Smirks, even. She put her hands on her hips. "What?"

Dean snorted a laugh. "You just did it again. You got between two Dominant werewolves who were about to fight and persuaded them to stand down. You did it without even thinking about it, on instinct. Face it." He pegged her shoulder. "You're an Alpha to the bone."

Chloe opened her mouth to deny it, then stopped. Because she had acted on instinct. And she'd done it before, getting between Dean and feral Marcus, between Coach and Marcus, even putting herself in the way of a bullet.

Alphas protect.

She'd thought she couldn't be an Alpha because she'd been last to Change. But maybe being an Alpha wasn't about being first. Maybe it was about putting others first.

Maybe I am an Alpha.

Something clicked inside her. Some jagged bit of herself that had scraped at her soul since she dropped to the bottom of the Pack hierarchy finally fit. With it came peace and acceptance. This was who she was.

Rick scowled. He appeared to be the sole holdout. "She's certainly proven that she's brave, but she is young. For the Pack's male Alpha we'll need someone older to counteract her inexperience." He directed his last remark at Marcus. Obviously, he saw himself as the next Alpha.

Marcus looked to Chloe, clearly asking her if she wanted him to Challenge the older, stronger werewolf.

As much as the idea of them being Alpha couple together appealed to her, Marcus wasn't ready. Even if he could take out Rick—a big if—he wouldn't make a good Alpha. At least not yet. He needed recovery time, time to get used to living human again. In fact, she doubted he would ever be completely normal. He would always be wild.

She shook her head at him, and he subsided.

"Are there any other candidates for male Alpha?" Chloe asked.

If there were, Rick subdued them all with his glare.

"Does anyone else wish to add something?" Chloe asked. She looked at Judy, trusting her to speak out if this was a bad idea.

Silence.

"Then I'll be your new Alpha with Aunt Laurie as my Beta." Her voice shook with emotion. "I promise to work for the good of the Pack, and to seek advice from older and wiser members when I'm in over my head." Like, for instance, on how to call off the logging deal, and how to arrange a guardian for Ilona.

Polite applause.

"Before I accept, I do have one condition." Chloe put on an Alpha face and made her stare direct and challenging. The Pack fell silent, waiting. "Marcus Jennings is hereby a full member of this Pack. I won't tolerate any talk of him being banished or executed as a feral." She bared her teeth.

"Yes, Alpha." The murmur of many voices came back to her.

Another wave of tiredness hit Chloe. She wanted to crash so bad. "Okay, meeting over. The position of male Beta and everything else can wait until tomorrow."

And they obeyed her. What a weird head-rush.

Her mother insisted on feeding everyone a substantial snack before bed to make up for all the calories burned fighting and Changing. Bizarrely, it was only ten o'clock, but it felt much later.

Her parents trooped off first, tactfully leaving Marcus and Chloe alone in the kitchen. Though with werewolf hearing being what it was, alone did not mean total privacy.

Chloe wanted the full story on what had happened in Baba Yaga's hut, but that could wait. Right now she craved—no, needed—the reassurance of touch.

For once Marcus was wearing a shirt, but he obligingly pulled it off when she pushed it up. Her hands traced his ribcage, searching for new scars and kissing them. She laid her ear over his chest and listened to his heartbeat, exulting in the warmth of his skin. He was whole and so was she. They'd survived.

The need to celebrate their survival grew inside her. She wrapped her arms around him, enjoying the way the strong muscles in his back flexed as he embraced her in turn. He couldn't hold her tight enough to suit her. She lifted her head, nuzzling his cheeks, then dived into a more human kiss.

They kissed and kissed and kissed, bodies locked together—until her dad pointedly cleared his throat from down the hall.

Smiling, breathless, they separated and went to their bedrooms. After changing into pajamas, Chloe opened her door in silent invitation. Two minutes later, Marcus trotted inside in wolf form and lay across the foot of her bed.

Chloe drifted off to sleep, knowing he would be there all night and at her side in the day. He belonged to her, and she to him. They were Pack.

The End

ACKNOWLEDGEMENTS

Feral is an expansion of a short story that I wrote for *Tesseracts Fifteen: A Case of Quite Curious Tales* which was published by EDGE Books and edited by Julie Czerneda and Susan MacGregor. This novel would probably not exist if not for the anthology. In writing the short story, I fell in love with both Chloe and Marcus and wanted to tell more of their story.

Thanks are also due to my long-running Edmonton writers' group. Aaron Humphrey, J.Y.T. Kennedy and T.K. Boomer all read the novel in its entirety and gave me much-needed feedback.